WINTER'S RETURN

WINTER BLACK SERIES: BOOK TEN

MARY STONE

To all those who need, and deserve, a fresh start.

DESCRIPTION

Jingle all the way...to murder.

When FBI Special Agent Winter Black enters a luxurious Montana cabin two days before Christmas, she's excited because all the people she loves will be joining her soon. Her joy is dashed when an unexpected blizzard hits the area, leaving her stranded and without any means of communication.

And she's not alone.

Instead of her friends and family arriving, a momma cat shows up at the cabin's door, begging for help. Braving the snow, Winter finds more than just the feline's litter.

She finds a dead body.

With nowhere to run and thrust into a game of psychological warfare by a killer she can't see, Winter's hope for a bright and shiny Christmas turns into a fight for her life.

Winter's Black Christmas by Mary Stone, is a reminder that both dreams and nightmares come from the same place...your mind.

1

Bobby Burner dropped a fresh ice cube into his glass of Johnnie Walker and surveyed the spectacle surrounding him. Elite Motors's annual Halloween party was in full swing, with costumed bodies filling up almost every inch of his showroom floor.

It made Bobby happy to watch his employees and their significant others laughing together in little groups because a happy employee worked harder and made him more money. Lucky for him, the entire crew appeared to be ecstatic tonight. They were socializing and throwing back enough free booze to drown a herd of elephants while a bass beat rattled the windows.

The party was awesome…as usual. Bobby wouldn't allow for anything else.

A whiz of motion by the electric blue Stingray caught his eye, and Bobby barely managed to hold back a laugh. Paul from accounting was already busting out his rusty backspin moves. Truth be told, the geeky accountant wasn't that bad.

"Hey, you break it, you buy it!"

Bobby's joke drew a few laughs from a nearby group that

included his "sexy mouse" receptionist. While he normally detested rodents, Crystal, wearing a faux fur minidress with a plunging neckline and fuzzy little ears, was an exception to his vermin aversion.

"Remember, Crys," he winked over his shoulder as he swaggered away, "you're off duty tonight. Make sure you have some fun. I can remind you what that is, in case you've forgotten."

After saluting her with his whiskey, he turned and continued cutting across the polished showroom floor in search of his errant wife. Where the hell was she? He didn't have to look for long because her uniquely resounding giggles drew his attention toward a cozy spot behind a red Porsche pickup.

Tawny, his devoted wife of thirteen years, had her breasts pressed up against his youngest salesman's arm. Chad, the dashing employee she'd sidled up to, grinned like a damned Cheshire cat as he shared some riveting tale. The twenty-two-year-old douchebag didn't appear to care that Bobby had a front-row seat to the scandalous interaction.

Truth be told, Bobby didn't give a shit either. He'd understood the minute his wife donned the skintight, latex Catwoman bodysuit that she'd be out for blood that evening.

Young blood.

Making the matter even richer, Chad was dressed as Batman. That would no doubt be Tawny's drunken defense when she and Bobby were having it out at midnight. He could almost hear her now…

"What was I supposed to do, Bobby? It was fate.*"* She'd draw out the vowel of the last word long enough to make him want to puke. *"If you'd wanted me to hang on your arm, you should've worn the Batman costume I brought home instead of dressing up as boring old James Bond."*

Tawny would convince herself—had already convinced

herself, Bobby was sure—that it was *his* fault she'd all but ignored him for the duration of the party. It was always his fault, no matter the time or circumstances.

The bitch.

He waited for a fiery, jealous rage to consume his entire being, but all he felt was the pinpoint burn of indigestion in his gut. Maybe it was the four stiff drinks talking or the decade plus of Tawny making it clear that having a husband and kids didn't equal settling down, but at that moment, Bobby was certain he'd divorce her five times over before he got rid of Chad.

That kid could sell a damn car.

"Here's to priorities!" Bobby raised his whiskey in a mock toast to the happy couple before swigging a gulp. As far as his priorities went, keeping his dealership empire alive and well topped the list.

"Hey!" Chad's vainglorious voice called out. "Bossman, toss me another beer, will ya?"

The youngster slurred his words and flashed a drunken smile at no one in particular, missing the hostile glare that passed between Tawny and his boss. Bobby retreated to grab a can and lobbed it at Chad's head, angling it so it'd be sure to miss the Porsche.

"Drink as many as you want, kid." He stalked by them toward the exit, grinding his teeth and muttering under his breath. "Then go play in traffic, you egotistical little shit."

Maybe he was more upset about the Tawny situation than he preferred to admit.

Shoving open the door and stepping into the brisk October air, Bobby focused on the fleet of sleek, top-of-the-line luxury vehicles before him. Even though it was a week before All Hallows' Eve, the Texas air was chillier than normal. The gleam of chrome and steel beneath the overhead lights served as an instant mood boost, heating him up.

Money. Money. Money.

Retirement from playing minor league baseball had opened up a whole new world of financial prosperity, but for Bobby, it was never enough. The lucrative empire of Elite Motors would be Bobby's legacy, and he intended it to be a massive one. His sons wouldn't have to worry about money for a single second of their lives.

Pride swelled in his chest as he stumbled forward, sloshing his drink and sweeping his arms wide. The vision of his automotive kingdom spurred inebriated tears to spring to his eyes. "You've done good, Bob. You've done—"

A flash of movement toward the back of the lot cut him short. Apparently, he wasn't the only poor soul who'd needed a break from the festivities.

When Bobby swiped the moisture from his eyes, though, an uneasy tingling needled his scalp. The person skulking around the used cars was no party guest. They wore an over-sized hooded sweatshirt that concealed their face, and their bent posture and skittish movements announced less-than-lawful intentions.

He sucked in a breath, standing straighter with the action.

Some punk's trying to steal one of my cars while everyone gets wasted on the showroom floor.

Kind of genius, really. No one would expect a robbery with so many people present.

Whiskey-fueled adrenaline surged through Bobby's veins. Whoever the bastard was, he'd jacked with the wrong guy. Bobby Burner reigned supreme over his automotive kingdom, and no little two-bit hoodlum was going to mess with that.

He charged forward like he was sprinting for home base, letting out a bark that was sure to send the moron running. "What the hell do you think you're doing, asshole?"

As he drew closer, a wave of smug masculinity washed

over him as he closed in on the little shit. The sensation dissipated the second the intruder whirled and thwacked him in the ribs with a brutal swing of a baseball bat.

Pain exploded in Bobby's side, dropping him like a stone to the hard pavement. Sprawled on his back, Bobby struggled to focus on the face looming above him, but the agony tearing at his ribs blurred his vision.

Move. You need to move.

Panting from the pain, he rolled himself onto his hands and knees, gasping for enough air to offer the bat-wielding psycho whatever he wanted. Cars, money, a hot night with Tawny. Anything to give Bobby a minute to recover and recalibrate.

I need help. I can't breathe. I have to—

Hissing air was Bobby's only warning that the bat was moving through air again. He remembered the sound from his baseball days.

The best days of my life.

Instead of connecting with a little white ball, the bat slammed into his skull an instant later, igniting a starburst of electric pain that silenced his racing thoughts for good.

2

Winter Black-Dalton leaned over the porch railing, sipping a mocha latte and savoring the cool January air while chirping birds serenaded her from a canopy of live oaks. Down the street to the west, a small gathering of children waited at the neighborhood bus stop, exuberant and carefree. Their laughter carried to Winter's ears and prompted her to grin in return.

In the opposite direction, a woman pushing a stroller stopped on the sidewalk to chat with an elderly couple walking a pair of basset hounds that Winter had already had the pleasure of meeting.

All in all, experiencing the peaceful Austin, Texas morning felt a little like being transplanted into a dreamworld.

Just one week of living in the Destiny Bluff subdivision had provided ample time for Winter to witness the community's congeniality. Neighbors rushed to help each other carry groceries inside. Friendly faces hollered across the street, offering fresh barbecue off their grills. Even in January, the lawns were well tended. Of course, there was no ocean or beach, but the happy little subdivision was still its own type of—

"Paradise." Noah Dalton spoke the word softly behind her, sliding his arms around her waist. "I always told you Texas was paradise, darlin'."

Winter turned in his arms, careful not to spill her drink. "You did. And I never doubted that, for *you*, it was." Smiling and leaning into his tall frame, she cupped a hand to his cheek. "Just wouldn't have guessed that, someday, I'd be standing here agreeing with you."

Noah planted a kiss on her forehead before stepping back and straightening his tie. "Well? Do I look like a seasoned FBI agent ready to defend the Texan citizens from whatever darkness lurks their way?"

She laughed and ran a hand down the silky tie. "Yes...but you *sound* like the voice-over for a testosterone-fueled movie premiere. My advice would be to use sign language for the rest of the day."

Noah's theatrical sigh was loud enough to be heard two blocks over. "Well, there goes my first-day confidence."

Stretching on her tiptoes, she pressed an apologetic smooch to the corner of his mouth. "Teasing. You're going to do great. Amazing. Jaws will drop at the sight of my dashing, intelligent husband and all of his federal agent wisdom."

He chuckled as he grabbed his briefcase and inched down the porch steps backward. "And the world will *tremble* as Winter Black, P.I., forges her new path of ruthless investigation across the bustling Texas landscape."

"Seriously." She shook her head when Noah turned toward the driveway and nearly tripped over his own two feet. "You're going way overboard with the dramatic-flair thing."

Winking, he blew her a kiss before disappearing into his truck and cruising down the street. The multiple friendly waves he gave to neighbors as he passed filled her with another ripple of satisfaction.

I'm glad to be here.

They'd made the right decision to move. Relocation had allowed them to leave painful memories behind in Virginia while also enabling them to form their own little family haven right there in Austin. Noah's sister, Lucy Dalton, was already an Austin resident, and with a little persistence, Winter had convinced her grandparents to make the move as well.

Now, Gramma Beth and Grampa Jack lived just four blocks away in the same subdivision.

She sipped her coffee, welcoming the absence of the claustrophobic worry that had marked so much of their last year in Virginia. Texas was a fresh start, but the key factor fueling a newfound sense of peace was the knowledge of what—or *who*— was locked away in a secret subterranean dungeon. No more waiting around wondering when her serial killer little brother would strike next. No more getting dragged into his sick games or fretting over which innocent lives he'd end just to upset her.

The bloodthirsty reign of Justin Black was over, and every single person on the planet was better off for it.

Especially her and Noah.

Cupping the warm mug between her hands, Winter turned to survey their new home. The classic, white two-story craftsman came complete with navy blue shutters and a white picket fence. A porch swing hung to the left of the front door. On the right side, a small army of terracotta pots waited for Noah to test out his green thumb once the warmer weather arrived.

He'd promised her a rose garden as well. The idea appealed to Winter, as long as he followed one simple request.

The flowers could be any color but red.

A shiver crept down Winter's spine, delivering a stab of apprehension in the otherwise peaceful morning. When she was just thirteen years old, a sick man named Douglas Kilroy —or The Preacher—had stolen Winter's family. He'd murdered her parents, kidnapped Justin, and gifted her with a massive head wound before leaving her for dead.

Emergency brain surgery had saved her life, but Winter had never been the same after that day. In addition to her trauma and loss, she'd gained an unwanted ability that scientifically wasn't possible. Sometimes, it was as simple as an outline or glow of red around an object or place, alerting her to clues and information that often proved helpful in solving cases.

"And other times, it causes migraines from Hades."

Absently rubbing her temples, Winter counted her blessings that she hadn't experienced a single episode since moving to Texas. Yet.

The blindingly painful attacks—always accompanied by a nosebleed—intensified until she blacked out. That was when the visions started. A reel of footage played out, sometimes making perfect sense, but too often, foggy and confusing instead.

The special abilities were the aftermath of that fateful night long ago, and a small part of Winter prayed that with the clean break from her past, maybe she'd left behind her curse of a sixth sense as well.

Focus. Freak ability or no freak ability, this is your first day at a new job. Get to work.

Stepping inside, Winter strode through the home, admiring—for the umpteenth time—the original hardwood flooring, arched doorways, and sturdy framework. "We picked a good one."

Her statement echoed off the mostly undecorated walls

and bounced around rooms full of half-unpacked boxes. "We'll get you all set up, slowly but surely." Although so far, "slowly" seemed to be in the driver's seat.

Winter continued down the hallway to the repurposed first-floor bedroom and surveyed the space with satisfaction. Modest as it was, her office was ready for business.

She only hoped that she was too.

Pausing in the doorway, she fought off an excited shiver and tried to process the fact that she was no longer a special agent for the FBI. Instead, she was the official owner of Black Investigations, licensed by the Texas Department of Public Safety and Private Security Board to legally operate as an independent private investigator.

A fresh start that was also solitary.

Even her name was solitary when it came to the business. Noah had insisted she use her maiden name as her professional one, because, "Darlin', we're a team in every single way, but this business is all you. I'll support you a thousand percent and with my last breath, whether you have my last name or not."

She'd chosen the career change, but that didn't make it any less daunting to step into the P.I. role. Winter was accustomed to operating with the support of a tight-knit squad of talented, intelligent, and highly trained colleagues.

Right about now, her old team would be filing into the Richmond Field Office, greeting each other, and preparing for a new case surrounding a new psychopath. Her best friend, Autumn Trent, would—

Miss them later. It's. Time. To. Work.

Taking a deep breath to tame the sudden pinch of sadness, Winter crossed over to her desk and settled into the rolling chair. The red flashing light on her desk phone signaled voicemails to check.

Looks like that painful advertising budget was a smart decision after all.

She might be alone in her new career, but hopefully, she wouldn't be bored.

"Here goes nothing." Winter put the message system on speaker and pressed play.

"You have...seventeen...new messages."

Her eyes widened as the robotic voice delivered the report. "Seventeen? Already?"

Glancing at the calendar to double-check that her ads had only been live for four days, Winter grabbed a pen and began taking notes as the messages played.

The first one was from a local car insurance company requesting assistance with proving a claim fraud. Next came a man who was certain his ex-wife was blowing child support on manicures and shopping extravaganzas. The third was a woman who left her number and no other information whatsoever.

Some of her initial excitement faded. So far, so blah. "Come on, give me something good."

The fourth call was another insurance claim, but the fifth call granted Winter's wish.

"My name is Mahoney Fitzgerald, and I am willing to pay whatever it takes *to gain your services."* The man's voice held an unmistakable edge of desperation. *"I have...um...well, a situation has come about in my personal life that must be addressed. Immediately. Please call me back as soon as you possibly can. My number is..."*

Winter yanked the notepad closer and jotted down the number. She didn't need a sixth sense to detect the caller's misery. Something had gone horribly wrong in his world, and there was no denying that her interest was piqued. Inhaling a cleansing breath to calm her nerves, she placed the return call.

Not two full rings passed before her first prospective client picked up. "Mahoney Fitzgerald."

"Mr. Fitzgerald." She injected all the confidence she'd gained over the years into her phone voice. "Winter Black here, returning your call to Black Investigations. Do you have a moment to discuss your case?"

Boisterous laughter, a blatant contrast to the palpable angst in the man's voicemail, boomed through the speaker. "Of course I don't. I'm a very busy and important man, Miss Black. Handsome, too, in case you were wondering."

Winter fought the gag climbing up her throat. "It's Mrs. Black-Dalton, but you can call me Mrs. Black." Her business might be built on her name alone, but she loved being able to knock this bastard down a few pegs with her married moniker. "If you'd like to call me back at a better time—"

"No!" He all but yelped the word. "Now works. And please, call me Fitz."

"Okay. Fitz." A few ideas for nicknames were already forming on Winter's tongue, none of them as benevolent as Fitz. "Can you give me a little insight into your situation?"

Her wooden wall clock ticked off the seconds that followed. Just as she began to wonder if Fitz had either hung up or passed out cold, his voice started booming again. "My girlfriend has disappeared. She just stopped communicating two weeks ago, and I'm...I'm scared for her. I think something horrible has happened to her."

Winter swallowed an exasperated groan. So much for the promise of an exciting case. If she understood correctly, Fitz wanted her to track down a girl who'd ghosted him.

No shock there. She'd spent all of forty seconds talking to the man and could already understand the temptation.

Her grip on the pen tightened. *Keep it professional. You can use this call as practice for real clients.*

"What's your girlfriend's age?"

"Thirty-one."

An adult. That was good, but it also made what she was about to say even harder for her potential client to hear.

"It isn't unheard of for an individual to take off on their own. This happens more often than you might think and for a multitude of reasons. Could you tell me exactly what reason you have to believe she's been harmed?"

She doodled a little ghost next to Fitz's number while she waited for him to answer.

After another few seconds slipped by, Fitz cleared his throat. "See, that's the weird thing. Everyone who knows her," he blew out a long breath that whistled over the phone's speaker, "at least, the people I met while she was standing *right next to me*...are trying to convince me that she never existed at all."

3

P arked behind a plain brown desk in his new office, Noah swiveled his hips from side to side in the unfamiliar chair.

Creak creak.

There was a definite creak happening every time he moved, and it was getting louder with each motion.

New guy gets the old chair. Alrighty then.

He shifted his weight again. *Creak.* Three minutes and a screwdriver would more than likely fix the situation. Maybe a little grease. In fact, Noah was almost positive he had a bottle in his truck.

Now that he'd heard the noise, it would drive him to distraction until it was fixed. Maybe he could—

"You must be Special Agent Dalton." A female voice laden with a thick Southern accent interrupted his seating dilemma. "I'm Special Agent Eve Taggart, your new partner."

Standing, Noah offered his hand. "Pleased to meet you, Agent Taggart."

And he was. When he'd first arrived at the Austin FBI Resident Agency that morning, the front desk agent, Mindy

Lou Steiner, had led him to the small office space with two desks facing each other and no window to speak of. She'd informed him that his boss, Supervisory Special Agent Weston Falkner, was currently in a meeting and that Agent Taggart, who he'd be sharing the office with, was running a bit late due to one of her kids' dental appointments.

Noah had thanked Agent Steiner and settled into the empty spot, grateful for a few moments of privacy to take in the surroundings and gather his thoughts. Thirty minutes later, however, he'd overthought his pending greetings to the point of inspiring more anxiety in his stomach than he'd experienced when first entering the building.

With Agent Taggart's arrival, his first-day jitters diminished. The woman was a good two inches shorter than Winter—who, at barely five-seven, was no giant herself—and greeted him with a wide, warm smile that he didn't doubt for a second was genuine.

She shook his hand and proceeded to take the seat across from him. "Guess you were probably expecting a little bit more than this tiny gerbil cage, huh?"

Gathering up her long, blonde hair, she effortlessly twisted it into a bun on top of her head and laughed as Noah struggled for the right words.

"What? No, of course not." He winced. Even he could hear the forced cheerfulness in his tone. "This is fine. Good. It's, um…peaceful. I really like the…uh," his desperate gaze swept the barren room and settled on a sad faux plant tucked into the far corner, "bamboo?"

After glancing at the eyesore, Agent Taggart laughed even harder. "Oh, I see you've met Pokey. That thing was here when I came, and since I never got around to dumping it, I named it instead. Also, you're a good sport, but I've seen pictures of the Richmond Field Office. Y'all have a nice setup over there. We're more of an efficiency establishment here at the resident agency. San Antonio, they've got the impressive field office thing happening. I'm surprised you chose to transfer here."

Noah waved off her comment, despite the fact that having no view of the outside world was already making him a bit stir-crazy. "I've got family in Austin. It was the best fit for me and my wife. I'm curious, though, about where the rest of the Violent Crimes Division agents are located?"

"Oh, they're all just down the hall." Agent Taggart pulled an oversized purple water bottle from her purse and sucked a long drink from the straw. "There's just four more of us, and they all split a slightly bigger office. They even have a *window.*"

Bastards. "What about SSA Falkner?"

"He's straight across the hall. He gets his own office, but I like to think of it as more of a glorified closet. No window for him."

Appreciative that his new partner displayed a healthy sense of humor, Noah didn't have a chance to respond before a knock rattled the door. His new boss loomed on the threshold. "Agent Dalton. Agent Taggart."

Without waiting for an invitation, SSA Weston Falkner strode a few steps into their office. Unlike Noah's new officemate, the weathered face beneath the SSA's shock of white hair was devoid of humor.

Their conversation during Noah's transfer interview process had been short and to the point. He'd left the meeting without gaining much insight into his new superior's personality other than the fact that SSA Falkner came off a tad stern.

As the man stood before him now, stiff, unsmiling, and sporting the same no-nonsense buzz cut and chilly blue eyes, Noah understood that he'd read SSA Falkner accurately the first time. Expecting or hoping for any spontaneous displays of warmth would be foolish.

"We're happy to have you, Agent Dalton." SSA Falkner didn't offer a handshake. "The atmosphere here may not be what you've grown accustomed to in Richmond, but trust that you're surrounded by hardworking individuals. I see that you've already met your new partner."

Offering a broad grin despite SSA Falkner's severe expression, Noah smoothed his collar and nodded. "I have. I believe we're going to get along great. Eager to get started."

SSA Falkner slid his hands into his suit jacket, eyeing Noah warily. "Glad to hear it. You'll be working most cases solely with Agent Taggart. We tend to work in pairs here, and our emphasis is on a serious, productive working environment. Austin's Violent Crimes Division isn't concerned with the fantastic 'super-team hijinks' you and your Virginia crew are known for."

Biting his cheek until it bled to stop the spurt of laughter triggered by the word "hijinks," Noah attempted to find humor in the thinly veiled jab. "It *was* kind of exhausting being a part of the Richmond Avengers. Way too much pressure. And the fanbase? There were some crazies in that group for sure."

While Agent Taggart made a suspicious little hiccupping noise before swigging another sip of water, not even a hint of a smile appeared on SSA Falkner's face. If anything, the man looked constipated enough to need an IV of prune juice. "Agent Taggart has been briefed on the case you'll currently be working on. I'll let her fill you in and check back on the two of you later."

With that, Noah's new supervisor pivoted and exited the room, pulling the door closed behind him.

Agent Taggart waited a few seconds before letting out a low whistle. "Wow, you okay over there? That was a little painful to watch. Weston's not exactly what you'd call a people person, but he did approve your transfer, so he must think highly of you."

"That's nice to hear."

In reality, Noah wasn't convinced that Falkner thought any higher of him than he did of Pokey the Fake Bamboo Plant, but that was okay. This was only day one, and he was eager to show Falkner who he truly was.

Noah's old boss back in Richmond, Special Agent in Charge Max Osbourne, had been equally gruff on first acquaintance. Over time, though, the man had shown that he possessed a sense of humor, even if it only made the occasional special appearance.

His other superior in Virginia, Supervisory Special Agent Aiden Parrish, had likewise presented with a hard outer shell. In fact, Aiden had been Noah's least favorite person at the Bureau for some time before the two found common ground. Now, he could admit that they'd developed a friendship of sorts. Hell, he actually missed the man.

Sometimes.

"I'm sure it'll just take some time to develop the trust factor." Noah fought off a grimace. The last thing he wanted to do was spend his first day in the Austin VCD overanalyzing SSA Falkner. "Anyway, how about you brief me on what we're dealing with, and we get going?"

"Okay, but first things first." Leaning back in her chair, Agent Taggart crossed her arms and peered down her nose at him. "I expect you to call me Eve from here on out. None of this Agent Taggart crap. You good with that?"

He touched two fingers to his head in an informal salute. "Absolutely. Eve it is. And I'm Noah."

"Okay, Noah." She motioned to the corner. "And Pokey over there obviously prefers Pokey. Though he answers to Agent Bamboo too."

Noah directed a solemn nod at the plant. "Of course he does. I'd never expect any differently."

Her grin brightened the depressing room. At least the person he shared the tiny office dungeon with had a good sense of humor. Noah figured that Eve's sweetness balanced out SSA Falkner's icy interior just enough to make the workplace tolerable.

"Well, now that we've got that all figured out, I guess we'd best get down to business." She ran a thumb along the side of her water bottle as her expression turned serious. "This case we're workin', it's an ugly one. And unfortunately, it's all too common down here in the Lone Star State. Three minors, all girls, went missing on the same evening. One was found dead, and authorities suspect the other two were pulled into a statewide sex trafficking ring. Texas has the *third highest* rate of missing individuals in the entire country."

As she spoke, Eve's entire body stiffened. The topic obviously distressed her, and Noah couldn't help wondering if either of her children were female.

"Well." He snapped his laptop shut and rose from the chair, filling the space with the mother of all creaks. *Mental note...bring toolbox tomorrow.* "Where should we head to first?"

"Oh." A deep pink flush crawled up her neck as Eve held up her hand. "No, we're not going anywhere. I'm sorry, I should have started with that. This is an ongoing case, and the way it's developing so far." She sighed. "Or not developing, to be more accurate, it seems destined to be a cold one. We'll be working on it in-office until we get a fresh lead."

Every word out of her mouth was like another chain attaching to Noah's neck. He cast a longing glance at the door before settling back down in the squeaky chair.

In-office case. A depressing phrase if he'd ever heard one, and not how he'd choose to kick off his new job in Austin. Then again, anything was better than spending another half hour staring at the walls and wishing for a window to magically appear.

No wonder Eve had given a plastic plant a name.

She popped open her laptop and immediately began clacking away at the keys. "Just a friendly heads-up to add to all of that. Most of the cases you and I will be working together are going to fall somewhere within the missing persons category. It can become...well, it can wear you down."

A wistful ache grew in his chest as he imagined Winter and the Richmond "super-team hijinks."

Stop that. You and Winter chose this move, remember? Or more like, you poked Winter about moving to Texas for long enough that she finally caved.

They'd wanted a new beginning near family...and far removed from the memories of Justin Black.

You're a big boy, Agent Dalton. Now, put on your big boy pants and get to work.

Noah opened his own laptop and scooted his chair closer to the desk. "I'm not so easy to wear down." He cracked his knuckles. "Let's find those girls."

4

Winter sat on an ornate wooden bench in a quiet yet highly visible alcove of Lakeview Hills Park. Nearby, ducks quacked to one another as they swam across a manmade lake that was surrounded by vast stretches of emerald grass. Women in high-end activewear pushed fancy strollers and walked fluffy little dogs in sweaters.

Fitz lived in the expensive Lakeview Hills suburb, just an hour out of the Austin city limits. Since Winter wasn't exactly set up to receive clients in her office—it would be a cold day in hell before she invited a complete stranger into her home—they'd arranged a meeting on his turf.

The basic premise of Mahoney Fitzgerald's case fascinated her. His girlfriend was gone, and the people who knew her were claiming to have no clue that she'd ever existed.

As Winter scanned the park for Fitz's arrival, his plea over the phone looped through her mind.

"I know what you're thinking...I must be nuts. And I'm telling you that I am a lot of damn things, plenty of them deserving the criticism and judgment of my peers, but I am not crazy. Do you hear me? I'm. Not. Crazy. Something horrible has happened to her."

Winter had no reason to believe him, and she certainly wasn't obligated to take his case. Yet she couldn't deny that, deep down, a part of her was screaming to give him a chance. Her own gut instinct was one of the few things she had full confidence in.

For that reason alone, she'd agreed to consider the case and made the drive to Lakeview Hills.

A child screeched, drawing Winter back to the park bench. As she gathered the paperwork she needed Fitz to sign before discussing his dilemma in any greater detail, footsteps crunched across the dry winter grass.

Straightening the papers, she lifted her head to study the man who approached. In person, Mahoney closely resembled the photos she'd found online before leaving the house, and his demeanor was an exact match to the image her imagination had conjured.

Mahoney Fitzgerald swaggered rather than walked. His blond hair, blue eyes, and classic bone structure made up a handsome face, and the half-smirk on his lips told the world that he was very much aware of just how pretty he was. A simple yet crisp white button-down shirt over pressed gray slacks—Winter guessed both items had cost a small fortune—polished black leather loafers and the gleam of an expensive watch all quietly declared to the world that Mahoney came from money.

A lot of money.

"Thank you so very much for meeting with me and taking my case." Extending a hand, Fitz's casual hair flip and seductive smile seemed at odds with his predicament. Appreciation glinted in his blue eyes as they roved over her slim-fit jeans and soft gray jacket. "I must say, Mrs. Black-Dalton, that you are absolutely striking."

Winter dropped his hand like it was a snake and

narrowed her eyes. "You should be aware right off the bat that I'm here to investigate your case and nothing more. I will not tolerate flirting, come-ons, or any other inappropriate machismo behavior. Do you understand?"

Fitz bowed his head, though she doubted he experienced a shred of remorse. "My apologies. I only meant to compliment you."

Freaking gaslighter.

She rapped the clipboard with her knuckles. "I don't need your compliments. I do, however, need you to sign these documents and retainers. After that's completed, you can describe your situation in detail. While you do that, if you can manage to keep things completely professional, we'll formulate a game plan."

Dropping to the bench beside her and accepting the paperwork, Fitz appeared to resign himself to the duty at hand. While his pen scratched across the pages, she watched a duck waddle over to inspect a tidbit on the grass and wondered how Noah was faring.

She pulled out her phone and typed a silly message, biting her lip as her finger hovered over "send."

Leave him alone. He's probably out in the field already, halfway to solving a big case. He doesn't need you distracting him on his first day.

With a sharp pang, Winter deleted the text. Not even five minutes into meeting her first client, and she was already experiencing FOMO about Noah's new job with the Austin Feds. Instead of having a Fear Of Missing Out, she needed to get a grip.

"All done." Fitz handed her the documents along with a check for the retainer fee.

After a cursory inspection to ensure all the pages were signed, Winter tucked the papers into her messenger bag style briefcase and snapped it shut. "Okay. Start from the beginning."

All bravado drained from Fitz's face as he tipped back his head and stared at a puffy patch of clouds. "I met her three months ago at a bar. An upscale bar, obviously."

Winter fought the eye roll and gag that threatened to twist her features.

"Sandra Smith." Fitz grinned for a brief moment. "Beautiful woman. Long blonde hair. Big brown eyes. Gorgeous smile. Great ti...uh, legs. We really hit it off, and I'm not a 'hit it off' type of guy, you know?"

No shit.

The corners of her mouth twitched upward, but Winter somehow managed to keep a neutral expression. "I can imagine."

Fitz nodded. "Right. Well, I fell in love with her. That's not something I'm normally known for either. I'm a thirty-eight-year-old man who'd never been in love and never had a problem with that fact...until Sandra. Things were great, and then she just disappeared. Two whole weeks and I can't find her anywhere."

No obvious deceit in Fitz's voice, but that didn't mean much. She'd met many an individual capable of spewing rainbows and unicorns through their lying teeth. "You mentioned that everyone tried to convince you she didn't exist...could you expound upon that?"

Fitz fidgeted with his watch clasp. "Yeah. At first, when she wasn't answering my calls and texts, I'd assumed she was super busy. She said she ran an online fashion business or something...I don't remember exactly. Toward the end of the first week, though, I was beginning to think she was ghosting me."

Well, well, would you look at that? Maybe Fitz doesn't believe he's irresistible after all.

"Fair assumption."

Fitz's wince almost made her feel bad about the remark. Almost.

"I kept calling, but then her phone stopped working altogether." His posture sagged like a windless sail. "I couldn't tell if she'd gotten a new number or just blocked me. And I got angry. I decided to go to her apartment and stop the bullshit. If she was breaking up with me, she was at least going to have to tell me to my face."

Winter lifted an eyebrow. "You waited an entire week to seek her out? Why?"

He picked at an invisible scab on his wrist. "I've never had to chase a woman before. I wasn't keen on the idea this time either, but Sandra is different. So I went to her place, her apartment that I've been inside of several times, and some middle-aged guy with *kids* in the background opened the door. He swore he didn't know who I was talking about. He said he and his family had lived in that apartment for the last three years, and he got super angry when I challenged him on that fact."

Winter pressed her lips together, envisioning the scene. It was a bizarre picture at best.

"Go on."

"He called the property manager up to Sandra's place," Fitz threw his arms in the air, "and that dude backed him up. Said he'd never heard of anyone named Sandra Smith and told me to get lost or he'd call the cops."

She leaned back against the bench, skepticism brewing in her brain. So far, his story sounded like the plot of a new Jason Bourne film.

On the flipside, so did half of Winter's life. "So, you're saying a random man with children and the property manager of the building are in cahoots against you?"

Fitz slapped his palms on the bench, shaking the entire

structure. "It's not just them! Sandra's mother, Patricia, lives in a hospice care facility, and I've met her twice. *Twice.* When I went to ask her about Sandra's whereabouts, the lady had the nerve to tell me she's never met me before and *doesn't have a daughter!*"

His voice rose, drawing alarmed glances from two older women on the lake path. They paused to wrinkle their noses at him before speed-walking away.

Winter jerked her head in their direction. "Let's keep it down before one of the locals calls the cops. As far as Sandra's mother...that could possibly be a side effect of medication, depending on what she's receiving hospice care for. Do you—"

"She's perfectly lucid." Clipped vowels demonstrated Fitz's frustration. "She's *lying*. The doctor and nurses I met there are lying too. It's like Sandra disappeared into thin air, and everyone wants me to believe she was never real to begin with. That there's something wrong with *me*."

Having dealt with a fair share of psychopaths throughout her career, Winter was aware of the warning flares shooting up around Mahoney Fitzgerald's claims. With a casual motion, she patted the reassuring bulge beneath her jacket.

Her new client wasn't giving off dangerous vibes. Yet. History had taught her, though, that a little healthy suspicion never went amiss. "But you think they're wrong."

"Yes!" He raked clawed fingers across his scalp before tugging at his hair. "Someone is messing with me. They've done something to Sandra. I can feel it."

"If what you're telling me is true," Winter employed the gentlest tone she could muster, "then it sounds like a lot of people are messing with you."

"Yeah." Fitz fell silent, his mouth drooping at the edges.

Winter groped for a delicate way to pose the follow-up

question. "What about your family? Their perspective could help. What's their take on Sandra's disappearance?"

"I'm not close to them." Fitz's tone rang hollow. "They hadn't even met Sandra yet, and when I tried to talk to them about the whole thing, they just laughed it off. Said I must have taken a night of partying too far. Acted like Sandra was nothing more than a bad acid trip. I haven't let it go, though, and now they're changing their tune."

Despite her concern about Fitz's implied drug use, Winter perked up. "They're beginning to believe you?"

Laughter bubbled out of Fitz's throat without a hint of merriment. "Nope. They've suggested that maybe I should get some help. I'm pretty sure if I keep bringing Sandra up, they're gonna try to have me committed. They've got the money and power to make it happen too." His voice hitched as he sank back onto the bench. "You...you have to help me."

Winter searched his glistening blue eyes for any signs of madness but found desperation instead. She was familiar with insanity. Too familiar. A lost mind was incapable of blending into the background, no matter how hard its owner tried to embody the image of "normal." A shift here, a crack there, and eventually, the walls came tumbling down without fail. Lunacy unleashed.

Mahoney Fitzgerald hadn't lost touch with reality. His assertions were absurd but not beyond the realm of possibility.

Her limbs buzzed with that same adrenaline rush she'd experienced numerous times throughout her career. Maybe she was hovering on the verge of lunacy herself, but she believed him. Or, more accurately, she believed that he believed his story.

"I'll help you. We'll get to the bottom of this."

"Thank you." Relief saturated his voice. When devoid of

an arrogant smirk, Fitz's features softened, hinting at a hidden vulnerability.

Careful, or before long, you'll be pulling out a violin for poor little Richie Rich.

"You're welcome."

Over near the lake path, a toddler screeched as he chased after a duck. Winter idly tracked their movement while considering her first move.

"I need any photos you took of Sandra or the two of you together. I also need a list of every establishment you went to with Sandra, in chronological order, if possible." She watched him jot the information down in his phone. "I need a list of any social media platforms you have a profile on as well as any Sandra might have told you she used. I'll need screenshots of all the messages you two exchanged. Don't leave anything out."

But if he sends a dick pic, I'll murder him.

"I don't have many pictures of the two of us together, but I'll send you everything I have."

Winter stood, ready to sink her teeth into this mystery. "Terrific. I also need the dates you visited both her apartment and the hospice center. My email is on the card, so please send everything as you get it. Don't wait until you've gathered all the information to send at once."

He seemed pleased and much more relaxed, but there was still something nervy going on with him. She wasn't prepared for the next words that fell out of Fitz's mouth.

"You are *the* Winter Black...correct? FBI? With the brother and...all that?" Fitz sputtered out the questions as though he'd been waiting to ask for decades.

Winter rubbed her temple and swallowed a groan. No telling what kind of ground "all that" covered or just how far her reputation proceeded her.

Despite a twinge of curiosity, she decided it was best not

to ask. "Yes. I'm *that* Winter Black. And on that note, I'm going to take my leave and get to work. I'll call you when I have an update."

Hoisting her messenger bag, Winter shook her head as she crossed the grass toward the parking lot where her brand-new Honda Pilot waited for her.

Apparently, even moving fifteen hundred miles away to Texas isn't enough to escape who I am...or what I've done.

5

I stared at my sweet Wally's cherubic face, forgetting for a second just how badly the world had wronged us. He giggled at a flatscreen television big enough to outfit an average-sized movie theater.

My husband and I had hired a celebrity interior decorator to create a dreamland playroom for Wally. A mini Disney World all his own, with life-sized cutouts and plushies of Mickey and friends and colorful murals splashed across every wall. Even though he couldn't hear his favorite characters' voices on the cinema-esque display, he was perfectly content to read along with the captions.

At just thirteen, Wally had learned to accept who he was. How I admired him for that...because I could never do the same.

No matter that I'd entered into my thirty-eighth year of life and the time for reconciliation with the universe was running short. This existence and I would never be friends... would never make peace.

I leaned over the arm of Wally's custom-designed recliner, ruffling his carrot-red hair that was so much like my own and drinking in the fruity scent of his strawberry shampoo. "Miss Anthony will be here soon, Wallace. I think she's bringing a new map today."

Easily reading my lips after years of practice, Wally broke into a dimpled grin and let out a quiet sound—somewhere between a hum and a grunt—in an attempt to express his delight. My son loved maps. Traveling the world was his dream, and researching new destinations was his passion.

While my husband and I could certainly afford to send Wallace anywhere he wanted to go, travel for him would be challenging...were he ever to take trips at all. He'd require a tremendous amount of assistance, and the thought of all the curious, insensitive stares fellow travelers would inflict upon my precious baby broke my heart.

My stomach lurched the way it often did when I concentrated too deeply on Wally's undeserved obstacles. At the simple childhood joys denied him.

Such a handsome face my son possessed. I always tried to focus on that fact—on his beautiful chocolate brown eyes— and not allow myself to ache for the bone-thin arms hanging over the armrests or his propped-up toothpick legs swallowed whole by even the slimmest style of pants. Against all odds, he was a happy child.

I had no right to rob him of that innocence.

Let him be happy. Keep your dark, poisonous snake of a soul to yourself. He deserves that much...and so much more.

The doorbell pealed its alert throughout my expansive home, and I knew our butler would be answering the door and guiding Miss Anthony to Wally's quarters in short time.

I rose, planting a kiss on the top of my son's silky red hair before pulling far enough back so that he could see my mouth. "You be a good boy and have a great day, okay? I'll have Chef add some extra bacon to your cheeseburger for lunch."

Another sweet indiscernible murmur from Wally. He loved bacon.

Miss Anthony's entrance was my cue to exit. Wearing her usual wide smile and soft-hued sweater vest, the thirty-one-year-old private tutor greeted me and immediately went to tend to Wally. Her favorite student, as she always told me.

He better be. We paid her enough to ensure that he was her only student as well.

I made my way through the halls, ignoring the elaborate paintings my husband collected and the fresh bouquets of flowers he insisted on displaying throughout our home.

"Nature is good for the spirit."

My husband was always telling me that. As if a few more vases full of roses or lilies would cure what ailed our family. The concept was endearing...but one-hundred-percent flawed.

He used the term "radical positivity" to describe his approach. I preferred the term bullshit. Together, we formed the perfect yin-yang.

Our baby boy had entered the world with a rare disease—Jervell and Lange-Nielsen Syndrome—that rendered him deaf, nearly mute, and with an abnormal electrical system of the heart. He was prone to fainting and at a very high risk of sudden death. For thirteen years, I'd spent every waking second terrified that this was the year, the month, the day, the moment when his heart said *no more.*

So far, that day hadn't come. Fragile as glass, Wally could possibly live out a normal life span. Or he could fall asleep during his lessons with Miss Anthony and never wake up.

That was his reality. Our reality. My reality.

My heels clicked on marble as I entered the massive foyer and dragged my fingernails along the edge of an antique coatrack. The financial wealth my partner and I possessed enabled us to make Wally's daily lifestyle comfortable, considering his challenges. He was afforded the best treatments, doctors, tutors, and so on. We eased his obstacles in every way we knew how.

No amount of money, however, would magically allow Wally to hear…to speak clearly. We couldn't buy him a normal day at the park to run around and roughhouse with friends like the average thirteen-year-old boy.

We couldn't purchase our son a typical childhood or finance a predictable future.

Often—more often than I wanted to admit—just being near Wally hurt so much I could barely squeeze air into my lungs. My stomach would wrench about in agony, my mind unable to make peace between the infinite love I possessed for my child and the utter uselessness of those affections in the grand scheme of things.

I couldn't fix Wallace. I couldn't make him whole. I couldn't change a damn thing.

Halting opposite the sweeping mahogany staircase that curved up to the second floor, I closed my eyes as the image materialized again. My mother, lying dead at the bottom of my childhood home's staircase. Her unblinking eyes had been open wide—too wide—as she'd gazed right through me. At eight years old, I'd still understood what that empty, hollow stare meant.

My mother hadn't seen me at all. She would never see anything again.

"You little rat! Look what you made me do!"

His voice still clamored through my head like a death knell. No matter how hard I tried, I'd come to accept that this was another reality I could never change. My father's vitriol would burn my ears for all eternity, despite the fact that he'd spewed the words over thirty years ago.

Nor could I change the horrors that came after my mother's death, like foster care. Fists I didn't deserve. Bruises I couldn't explain. Greedy, sick hands that had no right to touch me as they did.

Sagging against a side table, I forced myself to inhale steady, even breaths. There was no time for a breakdown today, and I wasn't that girl anymore.

I had survived all that. Married a rich and endlessly kind —and optimistic—man.

And received the ultimate knife to the heart when my boy was born already broken. This world hates me. It always has. It always will.

The walls shrank around me. A pitcher of daisies blurred on the windowsill. Biting my tongue until it bled, I forced myself to think of anyone, *anything* else.

My mind knew exactly where to take me, and for the first time that day, my shoulders relaxed as I time-traveled to that beautiful night nearly three months ago. I smiled as the brilliant crack of the bat against Bobby Burner's skull reverberated up my arms.

When I blinked back to awareness, I found a daisy clenched in my fist, its petals crushed and limp. I opened my hand and let them fall to the floor.

Murdering an innocent flower wouldn't fix what was wrong with my life. Neither had offing an utter douchebag like Bobby.

"But Jesus," my whisper sent a thrill of goose bumps down both arms, "did it feel amazing."

And I needed a little more amazing in my life.

6

Winter drove straight home and performed an immediate cyber check on her new client. Before meeting him, she'd scanned the internet just long enough to locate photos of Mahoney Fitzgerald to ensure the person who showed was actually him. Now, she wanted to dig a little deeper.

A slew of articles and posts popped up, most mentioning that Fitz was the wealthy son of an even wealthier couple—Warren and Laurel Fitzgerald—who'd grown up in the lap of luxury and privilege just two hours north of Austin. His hometown of Huntstown, Texas, was full of upper-class elitists.

While that explained the man's initial arrogance, those results proved nothing in regard to his missing girlfriend.

Winter dove into numerous databases—both public and private—and scrolled through the entries. As Fitz's P.I., locating Sandra Smith was her responsibility, plus an additional factor drove her motivation to find the woman.

Her gut.

A strong and immediate sense that Fitz was telling the

truth, despite the outlandishness of his claims, pushed her to prove him correct as quickly as possible. Yet despite the hundreds of Sandra Smiths that showed up in Winter's facial recognition search results, none of them were *Fitz's* Sandra, based on the pictures he'd given Winter.

"You can't hide forever." Clicking from image to image, Winter's frustration mounted. "No one's invisible in the digital age."

Even as she muttered the words, Winter was aware that they weren't exactly true. If Sandra had kept her nose clean legally and stayed off social media altogether, finding her could prove much harder, especially without the FBI resources she'd had access to only a few months ago. Added to that was the possible factor of plastic surgery…either before or after she met Fitz.

And there was always the other obvious alternative that the woman didn't exist at all. Or at least not as Fitz believed she did.

Bzzz. Bzzz.

Glancing at her screen, Winter blurted an unflattering word before placing the incoming call on speaker and praying for patience. "Hello, Fitz. Haven't found her yet, but I'm working on it."

"That's not what I'm calling about." Fitz's flat monotone reminded Winter of a victim experiencing shock. "Rat. A dead rat."

"Excuse me?" Winter wasn't sure how to mentally file the information.

Clearing his throat, Fitz repeated his statement. "A dead rat. I got home, and there was a dead rat outside of my property gate. Right at the entrance. Smack dab in the middle of the drive. And…I'm almost sure its neck is broken. It's twisted all weird, you know?"

An uneasy sensation tickled her spine. Maybe her gut was

off and Mahoney Fitzgerald was in the midst of a complete mental break after all. "Fitz, I'm not sure I'm following along here."

"I think it's a warning." His rapid breathing grew audible. "A threat. Whoever took Sandra...maybe they don't want me talking to you. Or maybe this is what they've done to her. Or what they're going to do to me." He swallowed so hard she heard the thickness of it as he gulped. "Winter, I think I'm next."

Dramatic much? Or correct?

Envisioning the ill-fated rodent, Winter couldn't quite bring herself to make the logistical leap. "A dead rat in Texas is far from hard evidence of foul play. I understand that you're under an abnormal amount of stress right now, but let's try to put this into perspective."

"It's a sign." The tone of his voice told Winter that her new client intended to cling to his theory. "When the person *you* love vanishes into thin air, you can talk to me about perspective."

Winter fought the deep sigh welling in her chest. "I'm on your team. Don't forget that. Finding Sandra might not be a quick process, but proving she exists should be relatively simple. The modern-day world isn't designed to make disappearing an easy task. We have surveillance cameras, security footage, paper, and cyber trails. All these things are on our side."

Now didn't seem like the right moment to mention her facial-recognition search failure.

"Right. Okay." Her client seemed to resign himself to her assurances. "As soon as you find anything..."

"I'll call you. In the meantime, take photos of the rat from several angles and send them to me." For a moment, Winter wondered if there might be a local veterinarian who could do a rat autopsy but shook the idea from her head just as quickly.

"Okay. Should I keep its body?" Her client must have been having similar thoughts.

Winter shivered at the notion and tossed out the thought she'd had a moment before, knowing the idea was ridiculous. "Unless you want to pay for an autopsy, I don't think—"

"I can do that!"

Sighing, Winter forgot she was dealing with Richie Rich for a moment. "I can call around to some local vets to see if any of them could perform a post-mortem." She clapped a hand over her mouth when she nearly laughed out loud. Another thought occurred to her. "Do you have security cameras at that gate?"

"Yes." It wasn't an excited sounding affirmation. "But I've already looked, and whoever murdered the poor rodent must have waited for the camera's blind spot. One minute the driveway is empty, and when the camera swings back, the rat is there."

"Can you download and send me the footage for the hour preceding and the hour following the rat's appearance?"

"Yeah. Give me a few minutes and I'll email it."

"Thanks. I'll call this evening with an update."

Trying not to consider the fact that she very well might be making an update call at the end of the day with no actual update to give, Winter pressed the end button.

If Noah were here, she'd immediately bounce ideas off him. They'd whirl up a conjecture storm together. Theorize until their faces turned blue.

Noah is probably having a blast right this minute, working a brand-new federal case with his brand-new federal agent partner.

Catching the sad-sack trajectory of her thoughts, she gave a decisive shake of her head. "Oh no, you don't. No boarding the self-pity train for you. Especially not after sinking all that money into your ad campaign."

Change was tough, but she was confident she'd made the right decision to switch career paths. The stress had been taking a hit on her physical and mental wellness.

Good pep talk. Now get your whiney butt back to work.

She gathered the photos of Sandra and laid them neatly side by side.

There were just five snapshots of Fitz's girlfriend. According to him, she wasn't big on picture-taking, so the only photos he had were shot at home with his phone. The fact was slightly maddening, as just one picture of Sandra in her mother's hospice room would have gone a long way to prove Fitz's story.

Or how about a double selfie of the happy couple in Sandra's apartment? You know, the one Fitz swore she'd lived in.

Pushing a stray strand of black hair behind her ear, Winter examined any element of the case that might prove her client wasn't lying.

He claimed to have the code to the building's front door, which fit with his story. Unless he'd followed someone in, how else would he gain access to confront the family living in Sandra's apartment?

Either way, possessing the code wasn't the slam dunk Fitz wanted it to be. In the rest of the world's eyes, that knowledge only proved that he'd managed to gain access to the keycode of a specific building.

"It doesn't prove that the person in the pictures is Sandra Smith. Or that Sandra Smith lived in that building. Or that Sandra Smith was the individual who gave you the code." Winter sighed. "And now I'm talking to myself again."

Better than not talking to anyone at all.

Pulling herself out of her momentary pity party, Winter studied the photos of the blonde woman for another minute.

Frowning, she pushed away from the desk. There was another concern hovering over Fitz's case that she couldn't ignore. He'd mentioned his family joking about Sandra being a delusion from a bad acid trip.

Mahoney was a thirty-eight-year-old man. If he was using illicit drugs now, he'd likely been dabbling for quite some time. Maybe long enough to cause brain damage...or saddle him with a criminal record.

Frustrated, Winter pushed the idea aside. That type of data would have shown up in her initial search. If he'd ever landed himself into any legal troubles, someone had wiped the black marks from his record. Judging from the number of zeros in his bank account, the Fitzgerald family possessed the power to make just about any slate as clean as they wanted.

Bzzzz. Bzzzz.

Fully expecting another semi-hysterical call from Fitz, Winter glanced down at her phone screen and smiled at the name accompanying the alert.

Autumn Trent.

Winter accepted the call, lowering her voice to a professional tenor. "Black Investigations. How may I help you?"

"Hi, yes, this is Special Agent Autumn Trent," her best friend's tone bubbled with playfulness, "and I think I'm being followed. This man, who *claims* his name is Aiden, is everywhere I go. He was at my apartment when I left for work, and now...he's at my *job*. Please. Help me."

Twirling in her rolling chair, Winter didn't miss a beat. "Ah. I think I can solve this mystery without lifting a finger. You see, Agent Trent, you made the ill-advised decision to fall in love with your boss. So, that Aiden guy? He's your boyfriend *and* your workplace superior, and I doubt he'll be leaving you alone anytime soon. In layman's terms, you're screwed."

Autumn's gasp filled the room. "Hey! No need to bring my sex life into this."

Winter slapped a hand over her eyes. "Wow. I really did not need that visual of Aiden in my head, like, ever."

The belly laugh her friend released across the airwaves served as a balm for all of Winter's anxiety. "See? You've already solved your first case. You're a natural."

Winter didn't attempt to fight the wave of melancholy that swept over her. She'd only left Richmond nine days ago and yet already missed Autumn something fierce. "If I ever need backup, I'm flying you in."

"You'd better." Autumn's voice wavered a bit, betraying her own emotions. "I'd never forgive you if you didn't."

The other woman's fierce loyalty had originally caught Winter by surprise. Autumn was the first real best friend she'd made in twenty-eight years of life on planet Earth. Aside from Noah, Winter trusted no one more, and the physical distance separating them now resonated as a painful stab deep in her chest. "Everybody okay?"

Winter needed to get to work, but at the moment, concerns about what the Richmond team had endured over the last six months overrode all else. None of her former teammates had emerged unscathed from their last major case together in August. That shitshow had started with the kidnapping and torture of Autumn's long-lost sister and ended in the betrayal and death of one of their fellow agents.

"Fine. Good." Autumn was probably bobbing her head, attempting to reassure herself along with Winter. "And you? You gonna make it out there in God's country?"

Glancing out a tall window facing their spacious backyard, Winter didn't hesitate to answer. "I'll be just fine, but I'm already missing you like crazy."

After a quiet moment, Autumn sniffed. "Ditto. I gotta get to work. Being the boss's girlfriend apparently doesn't mean you get an extra-long lunch break. But I thought, as someone who knows and loves you, I'd take it upon myself to tell you on your first day that you're going to kick major ass."

Winter swallowed the lump in her throat. "I'll call you soon."

Autumn gave a faux haughty snort. "You better."

It was as though Autumn Trent had read her emotional state from fifteen hundred miles away. Placing the phone back on the desk, Winter admitted to herself that, after everything the two of them had experienced—together or otherwise—she wouldn't be surprised if Autumn *had* distance-analyzed her.

Just like Winter, her best friend's hellish backstory included emergency brain surgery as a child. Autumn had even gained an otherworldly ability following her operation too…like Winter, yet different. Autumn's gift didn't include migraines, visions, or glowing red clues. Instead, she could garner the emotional state of any individual with the simple touch of her hand.

Gift or curse? That's the question we will never fully be able to answer.

A sudden fit of restlessness seized her. Computer hunting wasn't exactly going her way, and she'd never enjoyed sitting still for long periods of time. Fieldwork was her jam. Getting out in the field was her best bet to obtain video footage of Fitz and Sandra together, and Winter needed to meet with the people who had, or by their own claim had most certainly not, spoken to both of them together.

Stuffing the photos into a folder, Winter bolted from the chair and grabbed her messenger bag.

If Mahoney was telling the god's honest truth, then a lot of people were lying like dogs…and lies could only survive for so long out in the open air.

7

The vast blue Texas sky soothed Fitz's nerves as he steered the flashy little sports car down the highway. After spending the last few hours trying—and failing—to occupy his mind with anything other than the plight of his missing girlfriend, the echoes of his pacing feet throughout his empty house had finally driven him to leave.

He'd needed to get out. Breathe some fresh air.

The thought of lounging around doing nothing all day while Winter Black investigated Sandra's disappearance had begun to make him as crazy as everyone assumed he already was. He'd taken leave from the stockbroker firm he owned due to his inability to concentrate on business, and all that free time was backfiring.

His parents only lived an hour away in Huntstown, Texas, and despite their growing concern about his mental state, the idea of spending the afternoon in his childhood home was comforting. Maybe there, he could pretend for five seconds that everything was fine. Make-believe that an entire human hadn't just evaporated out of his life like a cloud of cigarette smoke drifting away on a breeze.

Blasting Pearl Jam through the Porsche speakers, Fitz flew down the highway and tried to pretend he was on his way to a party to throw back some beers with his buddies. There'd be harder stuff to snort or eat in the back rooms—there always was—and plenty of hotties to cuddle up with. He'd binge his way into euphoria and end the night with a blackout, waking the next morning and resuming life fit as a fiddle...with the aid of an upper or two or ten.

The next night would follow the same schedule.

"You're not twenty-five anymore, dipshit." Fitz murmured the words while Eddie Vedder crooned on about finding a better man. "Grow the fuck up. *Grow the fuck up.*"

As he crossed into the Huntstown city limits, Fitz was positive that nothing had changed in the uptight land of corporate assholes since his last visit. Most of the men who lived in this dandy jewel of a town believed themselves to be extraordinarily successful, but their real talent was never so well displayed as when they acted like dicks toward their nauseating Stepford wives.

Turning onto his parents' lane, Fitz braked and waited for the massive metal gate to swing open while the aging guard sat in the kiosk and raked Fitz with a disdainful glare.

Good ole Ralph. Hates me just as much now as he ever did.

Considering the dozens of times Fitz had snuck past Ralph's ever-watchful eye as a rule-shunning teen and the blistering lectures Warren Fitzgerald had delivered to the guard for "allowing" such shenanigans to occur, Fitz didn't blame the man.

He'd been a little shit as an adolescent. And admittedly, not much had changed in the two decades since then.

But Sandra. I was changing for Sandra. I'd do anything for her.

Fitz parked the Porsche and walked up to the estate's wraparound porch. His mother answered the ring, which was a task she seldom took upon herself unless she was passing by the expansive double-door entrance at the precise second the bell chimed, though she rarely opened the door under those circumstances either. Yet there she was, dolled up in a hot pink "day dress" as she liked to call them. They were really just less formal evening gowns, with his mom modeling a different ridiculous ensemble every single day.

Laurel Fitzgerald lived her life prepared for the red carpet at a movie premiere. Her footwear always boasted impractical high heels. She never left her room without her platinum-blonde locks styled to perfection and a professional makeup job covering every inch of her natural face.

"Fitzy!" She stood on her tiptoes, and he bent down so she could kiss his cheek. "I had no idea you were stopping by today. Come. Have some tea with your mother. Can you believe it's nearly three o'clock in the afternoon, and I haven't had a single sip of my blackberry oolong? Scandalous."

Clacking her way across the marble floors, Laurel didn't seem to notice or care if her youngest child followed or not. Fitz battled the wave of resentment he'd fought since childhood as he trailed behind, wishing he could tell her that truly scandalous was the activity he'd caught her performing on the pool boy fifteen years ago.

No one gave a single shit about her oolong consumption.

"Where's Dad?" Fitz dropped onto the floral settee in his mother's sitting room while she busied herself with china cups and pitchers that the maid had set out in meticulous order. "Still locked in his office and drowning in denial over his retirement?"

Laurel clucked her tongue. "Don't make fun of your father, dear. It's unbecoming. He said he had some stocks and bonds or something very important like that to go over today. I never ask for too much information. You know all that serious business goes over my head."

Accepting the tiny cup she offered, Fitz decided to do something he rarely dared under his parents' roof. He called bullshit. "Not much of anything seemed to go over your head when you graduated summa cum laude from Yale with a bachelor's degree."

For a heartbeat or two, his mother's congenial demeanor, which she'd worn like sticky-sweet faux armor for the entirety of his life, cracked. Narrowing her blue eyes, she sipped oolong before making the declaration he'd anticipated. "You know I gave up all that nonsense when your sister came along. Best decision of my life."

Fitz grimaced and tasted his own tea. What he knew was that his mother deeply resented his older sister, Laurel-Anne, for existing at all. Making the matter worse, Laurel-Anne had cruised through high school and practically flown through her doctorate of psychiatry, the exact degree Laurel had pursued before meeting Warren Fitzgerald and getting knocked up with a baby she'd never wanted.

"Right." Fitz chugged the contents of his cup in one gulp. "How is Laurel-Anne these days?"

His mother arched a perfectly tweezed brow. "Well, you would know if you ever checked in on her. I don't approve of this distance you two have developed over the years. It isn't healthy. If hell freezes over one day and you both actually produce a few grandchildren, you'll want them to be close."

The smile on her face didn't fool Fitz, just like her dulcet tones did nothing to camouflage the pointed sentiment. It drove his mother batshit insane that neither of her offspring had provided her with an outlet for her focus aside from the ever-deepening wrinkles in her forehead, the rising cost of Botox, and her unfulfilled dreams.

Fitz set his cup in the dainty saucer and leaned back against the stiff velvet couch. "I was actually considering all of that. Settling down. A family. I could see myself having that with Sandra. But now I—"

"Oh, Fitzy." Laurel Fitzgerald waved his words away like she was shooing a fly. "Let's not spoil the afternoon with all that silliness. Please? For your mother's sake?"

Pure anger boiled in his belly. He wasn't supposed to talk about his girlfriend, whom he'd realized was the love of his life before she went missing, because doing so would upset his mother.

I mean, who gives a shit how I'm feeling? I'm just your child. No big. Just the fruit of your damn loins who lost the only woman I've ever loved. No, really, Mom, don't worry about all that. I'll be fine.

There were many good reasons why Fitz hadn't yet introduced Sandra to his parents, and today, his mother seemed hell-bent on reminding him of every single one. Dipping his head in acquiescence, he managed a small smile. "Sure. Let's talk about something else."

Warren and Laurel didn't believe that Sandra was real. His mother had been the first to pose the possibility that perhaps his girlfriend was the result of a hallucinogenic episode gone wrong. Little Fitzy had always gambled around a bit too much with the recreational substances, after all.

His father had declared that the woman was one of Fitz's many whores who'd probably played his son like a fiddle and taken off, and that Fitz was lucky he hadn't lost part of his fortune in the ruse.

Fitz had always been the prankster. The problem child. The pain-in-the-ass younger brother. The missing-girlfriend story wasn't his first far-fetched tale, and it wouldn't be the last.

Between the two of them, Fitz's parents had agreed that, at best, the matter was an embarrassing misunderstanding that should be kept quiet for the sake of the Fitzgerald family's good name. And at worst, well…they refused to entertain that thought.

"What should we talk about? What's the latest gossip?"

Resting his chin on his hand, Fitz feigned interest in the next words to pass his mother's perfectly lined lips.

Laurel wasn't stupid enough to buy his act, but she was more than willing to pretend. In her mind, any deception undertaken to steer clear of Fitz's latest debacle was acceptable. The topic of "Sandra Smith's disappearing act" was to be avoided like the damn plague.

His mother tsked him yet again. "You know how I feel about gossip."

Fitz held his tongue. Sure, he knew how his mother felt about gossip. She needed it like the air she breathed…unless the subject involved her.

She took another tiny sip of oolong and brightened. "Oh, I know something you might find interesting, though." He very much doubted that but gave her an encouraging nod, nevertheless. "This morning, our groundskeeper found three dead rats on the edge of the estate property. Three. Just lying in a row on the grass near the backroad entry like some sort of group suicide."

Fitz's teeth snapped together with so much force he was surprised he didn't bite through his tongue. In order to stop his hands from shaking, he had to clench them together in his lap.

"What?"

His voice rasped like sandpaper against wood, but if his mother noted anything off about his behavior, she didn't comment. With a delicate shudder, she refilled her teacup. "Of course, he disposed of them immediately. He mentioned that their necks appeared to be broken. Isn't that the strangest thing? Well, as I'm sure you can imagine, I called the exterminator right away. He's combing the property as we speak."

Panic swelled in Fitz's chest as he envisioned the dead rat he'd found earlier in the day on the edge of *his* property. If he told his mother about the coincidence, she *might* begin to believe that something sinister—and very much real—was happening.

She might also become even more convinced that he was losing his mind.

"Rats." Laurel shook her blonde head and gazed into her tea. "Deplorable. The last thing your father will stand for is a rodent infestation. He's a very busy man. All will be well, though. That's why we have exterminators. After all, someone has to keep the vermin at bay."

With another delicate shudder, she resumed sipping her tea as though nothing happened, switching topics to a bit of gossip she'd heard about a neighbor's daughter entering rehab.

Fitz tuned her out. His mind was too busy rewinding one of her previous statements.

"...he mentioned that their necks appeared to be broken. Isn't that the strangest thing..."

Picturing Sandra's lifeless body sprawled across his driveway when he returned home with her neck twisted at an unfixable angle, Fitz mumbled a hasty "excuse me" before sprinting for the nearest bathroom and vomiting all over his parents' spotless porcelain throne.

8

Peaceful Acres Hospice Care was a short drive from Winter's subdivision, and the moniker proved accurate. Despite its location in the middle of a not-so-quiet part of Austin's metro area, the facility sat on a large, wooded lot full of scenic views and boasted its own lake.

Soft, rounded stone walls gave the building a resort vibe, and for a split second, Winter forgot that she was visiting a place where sick people went to die. Shaking off the morbid thought, she crossed the parking lot with confident strides.

A few minutes with the right person inside should clear up Fitz's dilemma in no time. With a little luck, she'd wrap up the case by dinner.

"Hello!" A perky brunette bounced up from a desk chair when Winter cleared the front doors. "Welcome to Peaceful Acres Hospice Care, where we make every moment count. I'm Poppy. How can I help you today?"

Winter's own freakish existence meant little creeped her out these days, but she couldn't deny the chill racing down her spine at the paradoxically cheerful welcome. *Maybe Poppy missed the memo about the whole people dying thing.*

A quick flash of her P.I. license and former federal agent credentials sobered the receptionist up pronto. "Winter Black. Private Investigator. I'm looking to establish a rather basic fact for a client. He says he was here visiting a Patricia Smith on two specific dates. Assuming you have a visitor's log, I'd be grateful if you'd let me have a peek."

Poppy tapped a finger to her pointed chin. "Well, you're asking for confidential information, but..." her hazel eyes swept the empty reception area before sparkling with excitement, "holy cow. A federal agent walking through the doors. Monday afternoons will never be the same again."

She reached across her desk and plopped a thick sign-in book on the counter between them.

Winter slid the book closer. She wasn't sure Poppy understood the "former" aspect of her federal I.D., but she also wasn't about to waste the opportunity for an easy fix to prove or disprove Fitz's sanity. As she flipped through the pages in search of November thirteenth and December eleventh, Poppy's commentary provided a chirpy soundtrack.

Like a bird. On amphetamines.

"...and I wanted to find a place to work where I felt like I was making a difference, you know? This first week has been all the confirmation I needed. If I can bring just one smile to a single patient's face—"

Poppy's singsong blabbering cut without warning.

Uh oh. That's not a good sign.

Sensing a disturbance in the atmosphere, Winter lifted her head. Sure enough, a troubled expression froze the receptionist's features in place.

Winter paused her page flipping. "Is everything all right?"

Poppy sank back into the desk chair and pressed both hands to her chest. "Y-yes. It's just that I think I know why you're here. The only thing about Peaceful Acres that bothered me at all this first week was when one of the nurses told me about a man, Mr. Fitzgerald, I believe, who busted in here the day before I started and just went off shouting at everyone."

Not so much as flinching, Winter waited for Poppy to continue as she was sure there was more.

The receptionist leaned closer, dropping her voice to a conspiratorial volume. "Rumor has it, he was having a nervous breakdown, insisting he knew one of our patients or something and getting almost *violently* angry when the poor woman tried to tell him she'd never met him before. From what I was told, Dr. Newberry had to threaten to call the police just to get him to leave. You're here for *him*, aren't you?"

Seeing no reason to deny the truth, Winter nodded. "I am. Proving whether or not he was here when he claimed to be back in October and November seems easy enough."

Winter didn't add that Fitz had conveniently left out the heated nature of his most recent visit to Peaceful Acres a week ago. The bastard.

Bobbing her head up and down like her neck was one giant spring, Poppy paid rapt attention as Winter continued rifling through the pages to find the correct dates. The woman tipped the obnoxious side of the scale, but nothing about her roused Winter's suspicions that she was part of a grand scheme to take down Mahoney Fitzgerald.

Besides, if Poppy really had started the job just a week ago, she would have missed Fitz's visits—even the final one —altogether.

Winter located the sign-in for November thirteenth. Using her finger as a placeholder, she scanned each name, line by line. When that day produced no results, she paged ahead to December and repeated the process. Too many names to remember flashed before Winter's eyes, none of them belonging to Fitz.

Lost in thought, Winter tapped a finger against the paper. Maybe he'd signed in on the wrong page or left a wonky, illegible signature? That mistake, coupled with another misunderstanding, could explain the entire mess.

Or...in addition to cancer, maybe Sandra's mother suffered from the onset of some type of dementia. Or maybe the employees Fitz had met during his two visits with Sandra were absent on the day he'd returned to ask Patricia about her missing daughter.

Surely there was a reasonable explanation for her client's narrative other than the one suggesting he'd lost his damn mind. If such an explanation did exist, though, Winter had yet to discover it.

Something else she had yet to discover? Fitz's signature. It was nowhere to be found.

Poppy released an empathetic sigh. "He's not in there, huh." She twirled her pen back and forth, watching Winter's every move with unnerving dedication.

Winter gestured to the pair of computers sitting in front of Poppy. "Does Peaceful Acres keep any digital records of visitors in addition to the sign-in book?"

The receptionist shook her head with a frown. "I'm afraid not. They're old-school here."

Frustration rising in her chest, Winter's fingers moved faster, tearing through the book as she searched the entire last year for any sign of a "Sandra Smith." The woman would have been visiting her dying mother on a semi-regular basis and certainly on the specific dates that Fitz had listed. Sandra wouldn't send her new boyfriend to meet Patricia Smith alone.

The name never made an appearance, but Winter wasn't

ready to quit just yet. "To my understanding, Peaceful Acres has one residing doctor, yes?"

Poppy's rampant head bobbing resumed. "Absolutely. Dr. Newberry. We do have other specialists visit the patients based on their individual diagnoses and prescribed treatments, but Dr. Newberry runs this place all by himself. I could see if he has a free minute to speak with you?"

Honey caught more flies, and Winter had no problem spreading the sweet stuff like butter. "It's like you're reading my mind. I would love to have a chat with Dr. Newberry. Thank you."

Nearly bouncing with happiness at the mild flattery of a —former—federal agent in the flesh, Poppy tapped a button on her desk phone. "Dr. Newberry?"

"Yes, Poppy. What is it?" Dr. Newberry's deep voice was brisk but not unkind through the speaker.

Poppy grinned and puffed out her chest. "I have an FBI agent here who would like to speak with you if you have a moment."

The receptionist's giddy announcement managed to relay very little of the actual situation to the doctor. Plus, her statement was inaccurate.

Winter didn't bother correcting her. Maybe the exaggeration would speed up the process.

"I see." If he was at all flustered by the news of a Fed hanging out in the waiting area, Dr. Newberry's cool tone relayed none of the anxiety. "I'll be right there."

With a triumphant croak, Poppy waved a pencil to her right. "He'll be coming through that door, and I'll introduce you."

Mere seconds passed before a thin man in a white lab coat with prominent circles under his eyes and gray-streaked brown hair burst into the reception area. Homing in on Winter with a concerned crease between his eyes, the doctor had no chance to speak before Poppy followed through on her promise. "Dr. Newberry, this is Winter Black. She's a private investigator and federal agent—"

"*Former* federal agent." Winter hated to interject but knew the distinction was necessary. Getting nailed for impersonating an FBI agent her first time out the gate as a P.I. did not rank highly on her to-do list. "You can just call me Winter."

"Okay then." Dr. Newberry offered his hand. "A pleasure to meet you, Winter. How is it that I can help you today?"

While Winter shook the doctor's clammy hand, Poppy settled dutifully back down behind the computer screen as though she had no interest in their discussion whatsoever.

Yeah, right.

"I'm here on behalf of Mr. Mahoney Fitzgerald. There seems to be a rather large misunderstanding taking place between him and—"

"No misunderstanding at all." The physician's eyebrows knitted together. "That lunatic bombarded my facility, pushed his way into poor Mrs. Smith's room, and terrified the living daylights out of a *dying woman* with stage four cancer."

Another torrent of annoyance rippled through Winter, not only over Fitz's behavior but also his failure to inform her of said behavior before she bumbled into Peaceful Acres like an idiot.

Crossing his arms, Dr. Newberry took a deep, slow breath before speaking. "I nearly resorted to calling in law enforcement, but Mr. Fitzgerald left of his own accord when the word 'police' was mentioned. I wouldn't be surprised if he has a record or outstanding warrants he's trying to avoid."

The wisest move to make at the moment was a complete and total shifting of gears. "Would Mrs. Smith be available to discuss the incident?" Winter glanced around the sparse reception area. "Her take on what happened could shed some valuable light on the situation."

To her surprise, Dr. Newberry didn't hesitate before inclining his head. "I'll check on her. If you'll excuse me for a moment."

The doctor strode toward one of the many hallways. As soon as he disappeared around the bend, Poppy draped herself across the desk. "You see? You see how upset he got? One of the nurses told me Dr. Newberry never gets worked up about anything. That's how bad that little visit with Mr. Fitzgerald went."

Winter suspected that "one of the nurses" had told Poppy many things, and given the opportunity, the receptionist could spend a full day elaborating on those tales. As if to prove her right, the other woman started prattling on about a time when that same gossip source caught a patient climbing into a toilet to take a bath.

She uttered a silent *thank you* when Dr. Newberry's tall form reappeared on the horizon and prevented the story-time session from escalating.

"I'm sorry." He clasped his hands together. "She's sound asleep. Unfortunately, that's Mrs. Smith's norm these days. I'm hesitant to rouse her and disturb her peace of mind. Patricia's waking hours are often spent in excruciating pain."

The argument fizzled on Winter's tongue. Nope. Nuh-uh. Case or no case, she wasn't about to interrupt a dying woman's tranquil slumber. She'd need to find another way.

While she debated between scheduling a date to visit Mrs. Smith or performing repeated drop-ins until she lucked into a time when Sandra's "mother" was awake, Dr. Newberry slipped behind the reception desk and maneuvered the mouse. "Maybe this will help you. What days did Mr. Fitzgerald claim to have visited Peaceful Acres?"

A glimmer of optimism sparked in Winter's chest. "November thirteenth and December eleventh."

Tapping filled the room as Dr. Newberry's fingers flew across the keyboard. He stepped back and waved a hand toward the screen. "I've pulled up the camera footage from both dates. Our security surveillance covers the front door, the reception desk, and the hallway leading to Mrs. Smith's room. Feel free to peruse."

Taking the seat offered to her, Winter spent the next hour combing through all the footage with an eagle eye, Poppy providing commentary the entire time. No Fitz. She replayed the files at a slower speed. Still nada.

Fitz was never here.

Poppy let out a sympathetic huff from her position beside Winter. "That's weird, isn't it?"

Winter was saved from answering when Dr. Newberry returned. "Find anything?"

Poppy was shaking her head before Winter could even open her mouth. "Nothing at all. Craziest thing I've ever heard of."

Winter hoped her cheeks weren't as red as they felt. "But I appreciate you allowing me to look."

Dr. Newberry rubbed his chin. "You seem like a sharp young woman. Undoubtedly so, if you worked as a federal agent. I'm sorry to tell you, but there's nothing to see. The sole revelation you'll find here is that Mahoney Fitzgerald is a sad and disturbed individual. He doesn't need a private investigator...he needs professional help."

After thanking both the doctor and Poppy, Winter left the care center with doubt creeping through her mind.

Was Dr. Newberry right? Had excitement over an intriguing case led Winter's instincts astray her very first time working as a P.I.?

9

Regardless of its reputation for being the hallmark of happy families everywhere, dinnertime had become the most exhausting event of my day.

I sat opposite my husband in the high-backed chair, tucked into my usual place at the hand carved Bubinga dining table that easily seated twenty. The oversized capacity only served to make our little trio that much sadder. We clustered at one end like the loser guests at a wedding, the remaining empty stretch of wood a stark reminder of all the dinner parties we'd never host.

Even in the twenty-first century, people still acted like disabilities were contagious.

As my husband shared a work story in his usual soft, soothing tones, my chin nodded toward my chest.

"Honey, are you feeling okay?"

His slight increase in volume jarred me awake. I met his concerned frown with a reassuring smile. "I'm fine. I just didn't sleep that well last night. Go on, finish telling me about that client."

He started talking again while I did my best to stay alert.

Aware that I'd been doing too much—bleeding myself dry—I still had a role to play and an elite standard of care to provide for Wally. My son wouldn't suffer because of my new extracurricular activities.

Beside me, the crystal chandelier turned Wally's red hair into a luminous blaze. My heart squeezed at the intent expression on his pale face as he read his father's lips.

Chef emerged from the designer kitchen to serve an exquisite Beef Wellington, inspiring my husband to praise the dish for the duration of our half hour meal. Meanwhile, Wally was more enthralled with the Duchess potatoes, and I focused on the basic tasks of responding to every coo my son made and not dozing off in my chair.

The ruse was catching up with me now. Excusing myself and escaping to a small parlor in the back of the house as soon as possible, I poured a glass of one-hundred-dollar-per-bottle Cabernet and sank into the plush velvet of an armchair. All I needed was a quiet fifteen minutes to recharge or recalibrate. Re-anything.

A temporary reprieve from the rodents...human and otherwise.

"You little rat." Mumbling, I rested my cheek against the supple upholstery. "Look what you made me do..."

They deserved what they were getting. I was doing the right thing. Carrying out justice. Making them—I yawned as my lids grew heavier and heavier—making them all pay...

My heart hammered under my shirt as I dashed for the towering structure ahead. There was nowhere to hide on the elementary school playground, yet I'd run off like an idiot anyway. Ms. Kelley, our recess attendant, couldn't even see us now, and I didn't have any friends to stick up for me.

No one was going to help me out of this.

Rubber smacked against my cheek, knocking my head into the slide that I'd attempted to hide beneath. Bobby Burner never missed a dodgeball throw. Our gym teacher was always saying what a good arm Bobby had on him.

This wasn't gym class, though, and Bobby wasn't aiming for the teacher's approval. Instead, he'd taken on the challenge of knocking me out altogether.

"Take that, Gaggy von Dork!"

Bobby's next throw slammed into my ear. An excruciating ringing reverberated deep inside my brain as I crashed down into the wood chips, their jagged edges biting into my palms.

Pulling myself onto my hands and knees, I lifted my head, determined to fight back. Instead, I faced the arrival of Bobby's two best friends. The tallest boy—the leader of all the bullies and the meanest by far—barreled toward me with an evil grin and outstretched hands.

I stumbled to my feet and attempted to flee, but my blurred vision and limp legs fought against me. Before I could do anything at all, the head bully clutched at my pants, yanking them down. The small crowd of classmates that had gathered around watched as warm liquid gushed down my legs.

The bully pointed and howled with laughter. "Look at Gaggy von Dork...she peed herself!"

Answering laughter rose to a thunderous roar as I tugged my wet pants back up.

As I dripped onto the wood chips, hot, dark rage bubbled up in my throat, burning my humiliation away. I hated that jerk. I hated him more than anyone or anything in the whole entire world.

Ms. Kelley's voice boomed across the playground. "You kids get away from her! Right this instant!"

She was coming to my rescue, but that was too little, too late. This kid was going to pay for what he'd done to me. For my humiliation.

Still wobbly on my feet, I charged him, winding a fist back and socking him straight in the nose. Blood gushed from his face, as bright red as the paint in our teacher's art supplies.

The sight was the prettiest thing I'd ever seen. Beautiful artwork spraying from the face of an ugly, disgusting, horrible little—

Without warning, the scene changed, and I stood in the upstairs hallway of my childhood home. My father stomped toward me, a belt swinging from one hand. The whites of his eyes cracked with bulging red veins.

I froze in terror, sure that I was about to die as he shrieked with fury. "You little rat! Making a fool out of me in front of the entire town! You little disobedient rat!"

My mother flew up the stairs, her face flushed with panic as she took in the scene.

I whimpered in relief. She was coming to save me. She was coming to—

Bzzzz. Bzzzz.

Jolted awake and gasping for breath, I read the number on my phone screen as the vibrating alert persisted. This wasn't a call I'd been expecting.

I hit accept and smashed the phone to my ear, my immediate anger at the caller's audacity emitting as a hiss. "You've got to be kidding—"

"Listen to me!" The frantic tone caught me off guard. "We have a problem."

My fingertips numbed as fear pulsed an icy river through me. A moment later, I was back in control. Most problems were fixable with resources like ours. Wally's health was one of the few exceptions.

I'd come too far not to finish now. Whatever had gone wrong, I'd find a solution.

Even if that meant adding more names to my hitlist.

"Calm down and start at the beginning."

10

A luminescent glow spilled onto the sidewalk as Winter walked up from the driveway and into her new home. Warm, inviting light shone in similar fashion throughout the surrounding neighborhood, inspiring an echoing warmth in Winter's soul.

A pair of basset hounds and their elderly owners, Abraham and Ardis Ogilvie, were out for an evening stroll, and Winter lifted a hand of acknowledgment as they approached. Decked out in matching U.T. sweatshirts, the Ogilvies were the oldest and friendliest couple on the block. Their stumpy-legged, Dumbo-eared hounds, Bonnie and Clyde, were equally ancient and amiable.

Winter loved them all. And not just because Ardis had brought Winter and Noah a steaming burrito casserole the night of their arrival while Abraham filled them in on all the best local fishing spots.

"I'm making pies tomorrow." Ardis offered the tantalizing information while Clyde marked the closest streetlamp. "Do you and that husband of yours have any favorite flavors?"

Grinning, Winter imagined the look on Noah's face when

he returned home to a freshly baked pie the following evening. "Blueberry. Definitely blueberry."

Ardis's confident nod seemed to indicate that she'd predicted as much. "Blueberry it is."

Between Gramma Beth's cooking and Ardis Ogilvie's kindness, Winter was going to gain a truckload of proud Texan weight in no time. Noah, of course, wouldn't gain a pound. He'd inherited some obscure gene reserved for actual Texans that allowed him to eat like a horse while staying as fit as a Greek god.

As the Ogilvies strolled away, Winter mounted the porch steps, eager to see that husband of hers.

"Darlin'?" Noah's greeting carried down the hall from the kitchen. "I'd like to tell you that there's a homecooked meal waiting for you, but I'm no Gramma Beth."

In the cozy dining area, two neat place settings adorned their four-seater table. Noah flashed a sheepish grin as he pointed at the microwave and the empty frozen dinner boxes stacked on the counter beneath it.

He lifted a shoulder. "Give me...thirty-four more seconds, and this fettuccini Alfredo is all yours."

Winter strode over and planted a kiss on his cheek. "Sounds perfect."

Fifteen minutes and two mostly unfrozen plates of pasta later, tales of their first day experiences began to flow. Winter's surprise over the Texas missing persons statistics was matched by Noah's intrigue at the evaporated girlfriend of Mahoney Fitzgerald.

The cases weren't related, but they both fell into the same realm. AWOL human beings.

"I think," Noah stacked their dirty plates together, "that this Fitzgerald guy might be your first up-close glimpse of a Texas-sized mental breakdown. I get that you're obligated to act as though you believe him since he's paying you to do exactly that, but there has to be a huge part of you that presumes the guy is off his rocker, right?"

Winter traced a finger through the condensation on her water glass. "You would think so. Fitz's claims certainly fall into the 'might be a nutjob' category...but I was drawn to this case. That's the reason I took it to begin with. When have I ever been drawn to something for no reason?"

Leaning against the counter, Noah held up both hands. "I definitely have no argument for that. If your weirdo sixth-sense radar is going off, I'm the last person to challenge it. Have you had any headaches or anything?"

That was her husband's tactful way of asking if she'd experienced any red glows or blackout visions to provide a little magical enlightenment regarding Fitz's case. "Nope. I'm not so sure my freak abilities made the move with us."

Noah set down the fork he'd been scrubbing, locking his dark green eyes on Winter. "Would that be such a bad thing? If somehow...you'd left that part of your life behind too?"

His hopeful tone echoed her own, but Winter's gut told her she was far from free of her curse. "I'd love nothing more, but I'm not banking on any supernatural emancipation just yet."

She quashed the disappointed twinge that surfaced. *Being free from Justin is reward enough. Anything else is cake.*

Noah finished washing and returned to the table, sinking into his empty chair. "I don't blame you, darlin'."

Both of them were aware of the potential backlash involved in setting expectations...high or otherwise.

Winter's mind returned to Fitz's case. No matter what the outcome, her new client's distress wasn't faked. "One thing I keep reminding myself about is the fact that even if Fitz is insane, to him, this is all very real. Can you imagine how that would feel? You wake up one day, and poof, I'm just gone. Vanished without a trace. And when you go to ask my family about it, they claim they have no idea who you're talking about because I don't *exist*."

Noah flinched, his usually smiling mouth downturned into a pained expression. "Well. I guess I probably wouldn't feel like existin' myself at that point. Don't you go pulling a Sandra Smith on me."

Winter rose and circled the table, settling onto Noah's lap and wrapping her arms around his neck. "There's no doubt in my mind that you'd find me even if I evaporated right in front of you."

He returned the hug and nuzzled her neck. "Damn straight."

Though the newlywed smooching session that followed threatened to wipe the case clear from her brain, Winter couldn't let her mind shut down so soon. Pulling back, she checked the time on her phone. "I wanna go drive by the apartment building where Sandra supposedly lived. Maybe stop in at the café that Fitz says he and Sandra frequented as a pair. It's not even eight yet."

Noah chuckled as he ruffled her hair. "You're not on the Bureau's clock anymore. This is when you leave work at work and go catch an episode of *The Bachelor* or something. On the couch."

Laughter bubbled up in her throat as she stood and searched for her purse. "Our couch is covered in boxes, and our television isn't even hooked up yet. Besides, you know that's not how I operate. I may not be on the Bureau's clock, but I'm still on Winter Black's schedule."

Spasming into a fit of exaggerated coughs, Noah held up his ring finger. "Oh. Excuse me. I think you meant to say Winter Black-*Dalton*. Little flub up there, ma'am."

"Oops, my bad! How dare I?" Winter feigned a gasp of horror before breaking into a wide smile. "I'm going for a drive. Care to tag along?"

When Noah almost tripped over his own feet in his eagerness to follow her to the door, she laughed. The moral support was kind of nice, though. Even if this was her first official day of P.I. work as a solo detective, she didn't mind having her old partner in tow.

At some point, the guy had apparently grown on her. Go figure.

As they headed outside, Noah's earlier words about how he'd cope if she vanished drifted into her head.

"Well, I guess I probably wouldn't feel like existin' myself at that point."

A shiver fluttered over her skin. Telling herself to stop borrowing trouble, Winter brushed the sensation aside as she climbed into the big red truck Noah insisted on calling Beulah.

While her uneasiness subsided, the sensation never completely disappeared.

11

Noah performed a quick visual inspection while Winter parked. Sandra Smith's address led them to a three-story structure located in a tidy, well-lit neighborhood within the Austin city limits. The sun had already set, and the nearby streetlamps cast the building's whitewashed walls with a soft glow.

Clean sidewalks. Clipped shrubbery and trees. No men skulking around. Nothing whatsoever to indicate that this was a dangerous area where shady characters kidnapped innocent women and performed elaborate ruses to cover up their evil deeds.

Uneasiness gnawed at Noah's gut as he unclipped the seat belt. Despite Mahoney Fitzgerald managing to reel Winter into his case, Noah retained a healthy skepticism of his claims. Most of his concerns revolved around the man's mental health, but an even scarier possibility existed.

What if Fitzgerald wasn't off his rocker? What if he was rich, and bored, and stalking Winter as his new pastime...or worse? Winter wasn't Hollywood-celebrity famous, but she'd appeared in the news enough to garner a fanbase. And most individuals who became obsessed with a serial killer's sister were a few screws short themselves.

Noah would never come right out and say it, but he worried for Winter's safety. She was so hell-bent on solving her first case as a P.I. that she might have overlooked some serious red flags.

A dangerous calm descended over his body. *Maybe I need to meet this Mahoney guy. See how straight he keeps his story when there isn't a beautiful woman listening to him whine.*

Winter's elbow poked his ribs, snapping him free of his mulling. "Thoughts? It seems like this area is about as clean-cut as an urban residential neighborhood can be. Nothing visibly sketch at all."

"Agreed." Survival instincts prompted Noah to tweak his reflections before sharing them. If his wife could hear his over-protective, caveman musings, she'd rip him a new one. Newly-weds or not. "Everything appears on the up and up, but as you and I well know, that doesn't mean squat in the overall scheme of things. There could be eighteen meth labs and an illegal chicken fighting ring going on in that building as we speak."

She arched an eyebrow at him, the corners of her mouth twitching. "Meth labs and chicken fighting do often present as a pair."

"Right?" He peered out the windshield. "What was the apartment number again?"

"2G."

Making a quick calculation, Noah pointed toward the rear of the building. "Second floor. Toward the back. Nothing too complicated there. Have you considered just buzzing the people who live there now and trying to talk to them? It's not the coolest P.I. move ever, but it might work."

Winter shot the suggestion down with a firm shake of her head. "Fitz already did that, with horrible results. I don't want to piss the family off even more. Plus, I'm not ready to blow my cover yet. I might wind up needing to do a decent amount of surveillance here."

Recalling his long day of desk duty, Noah's legs twitched with the urge to jump out of the truck and sprint around the block just to get some exercise.

The creak of the driver's side door flying open indicated that Winter was equally antsy. "Fitz gave me the building code. We could probably take a quick look around the inside without anyone paying much attention. Just stay away from 2G."

"Yes, ma'am." He winked before scrambling out of his seat.

In street clothes, they blended in, strolling up the walkway hand in hand like any other couple. The goateed man who passed them on his way to the parking lot muttered a quiet, "Hey," and didn't spare them a second glance.

When they reached the entrance, Winter veered over to the digital keypad glowing on the wall while Noah tugged at the double doors. "Locked."

Winter nodded. "All right, Fitz, let's see if your code works."

She typed in the five-digit code. A loud buzzing emitted, followed by a click. Confusion mixed with a bit of awe twisted her features as she pulled the door open. "If someone is messing with Fitz and Sandra, they screwed up by leaving the security code the same. Fitz's possession of that detail gives his side of the story credibility."

He followed her into an unremarkable foyer, once again struck by how normal everything appeared. An elevator. A glass door panel that read "Main Office." A glowing red exit sign above a door marked with a staircase symbol. "It's possible that 'they' don't have access to the lock to make such a change."

"Or," Winter turned a slow circle in the middle of the entryway, "Fitz has been in the building, but he was so high he doesn't remember which woman he was with."

"Or maybe he was here with a man." With nothing out of the ordinary to inspect in the small lobby area, Noah crossed over to the metal mailbox grid dominating one wall. He scanned the names above each box. "I don't see a Smith listed anywhere. All you really have is Fitzgerald's word that Sandra Smith ever lived in that apartment. He could have gotten the number wrong. She could have lied about her name."

Winter braced her hands on her hips. "*Fitz* could be lying about her name, for that matter. Maybe he isn't crazy. Maybe he's just full of shit."

His jaw clenched. "For all we know, he could have come here and *killed* Sandra Smith." The direction of his conjectures continued their downward spiral. "Or he owns the whole damn building under an alias, and he's making the entire case up to stalk you. Have you considered the possibility that Fitz could be a serial killer?"

"Don't." Winter waved her index finger under his nose. "That thought has crossed my mind, and I can handle it if that's where this case leads me. It'd be far from my first encounter with a bona fide psychopath. I'm a big girl, Agent Dalton, and you're here as my companion and sounding board, not my bodyguard."

That *Agent Dalton* told Noah he was treading on dangerous ground.

Careful, buddy. Better back off before your newlywed butt is sleeping on the couch.

Adopting an easy grin, he swiped his knuckles over his

polo-clad chest and preened. "Whoa. Companion? Sounds important. I should have dressed nicer."

Winter's overly dramatic eye roll was the exact response he'd expected. "Yes. Your outfit is deplorable. I'm embarrassed to be seen with you. Can we focus now?"

"As you wish, darlin'. I mean, boss."

Winter snorted before walking down the hallway. Five doors faced each other on each side. None of them were cracked open or yielded any useful clues, so they hit the stairwell and repeated the process on the second floor. From the outside, the apartment marked 2G appeared identical to all the others.

The third floor was more of the same. Not so much as an interesting smudge on the walls or an odd wrinkle in the carpeting.

No security cameras either.

Noah shared that observation as they stepped into the elevator to ride instead of walk back down. "Unless they're the state-of-the-art fibers you can hide in the ceiling or something, I don't think there's any surveillance here at all."

Winter jabbed the button for the ground floor. "This building doesn't give off 'state of the art security' vibes. I'll leave a note for someone to call me on the office door and hope that the property manager takes the ASAP part of the message seriously."

Their descent stopped at the second floor. The doors slid open, allowing a twentysomething man with bleached blond hair that matched his pale skin and an "Ur Mom" shirt to board. He pushed the button and nodded. "Yo."

Noah echoed the absurd greeting with as much solemness as he could muster. "Yo." His wife's incredulous expression forced him to stare at his shoes to avoid laughing.

"You live on the second floor?"

Winter's voice yanked his head back up. If the other guy

was unnerved by her question, his face didn't show it. "Yeah, why? You thinking of moving in or something?"

The man's appreciative examination of his wife's legs made Noah want to smack him upside the head. More because it was a douche move than out of any concern for his wife's well-being. If Q-tip head stepped out of line, she'd flatten him like a pancake while Noah sat back and enjoyed the show.

Winter replied as a beep announced their arrival on the ground floor. "Yeah. A friend of mine used to live here and said it was pretty nice. Sandra Smith. Did you know her? Blonde, pretty. Lived in 2G."

The doors slid open, and Q-tip shrugged on his way out. "Sorry, not ringing a bell, but I don't hang with the other tenants. I got my own posse, you get what I'm sayin'?"

Noah was pretty sure he didn't get it. He also didn't care.

Winter's shoulders fell as she exited. "I do. Have a nice night."

"Word."

Together, they watched the resident swagger out of the building. Winter heaved a giant sigh. "Well, that was worthless."

"Oh, I don't know. I'm starting to think Sandra Smith might have taken off for parts unknown just to escape that dude."

Noah's grin broke free, earning him a playful shove. "Cute. Real cute. Here, let me leave my card, and then we can go."

He waited until her back was turned. "Word."

Her snicker echoed in the empty space.

As she scribbled out a note, Noah walked the perimeter and checked over every inch of the walls and ceiling. No hint of surveillance devices anywhere. "It's pretty unusual to have no cams anywhere, wouldn't you say?"

Winter finished taping her card to the door before motioning to the floor above them. "Not more unusual than an actual human woman vanishing into the ether. I mean, what's our standard for normal at this point?"

As he held the front door open, a fresh wave of doubt struck.

"Actual human woman" according to Mahoney Fitzgerald, who may have lost his marbles. Assuming he ever had any to begin with.

The notion tormented him during their short walk to the vehicle until Winter broke his train of thought with a suggestion. "Let's go get some coffee."

He blinked. "Caffeine? At this hour?"

She paused with one hand on the door. "Or we can check if that all-you-can-eat buffet down the street has an AARP discount."

"Smart-ass." As Noah ducked into the passenger seat, he couldn't help envisioning a long night of staring at the ceiling and cursing their ill-advised latte decision. Unlike Winter, he was expected to kick off the workday by a certain time.

Winter waited for him to buckle in before planting a sappy kiss on his cheek. "Don't worry, old man. We'll make yours decaf."

Even though he laughed along with the joke, a worry wormed its way into his head. Was this an indicator of things to come? The two of them, working different jobs on different schedules?

What if the trade-off for reducing Virginia-related stress by moving to Texas was heaping unintentional strain on their marriage?

We'll work it out.

They had to.

12

Cup and Go Café was set to close in fifteen minutes when Winter and Noah approached the entrance. Within walking distance from Sandra's apartment building, the restaurant was the place Fitz claimed that he and Sandra had frequented as a couple.

Winter caught Noah's eye before reaching for the door. "Remember, we're looking for a young server named Shay. Fitz said she waited on them more than once."

Noah nodded. "Copy that."

She entered first, perking up when the aroma of fresh coffee mixed with cinnamon and other spices reached her nose. Quaint wooden booths with rainbow-colored upholstery stretched along the walls, while little round tables with padded chairs filled in the middle.

Sliding into a booth near the front counter, Winter scrutinized the employee standing by the cash register. The woman had short, dark hair shaved up one side and a little gold stud in her nose.

"Not her," she murmured to Noah, who'd taken a seat across from her, "unless she's had a radical makeover since

Fitz was last here. He said Shay had long, dishwater blonde hair."

"What about the barista to her left?"

She pretended to peruse the menu above the counter before sneaking a peek, hope rising in her chest when she spotted the barista's messy bun. "Maybe. I wish one of them would turn so we could see if they're wearing name tags."

The barista finished wiping down a stainless-steel machine and turned to laugh at something the cashier said. Winter squinted at the black tag on her red polo and deflated. "Olivia. Rats."

Noah kicked her foot under the table. "Shh."

Within seconds, a server popped into view from some-where behind Winter's right shoulder. Her pasted-on smile did nothing to camouflage the bent posture and heavy eyes of an exhausted woman. "Hi. I'm Sue. Can I take your order?"

Even before the server introduced herself, Winter knew she wasn't Shay. The wrinkles creasing her forehead and fanning out from her eyes pegged her at fifty or older.

Deciding to make the most of the visit, Winter cast Noah a mischievous glance. "We'll take two mocha lattes with extra espresso, please."

As Sue ambled away, Noah groaned. "You and your broken decaf promises. I knew I couldn't trust you."

She stuck her tongue out at him while keeping a watchful eye on Sue. "I can't let you get sleepy on me. Drowsy counsel is no counsel at all."

He plucked a napkin from the holder and folded it into an airplane. "Be sure to remember that when I'm counseling you at three in the morning cuz I can't sleep."

"Duly noted."

Their playful bickering continued until Sue reapproached with two bowl-sized aqua cups. She set the steaming drinks in front of them and straightened. "Anything else for you folks?"

Winter was determined to gather at least a shred of helpful information from the evening's reconnaissance. "Actually, I was wondering when Shay's next shift is? I owe her a huge tip for the other day. Clumsy me dumped my entire latte on the floor, and she was such a sweetheart about cleaning it up. She deserves a special thank you."

A genuine smile stretched across the older woman's face. "Shay is the sweetest thing, I swear. She'll be in for the mid-shift tomorrow."

Winter battled a stab of disappointment. *Too bad she's not here now, but beggars can't be choosers.* "She really is a sweetie, right? Has she been working here a long time?"

She held her breath, hoping that the question wouldn't come across as too nosy. If it did, Sue didn't seem to notice. "Not long at all...I want to say, maybe three months or so? Long enough to become a favorite around here, though. Employees and customers both love her."

"I'm not surprised." *Three months.* Winter hid her rising excitement by lifting her cup and blowing on the steam. "Anyway, I won't keep you from getting ready to close up. Have a good one."

"You too."

Once the woman was out of earshot, Noah leaned over the table. "What is it? I can tell you're amped up by the sparkle in your eye."

This man knows me way too well.

Winter finished her sip of latte. "Three months. That's exactly how long Fitz says he was dating Sandra before she disappeared. Tell me that timeline doesn't seem like more than a coincidence?"

Noah sent his napkin airplane soaring an unimpressive two inches into the air before it collapsed between them. "It's suss for sure, but I'm thinking that security camera up there might be able to answer a question or two."

She followed his gaze to the security camera behind the cash register. "I'll drop in tomorrow during 'mid-shift' and try to speak with Shay. While I'm here, maybe I can see if the day manager will let me view the security footage for the last few months. If Shay denies ever meeting Fitz and Sandra, the camera might have a different story to tell."

"Or the footage will back up Shay's denial, just like the cameras at the hospice facility did, and you'll have more solid evidence that Fitzgerald is out of his damn mind."

After downing another few sips of mocha, Winter cocked her head. "Do you *want* him to be crazy? It seems like you're leaning hard in that direction."

Her husband reached across the table and squeezed her hand. "The sooner you know if this guy is playing you, the sooner you can drop him as a client."

The cashier called out and interrupted them. "I hate to hurry you folks, but we're closing shop in five minutes. You need to-go cups for the rest of those lattes?"

Before Winter could say yes, Noah shook his head. "No, we're good, thanks. My wife was just saying she was getting a little old to drink caffeine this late anyway."

His devilish grin informed Winter that he was entirely too pleased with himself. Narrowing her eyes, she returned his smile before tipping the cup back and downing the rest of her mocha.

When she replaced the empty cup in the saucer, Noah pretended to bow. "You win."

Her smile widened. "Don't worry. I know."

Shaking his head, Noah dropped enough money to cover the check and a generous tip on the table. He scooted out of the booth and held out his hand. "Ready?"

After debating downing the remaining half of his mocha

too, she accepted his hand and let him pull her up. She wrapped an arm around his waist as they exited the café. It went into position as if it belonged there.

Because it did.

Once they were outside and alone, Noah pressed a kiss to the top of her head. "I just want you to be safe, and working for a stupid-rich, drugged-out nutball doesn't really fall into the risk-free category."

She tickled his side. "Says the federal agent working in the Violent Crimes Division. Face it. Risk is our M.O."

Streetlights illuminated Noah's distressed expression, transforming his eyes into glowing green orbs. "Darlin', you say the word, and I'll find a different operation altogether."

He really means it too.

With a quick squeeze, Winter released him and headed for Beulah. Despite her husband's sweet offer, she doubted either of them would be pulling the trigger on changing their jobs anytime soon.

For better or worse, solving crimes was in their blood.

13

Fitz slumped on his couch, smoothing a hand over the leather cushion where Sandra used to sit. The hollow ache inside him grew. They'd spent most of their time together at his house, which was a veritable resort compared to her dinky apartment in the city.

It's not Sandra's apartment anymore. Maybe it was never Sandra's apartment to begin with. Maybe I'm actually having the nervous breakdown that everybody seems to believe I am.

"No!" He barked the declaration out loud despite being alone. "I'm not crazy. She's real. She was here."

To prove it, he swiped at his phone screen and pulled up the photos he'd snapped of Sandra during her visits. There weren't many, as she'd hated having her picture taken, but the few he did possess proved she existed. That she'd been in his house. Seated on his couch. Laughing. Smiling.

Real.

Fitz paused on an image of Sandra sitting on his patio wearing a baseball cap and sunglasses. The soft sheen of her skin gleamed like a lustrous pearl. On that particular day, he'd told her as much.

Sandra threw back her head, laughing as though he'd cracked the ultimate joke. "I remind you of a pearl? You have seen a real pearl before, right?"

"Yes." Fitz leaned to nuzzle her neck, reveling in the silken texture. "And you are by far more beautiful."

He lifted his head to silence her giggle with his lips. The kiss deepened, igniting a fire in them both. A few minutes later, he took her hand and led her to the bedroom...

His groin tightened at the memory of what came next. Sandra was the most passionate lover Fitz could ever remember sharing a bed with. Sex with her felt a little like being devoured. The experience was almost as if she stole pieces of his soul with every touch and planned to continue until she owned his entire body.

"I made love to you right here." Fitz slammed a fist into the cushions. "*Right here!*"

Fitz had shown his parents the images of Sandra, believing—initially—that Warren and Laurel Fitzgerald would back him up after viewing such clean-cut evidence.

Instead, they'd reacted with laughter. Unabashed laughter.

His father had claimed that a few shots of some blonde hussy on Fitz's sofa didn't make the rest of the elaborate tale true. Kinder but equally unconvinced, his mother had suggested that perhaps Fitz was getting his many lady friends mixed up.

Of course, she'd preferred that theory. That way, his mother could attribute Fitz's troubles to a partying, playboy lifestyle rather than deteriorating mental stability. While Laurel Fitzgerald might entertain a secret wish for her daughter to fail, the matriarch of their family was ill-equipped to handle her "Little Fitzy" succumbing to a nervous breakdown.

She needed him to be fine again so that *she* could be fine

again. Suffering of any sort was a phenomenon that Laurel Fitzgerald preferred for people to keep to themselves.

As Fitz's loving mother had informed him when he'd first insisted on relaying his current dilemma, *"Sharing distressing stories will only ruin someone else's peace of mind too. Why do such a cruel thing to an otherwise happy individual?"*

According to her, Fitz's behavior regarding Sandra's disappearance was downright selfish, and if he insisted on continuing to be miserable, he would have to do so alone.

Emotional support did not exist in the Fitzgerald family.

Closing his eyes, Fitz tried to envision either of his parents helping him search for Sandra, but the image evaded him. The notion was just too foreign.

He threw an arm over his eyes. "You did this to yourself."

All the years he'd spent lying to his parents and wreaking general havoc on the world around him had left a distinct "boy who cried wolf" cloud hanging over his head. For life.

He was a fuck-up. A goofball. Unreliable and impetuous.

That's why you hired a P.I. Let Winter Black do the work she's being paid to do and stop worrying about what Warren and Laurel believe.

Deciding to throw in the towel on the day, Fitz stood and headed for the digital lockbox near his front door. The property gates and all entrances were on lock twenty-four-seven, but lately, he'd experienced an uncontrollable urge to double check the security system before attempting to sleep.

After the device assured him of what he'd already known —that his property was shielded from any intruders and threats of harm—he headed to the foyer table where his housekeeper always left the mail in a neat stack.

On a normal night, he'd toss the random assortment of bills and advertisements into his briefcase for his assistant to deal with at work the following day. Taking time off meant that he'd need to handle the mail himself.

When he reached the table, more than the usual envelope pile awaited him. Sitting on the top of the pile was a plain white cardboard box with no return address.

Fear slithered down his spine.

What if it's a bomb?

Scrambling a step back, Fitz stared at the package while his heart pounded. "Okay, think this through. If someone is out to get me...blowing me up would be a great way to go about it. I should call the police."

As soon as he verbalized the thought, he started shaking his head. Right. Great idea. The cops would rush over and open the "bomb" for him. With his luck, the box would end up holding a scented candle or stuffed animal or maybe a giant purple dildo. Everyone would laugh at his psychotic paranoia over a harmless package.

Then you'll be on the police force's radar as a local lunatic, and your family will start packing your bags to ship you off to the insane asylum.

Thanks, but no thanks. "Screw it."

Fitz grabbed the package and marched into the kitchen. The dim light from the oven hood was enough for him to select a long, thin blade from the wooden block and slit the packing tape. When he peeled open the lid, he was ashamed by how badly his hands shook.

A second passed. Five seconds. Nothing ticked. Nothing exploded.

Relief over not blowing up into a million bloody pieces seeped through his body. *Aren't you glad you didn't call the cops?*

As his muscles relaxed, Fitz's curiosity over the contents of the package heightened. He pushed aside the thick brown packing paper and peered inside.

In the depths of the box was a group of long, thin objects that he couldn't quite make out.

"What the hell are those? Pencils? Why would anyone send pencils?"

Shaking his head, he carried the box over to the wall and flipped on the chandelier. The kitchen flooded with megawatt illumination, but it still took him a few moments to comprehend the sight before him.

"Those are...those are..."

A violent shudder racked his body. Acting on pure instinct, Fitz let out a bloodcurdling scream and chucked the box as far as he could.

Big mistake. The box flipped upside down in the air, freeing hundreds of wormlike entities to form a spectacular arc before they scattered across the polished marble floor.

Only the segmented pink gifts weren't worms at all...they were severed rat tails.

14

S louched behind the steering wheel in my parked van, I watched the windows of the white house for any signs of life. With its darker shutters, wide porch, and weepy live oaks, the home appeared as unassuming as all the rest on the quiet street.

I knew differently.

What was it about neat and tidy suburbia that made even individuals like me, who lived in veritable castles, envious? Unremarkable houses inhabited by unremarkable families. Kids riding their bikes too fast or skateboarding in the streets because they could. Middle-aged couples standing in their yards discussing the best awning replacement companies with genuine interest.

"And dogs. What is it about the middle class and dogs?"

Since arriving over an hour ago, I'd witnessed at least four of the slobbery beasts being taken for late-night walks. Thankfully, they hadn't witnessed me.

Between my tinted windows and the darkness of the late hour, I had no worries about staying hidden. I'd driven our minivan into town, aware that the vehicle alone would act as camouflage in a residential neighborhood.

No one was threatened by minivans. They were a soccer mom's trademark, and soccer moms didn't go around killing people.

A slow grin pulled at my lips, the first one all day. "Maybe they should. I'd watch that movie."

If for no other reason, the idea was pleasing because it punched a hole in the perfect canvas laid out before me. The upper middle class hid behind their monotonous lifestyles, using the painted image as a protective force field.

They were happy without being rich while unimpeded by the woes of being poor. Every day was predictable yet pleasant for its lack of surprise. No one expected greatness from suburbanites. Just...normal. Happy families living uneventful, sitcom-esque lives.

I called bullshit.

Any time four walls came together to make a home, chaos lived within. Perhaps the mayhem was of the quiet variety, like a high-functioning alcoholic parent who couldn't wait to be alone with the whiskey bottle every night. Or maybe it was the violent disarray of an abused wife who kept the makeup industry going with her constant need for cover-up.

Regardless, all homes and families came with their own private nightmares. The simpletons just possessed the best smokescreen. A luxury money couldn't buy.

An angry drumbeat started pounding through my head. "You thought you could hide away in the middle of nowheresville, Austin, like some kindergarten schoolteacher or plumber, but I found you, Agent Black."

Stupid bitch would ruin everything if I let her.

I wouldn't let her.

"If you're as smart as those articles try to make you

appear, you'll back off when you get my warning." I grinned as I thought about the little surprise she would soon discover. "I have enough on my plate without dealing with you."

If the federal agent-turned-private investigator continued to interfere, well...I'd just have to kill her.

When Winter Black and her husband pulled into their driveway an hour and a half ago, my parking spot half a block down had afforded me a decent view of the couple as they stood under their porch light.

She was gorgeous, of course. Even better than her pictures. Glossy, black hair glistened in the soft, incandescent glow against a face as pale as fresh milk. And her husband? Tall, dark, and ridiculously handsome.

Of course, he is. I should have expected nothing less.

I would have bet money that the asshole was an arrogant douche who'd winked his way through life and straight into a position of power. "He probably runs the FBI's narcissist unit."

From the little research I'd gathered before getting Wally to bed and heading for Austin, I knew that the couple didn't have children. Not yet anyway.

But when they do, it'll be a strapping boy. A mini law enforcement lumberjack with stupidly attractive features. Because that's how the world works.

Bitterness flowed through my veins, and I wanted to scream at the top of my lungs. It wasn't fair. How was this woman walking free among decent citizens? She was as crazy as her psychotic baby brother, I was sure of it.

And now, she was after me.

I'd passed the time in my minivan by reading about the heinous acts Winter Black had committed as a federal agent. She'd orphaned a young child and walked away from her deeds without a single criminal charge thrown her way.

Remembering those facts fanned the flames of my

outrage even higher. My left hand curled around the hunting knife stashed in the door pocket as I imagined plunging the blade into her black heart. Beating her skull into mush with my trusty baseball bat was equally tempting.

She doesn't deserve to ever have a child. She should be—

Ding-ding-d-ding.

Pissed at how badly my phone alarm had made me jump, I turned it off with an angry tap at the button. Sixty minutes had elapsed since the lights in Winter's home winked out. The couple was young and healthy, so I figured in extra time for sexytimes and cuddling. My patience was at an end, though.

Now it was time to act.

Glancing up and down the street, I patted the bag in the passenger seat to ensure the gift hadn't disappeared or fallen to the floor. The lump was exactly where I'd left it.

At a little before midnight, not a single light shone from any of the neighborhood windows. A few porch lamps were on, including Winter's, but that only helped me check that no one was in sight.

Ensuring that the hood of my sweatshirt was secured over my head, I pushed the thick glasses perched on my nose all the way up. A quick glance in the rearview mirror told me the thick pedo-stache was exactly where it was supposed to be.

Doorbell cameras were the bane of my existence. Which was why I drove this van...a purchase made under one of my numerous shell corporations.

I refused to get caught. That just wouldn't do.

Once I was sure my disguise was firmly in place, I turned over the ignition and shifted the van into drive. Leaving the lights off, I inched away from the curb.

Anger burned my throat as the van coasted closer to the target. In a way, Winter Black was just as bad as my tormentors on the playground. The woman traipsed around the world, wreaking havoc and destroying lives without a single care as to the destruction she left behind. She was a dangerous individual who'd never paid a cent for her sins.

She would pay now.

"And now you want to nose around in *my* business and mess with the vengeance that I've waited so long for? Steal the peace that this world owes me and Wally and every other broken soul who's been dragged through the trenches of hell by vile human specimens?" Icy rage poured over me as solidly as it had when I first learned the young P.I. was meddling in my business. "I think not."

As my anger grew, I hoped that Winter wouldn't heed my warning. The bitch deserved to die.

I rolled to a quiet stop at the end of the private investigator's driveway. Still no signs of life inside the house.

"Not a creature was stirring. Not even a..." I rolled my window down and flopped my present onto the pavement, "well, close enough. Welcome to the neighborhood."

Filled with adrenaline and joy after a successful delivery, I switched the radio to a nineties station and steered the van out of the neighborhood.

It wasn't the vengeance I wanted, but it was a pretty good start.

Images of me slamming my bat into Winter Black's pretty little head kept me company all the way home.

15

Winter's lungs burned as she darted down a hallway to her left. More mirrors. This place—this hell she was trapped in—was made entirely of the reflective glass. The walls, the floor, the ceiling. An endless parade of terrified Winters taunting her as she ran.

At the next fork, she veered right, the glittering nightmare world filled with her harsh gasps for air. Encased in the mirror, hellish images tracked her with hungry eyes. All of them and yet none of them Winter.

Still panting, she slowed her pace. Movement caught her attention, and she jumped, locking eyes with yet another alien version of herself.

This new version of Winter had short, choppy hair streaked with waxy red stripes paired with thick, black eyeliner. As soon as they locked eyes, fake-Winter bared her teeth and released an animalistic hiss.

Blood dripped from her hands. Her t-shirt. Her pants. Rivulets even trickled down one cheek.

Ice crystallized beneath Winter's skin. "What did you do? Oh god, what did you do?"

The mirror image responded by licking the blood off its fingers.

A soundless scream wedged in Winter's throat as terror punched her in the chest. She lunged forward and pounded her fist against the glass. The mirror rattled but held. "Why are you covered in blood? What did you do?"

The glass shimmered, undulating like waves and stretching like silver taffy. In the blink of an eye, the reflection pushed its way out of the mirror. Winter's body quaked as the apparition moved close enough that their noses touched and placed a ghostly, bloodied hand on her cheek.

"You know exactly what we did." *The specter's voice was like a snake slithering across Winter's skin.* "You know what we are."

"No." *The icy touch sent a shiver through Winter's entire body.* "No. You're lying. I don't know you. I don't!"

Mirror-Winter sputtered into laughter. The sound echoed up and down the hallway, with each reflection joining in on the merriment. As the din grew to a thunderous roar, Winter fell to her knees and covered her ears, tears spilling down her face in hot rivulets.

Just when she believed the house of mirrors would combust from the uproar, the laughter stopped as abruptly as a radio being turned off. Even as her mind rejected the total silence, a new noise appeared. It was low at first but grew louder with each beat of Winter's hammering pulse.

Something about the high-pitched squeaking that followed made Winter's skin crawl. She dropped her hands to find the origin of the noises.

Her reflection was gone.

The squeaks grew louder, and the floor began to quake. As she struggled to her feet, a small black dot appeared deep inside the closest mirror. Transfixed for reasons she didn't understand, she stood frozen as the dot started moving toward her.

With every passing heartbeat, the speck grew bigger. Four legs appeared as the shape picked up speed, approaching so fast that it almost appeared to be flying. Every single mirror filled with identical images as the squeaks turned deafening.

"Rats."

Winter's voice was drowned out by the feral screeching of—one hundred? one thousand?—large rodents. Spinning, she scanned the mirrors for one that contained an image of anything else.

Every reflection was the same. Every single one showed a dark gray rat, its head tilted at an awkward angle, devouring her with glowing red eyes.

"Broken. Your necks are all broken."

A wave of nausea churned her stomach as, in the mirror to her left, images of Greg and Andrea Stewart bound to camping chairs with their heads hanging at odd angles appeared. Their mouths opened into ghoulish smiles. "This is your fault."

Winter clapped her hands over her ears again and closed her eyes, unable to stand the sights and sounds a moment longer. "No! No, stop! Please!"

The cacophony of squeaks ceased. Shaking with fear, Winter peeked at the mirrors again. The rat reflection closest to her was...smiling.

Blood seeped from its snout as it spoke. "You know exactly what we did. You know what we are."

As she watched in horror, the red-eyed creature unhinged its jaw and released a single, ear-piercing note. A sharp crack rent the air, followed by another...and another. Fault lines spiderwebbed through the mirrors, and Winter barely had time to throw an arm over her face before glass exploded from every direction. Sharp jagged shanks attacked her skin as she cowered, convinced she was about to die.

When the shower of glass ceased, hope pulsed through Winter's chest. Maybe it was all over. The mirrors were broken, and she could finally escape.

She should have known better than to hope.

Even as she peeked through her fingers, she found an infinity of *glowing red eyes waiting. A scream burst from her throat as they bared their bloody teeth and charged.*

Winter jolted awake with her pulse pounding and coated in thick, sticky sweat. Throwing the covers back, she leapt from the bed and whirled around the room, scanning the floor for an approaching horde of vermin.

Nothing stirred but the soft sounds of her husband's snores.

She pressed a hand to her chest, waiting for her heart to quiet.

Just a nightmare. You've had them before.

This one felt different, though.

Her hands still trembled as she walked toward the floor-length mirror in the corner. Drawing in a deep breath, she stepped in front of the glass. Her proper carbon copy image stared back.

No blood on her pajama top. Or hands. Or face. No rats in sight.

As her muscles started to unwind, a crimson light flickered through the bedroom window. Her pulse accelerated again.

Shit.

Using the curtains as cover, Winter peeked out at the first manifestation of her "gift" that she'd experienced since moving to Texas.

"So much for leaving everything behind." Her voice barely rasped from her throat.

From her vantage point on the second floor, it was impossible to tell what the red glow was trying to show her. Wanting with all her being to slip back into bed, Winter instead threw a robe around herself, slipped into tennis shoes, and grabbed her gun from the bedside table.

She had to see…had to know.

The clock read 4:03 in the morning. Noah slumbered on,

facing the opposite way with one arm thrown over his head. She studied him for a few seconds before turning away. He'd be upset that she hadn't woken him up to help, but that was okay.

This was her curse. Her burden. Her choice.

Plus, his rumbling, cartoonish snores were too cute to disturb.

Moving swiftly through the house, a familiar warm rush of job-fueled adrenaline flooded her once again. Her exit through the front door was soundless, and she carefully scanned the porch, the yard, the street, before sprinting down the driveway.

The object's red glow had faded to a soft pinkish hue. As she knelt and activated her cell phone flashlight to get a better look, a one-two punch of recognition sent her scrambling backward so quickly she landed on her butt.

Covering her mouth, Winter concentrated on inhaling slow, deep breaths through her nose. Bile scalded her throat, but she managed to force it back down.

Whoever had left the dead rat in her driveway had separated the animal from its skin, giving the carcass a pinkish hue.

Whether or not the person had skinned the rodent before or after its little neck was broken, she couldn't say.

And didn't want to know.

Noah's reaction the next morning over their housewarming gift was every bit as unhappy as Winter had anticipated. After learning about the incident, he spent a good ten minutes alternating between grilling her over the exact details and admonishing her for not waking him.

Once the shock wore off, he wrapped his arms around her and held her close while whispering "please never leave me asleep like that again" into her hair. She'd held him just as tightly but hadn't managed to give him the assurance she knew he wanted.

By breakfast, they were both hell-bent on finding out who'd left the rat and why. Noah had to rush off to work before they could come up with any concrete ideas on how to do that. Sleepy from her early morning wakeup call, Winter didn't drag herself to her home office until right at ten.

The phone was trilling as she entered the room. She lunged for the receiver. "Black Investigations."

"I wondered if you could come meet me for brunch." The

strain in Fitz's voice was unmistakable. "There was a new development late last night that I'd like to discuss in person."

Winter debated asking if her anonymous admirer gifted him with a skinned rat as well before deciding against it. She hadn't completely rejected the possibility that her client had created the entire ruse of a missing girlfriend himself. Mahoney Fitzgerald could be an attention seeker, and if that were the case, who was to say he hadn't skinned and planted that rat himself? Breaking the news to him in person would allow her to assess his reaction.

"Okay. Where do you want to meet?"

She agreed to his suggestion of the Lakeview Hills Country Club and hit the road, parking in the visitor's section of the club's pristine lot upon arrival. The rolling green hills of a golf course extended to one side of a beautiful two-story stone and glass building, where a quartet of senior citizens wheeling pristine golf bags chatted as they headed inside.

Must be nice.

As Winter climbed out of her car and shut the door, a body materialized behind her.

Her hand flew to her gun as she jumped back. With a string of curses she barely managed to keep behind her teeth, she relaxed a moment later. "Jesus, Fitz. Did you invite me here to send me into cardiac arrest?"

He held up his hands before pacing the length of the car. Stubble grazed his chin, and he'd missed a button on his blue collared shirt. "I'm so sorry. I was watching for you outside the entrance. I can't...I can't sit still for more than two seconds at a time. It was a box, Winter. An *entire box* of them."

Having a decent idea of what "they" were, Winter asked anyway. "Rats?"

Fitz shuddered and thrust all ten fingers through his hair.

"Rat *tails*. Just the tails. So. Many. Tails. They came in the damn mail."

A shiver rippled through Winter's body. "So, first the dead rat with a broken neck at your front gate, and now, a box of rat tails."

"And…" Fitz glanced around the parking lot before speaking, "my mother said her groundskeeper found three dead rats, all with broken necks, left in a row on the edge of their property. Do you think my parents are in danger too? I'm freaking out. I'm losing my shit."

Winter's stomach tightened. "This won't make you feel any better, but you should be aware that someone left a skinned rat, complete with a broken neck, at the foot of my driveway at some point during the night."

Turning a ghostly shade of pale, Fitz wobbled on his feet and placed a hand on a nearby car to stop himself from falling. "Oh my god. You're serious. I am so sorry that happened to you, but do you see?" He straightened, his pale face reddening into anger. "This is proof that I'm being messed with. Whoever is trying to ruin me is targeting you now because I brought you in to prove my sanity."

Though she was beginning to agree with him, Winter played the situation as cool as possible. "This feels personal. It's a lot of disgusting work to drive all over the damn countryside depositing rats in specific locations. Whoever is doing this to you believes that it's worth the effort."

Fitz's brows knit together. "Meaning?"

"Meaning," Winter cast a longing gaze at the country club as her stomach growled, "they really, *really* hate you. So now you need to start thinking hard about who might want to destroy your life and get you locked up in a mental hospital."

Sagging against her car, Fitz snort-laughed loud enough to grab the attention of a couple in tennis whites as they headed for the club. "You might have to help me narrow that list down. It's quite impressive."

Winter fought the urge to snap at Fitz's unbelievable arrogance. "Fine. Think business enemies. Ex-girlfriends. Estranged family members. Anyone you might have screwed over worse than the rest, or who might have taken a lesser offense more personally."

"You're searching for a needle in a haystack. I've been pissing people off since the day I was born." Fitz's cocky grin flattened, and he pressed his hand to his stomach. "But no one else should have to pay the price for my decades of being a dick. Sandra is just an innocent bystander."

After the multitude of cases Winter had worked, her skepticism was thick. "You've only dated Sandra for three months. Only known her for three months. You don't have a lot of solid ground to work with where she's concerned. Maybe she's innocent. But you have to consider the possibility that maybe she isn't."

Fitz flushed a deeper red. "Sandra Smith is the kindest person I have ever met. I've been surrounded by horrible people my entire life, so I have to disagree with you. I have a *lot* to go on as far as recognizing when someone is good." He waved his hands in the air as he searched for more words. "Pure. She's everything I'm unfamiliar with. Everything I'm not."

Not for the first time, Winter took mental note of the fact that the privileged one percent of the population appeared to be anything but happy. Money and misery seemed to go hand in hand.

"Listen." Fitz's eyes misted over. "Sandra understood what I was, but she let me be myself. She brought out the best version of me. The Mahoney that I didn't even realize I could be. I didn't deserve that. I didn't deserve her."

"You're being too hard on—"

"I'm not." Vehemence heated his words as harshly as sorrow filled his eyes. "I'm a piece of shit, and I'm being punished for it. But Sandra is the one paying the price. We have to find her. I can't let this go until I know she's okay, even if she wants nothing to do with me anymore."

Reluctant sympathy welled in Winter's chest. The man had every reason to fear for his own safety, but all he cared about was Sandra's well-being. "Could I meet your parents?"

Horror shot across Fitz's features. "My parents? *Why?*"

"They might remember things you don't." Another stomach growl assailed her. "Feuds or falling outs you've had over the years that stood out to them. Or maybe there are family feuds that you're not even aware of. You might be surprised at how helpful their input could be."

Fitz released a few dry laughs. "And you might be surprised how easily Satan incarnate takes on the form of two rich-as-shit human beings."

Winter arched an eyebrow. "You know who I am. You know who my brother is. Evil family members aren't going to shock me."

He rubbed his jaw as he studied her. "Okay. You've got me there. If you ever want to talk about that—"

"I don't." Winter didn't add that she wouldn't confide in Mahoney Fitzgerald about a troublesome hangnail. "If a professional like me speaks with your parents about your case, they might begin to take your situation seriously. That's what you want, right? For them to know you aren't insane?"

Fitz stared up at the cloudy January sky. "What I want is Sandra back. But yes. I'd also prefer for my family to not lock me up in a looney bin. I'll try to set up a meeting."

While Fitz wandered around the parking lot making his call, Winter gave the country club a final, wistful glance. So much for that fancy brunch. She rubbed her complaining stomach and tried to recall the location of the nearest gas station with a minimart.

Maybe a deli sandwich or just the entire deli at this point.

Food.

Meat.

Winter moaned as pink, fleshy corpse flesh flashed through her mind. Swallowing a gag, Winter decided that food, in general, was a highly overrated necessity.

17

Noah sped down the hall of the resident agency, holding a coffee in each hand. He probably should have skipped the coffee run that morning since he'd already arrived a little late, but after that conversation with Winter, his body demanded caffeine.

No harm, no foul...as long as your new boss doesn't realize that you slipped out.

Picking up the pace, he rounded the corner toward the VCU offices and nearly collided with another employee.

"Sorry, I..." His voice trailed off as he stared straight into the icy blue eyes of SSA Falkner. *Dammit.* Noah cleared his throat, thanking the heavens that he hadn't spilled any searing hot liquids on his boss. "I just ran out for—"

"I know what you ran out for." SSA Falkner's frown deepened. "You went to get coffees for yourself and Agent Taggart. I also suspect that perhaps you had something else on your mind. Another non-job-related errand to run?"

Dropping his chin like a naughty preschooler, Noah searched for a sufficient reply. "I...um..."

The truth was that he *had* taken a rather large detour to

drive past Sandra Smith's apartment building on the off chance that he might spot her. The possibility existed that Fitz had misremembered the apartment number, and the woman still lived there.

If that were true...*boom!* Winter's first case could be solved. Just like that.

Of course, that still left the question of the skinned rat in their damn driveway...

SSA Falkner cleared his throat. "Your wife was also your partner in Richmond, correct?"

Uh oh. Where is this going?

"Yes." Noah refrained from the urge to duck his head, feeling a little like a naughty schoolboy about to be reprimanded by the principal.

If only the barista hadn't messed up his order. A few minutes faster, and he could have probably avoided the entire uncomfortable interaction.

As he studied Noah, Agent Falkner's expression gave away about as much as a stone. "There must have been a certain level of comfort in that. Always being nearby when the person you love is in danger."

"Not always."

The words slipped out before Noah could stop them. It took all his self-control not to fidget beneath his boss's shrewd blue gaze.

In the uncomfortable silence that followed, Noah wrestled with the urge to swig a giant gulp of his coffee. *You idiot. Don't do anything to remind him that you skipped out!*

Next time, Taggart could go on the caffeine run.

After several intensely uncomfortable moments, the SSA finally gave a solemn nod. "As I recall, there was an incident when your wife went missing. Kidnapped by her brother. Those types of traumas can be challenging to move past, but Agent Dalton, you do have to move past it."

Justin had taken Winter captive a year ago. Almost an entire freaking year had gone by since the maniac took the woman he loved.

In theory, that should have been plenty of time for Noah to recover from the vivid flashbacks...only he hadn't.

The memory of standing next to Aiden Parrish as they'd peered into a dumpster flashed through his head and sent chills erupting through his body. The terror that had wrenched at his insides as he'd peered over the edge, filled with certainty that Winter's cold, lifeless body awaited, was a feeling he never wanted to experience again.

He gripped the cups harder so that his hands wouldn't tremble at the memory. "Yes, I'm aware. I think I've moved past it as much as can be expected, I guess."

"You haven't." SSA Falkner's stern tone wasn't kind but held no cruelty either. "And that's also to be expected. In our world, however, you can't have one foot in the door. The Bureau requires your full concentration while you're on the clock. You know this."

Noah's tongue twisted into knots because...he did know. As much as he bristled at the implied criticism, his new boss was right.

Distractions led to mistakes. Mistakes led to devastating consequences. The FBI needed agents to give the job one hundred percent. If they didn't, people died.

Falkner turned toward his office door. "I'll be retiring soon because that's what the Bureau rules dictate, but I'd give anything to have a few more years with the badge. Many individuals try and fail to ever become agents. If I were you, I'd do some reevaluating." Falkner faced him again, his gaze just as cold, his countenance just as stern. "This career is highly sought after, but it isn't for everyone. You need to ask yourself if your heart is still in the work."

Noah's shoulders went back. *All this over a coffee run?* He'd devoted years of his life to the badge. "My track record speaks for itself. You hired me because I've been an excellent agent."

A ghost of a smile flitted across Falkner's harsh mouth. "You're speaking in the past tense. Did you mean to?"

Without waiting for a reply, his superior headed into his office. The door swung shut behind him while Noah stood frozen in the hallway.

Shit. Shit. Shit.

Even as he cursed himself and his bad luck, Noah had to be honest with himself. He didn't agree with SSA Falkner. The problem was simple. He didn't disagree with the man either.

Eve's voice rattled him from his trance. "Excuse me, partner, but I'm in deep need of that caffeine."

Rushing into their claustrophobic office, Noah couldn't remember a time in recent history when he'd felt so jaw-droppingly dumb. He handed off the cup and plopped into his chair.

"I didn't mean to eavesdrop on y'all," Eve sipped her coffee but her gaze over the rim was filled with compassion, "but these walls are thin. Falkner is just pushing you. He doesn't want you to quit, if that's what you took from the conversation. He wants you to make sure you're really here, is all."

Noah suspected that her interpretation of the conversation was correct. "Yeah, I get that. It's understandable. He's the boss. Just doing his job."

Eve regarded him over the top of her cup. "So, are you?"

As he processed the last few minutes in his mind, her question didn't register. "Am I what?"

Whirling a finger at their surroundings, Eve offered a gentle smile. "Are you really here anymore?"

Noah opened his mouth. Closed it again. He envisioned

Winter tiptoeing down their driveway toward a skinned, dead rat in the middle of the night. He pictured the delivery person hiding nearby, ready to spring a trap, and goose bumps raced along his skin.

All she had to do was wake me up.

That image vanished, replaced by one of Winter in her wedding dress, dazzling him damn near into a coma with her beauty. On that day—the day Winter became his wife—Noah understood that nothing in his life pre-Winter Black was real. She'd entered his world and breathed life into every corner of his soul.

He could have happily spent the rest of his life on that dance floor, holding her close and swaying to love songs.

"Knock knock, is anyone home?"

Realizing that he hadn't answered his partner for a questionably long period of time, Noah ran her last query through his mind again.

Am I still here? Really here? With the Bureau?

He met his partner's expectant gaze with a helpless shrug and gave the only answer he could. An honest one. "I don't know."

18

_____

The one-hour drive from Lakeview Hills to Huntstown, Texas, afforded Winter an adequate window to stuff her face full of gas station goodies. She blasted an upbeat pop song, praying it would drown out any unwanted thoughts of rodent surprises as she annihilated a turkey and pepper jack on rye...followed by an entire bag of trail mix...followed by a king-sized Snickers bar.

When she pulled up to the metal gate stationed outside of Warren and Laurel Fitzgerald's estate, the guard scrutinized her I.D. and private investigator license for a long time. Clearly unfazed by her former Fed credentials, his wrinkles seemed to sink even deeper into his face as he informed her that Mahoney was waiting up at the house and buzzed her in.

Waiting on the gate to slide open, Winter wondered how many times Fitz must have pissed the poor old guy off to earn that type of reaction.

Forget that. What's it like, showing up at your parents' home knowing that your presence isn't wanted...not even by security?

Creeping along the drive toward the Fitzgeralds' towering brick mansion of a home, Winter brushed the remaining crumbs off her lap and prepared for a conversation with two people described as "Satan incarnate."

A black Porsche sat at the top of the circular driveway. Winter parked behind it and hopped out. Fitz waited for her on the gorgeous stone-plated stairs that tiered to a wrap-around porch, his hands shoved into his pockets and his expression sober. He jerked his head toward the castle-like structure behind him. "You ready for this?"

Winter gave him a quick pat on the arm. "Believe it or not, I've dealt with a lot scarier situations."

Earning herself a small grin from the otherwise high-strung Mahoney Fitzgerald, Winter followed her client to a set of enormous double doors, surprised when he rang the bell and waited. Fitz had grown up here but was apparently uncomfortable traipsing in without an invitation.

A stiff-faced elderly man in a gray suit answered the door with a sniff. "Mr. Fitzgerald. Would you like me to see if Mrs. Fitzgerald is up to receiving company?"

Winter fought to keep the surprise off her face. *Wow. Another servant. And what kind of parents require their kids to make appointments before visiting?*

Fitz rubbed the back of his neck. "It's okay, Duncan. I let Mom know I was coming."

Duncan didn't budge. "Still, I think it's best if—"

"Who is it, Duncan?" A woman's voice trilled from somewhere behind the unyielding butler.

"Mr. Fitzgerald, ma'am."

"Yes, I'll take it from here. You're dismissed."

Without another word, Duncan executed a sharp pivot and disappeared from view. An attractive woman wearing full makeup and a floor-length, ruby-red dress appeared in the opening and held out an immaculately manicured hand to Winter. "You must be Fitzy's lawyer."

Fitzy? Winter choked back a laugh.

"Private investigator, Mother." Fitz cast Winter an apologetic glance. "This is my private investigator, Winter Black. I told you about her on the phone, and you agreed to meet with her, remember? We had this conversation a little over an hour ago."

Wiggling her fingers at Fitz, Laurel Fitzgerald giggled like a tween and opened the door wider to usher them inside. "Oh, you know what I meant. Silly Fitzy. Of course, this is your *private investigator*. It is an absolute pleasure to meet you, Miss Black."

"Just Winter." Correcting Laurel would have been a waste of time. "You can call me Winter. It's nice to meet you as well."

Laurel's silicon-enhanced red lips spread into a puffy smile. "Come. Warren is in the den. We'll join him there."

Fitz's mother clicked across the marble floor in three-inch heels, leading them with quick, mincing steps. Winter took in the massive curving staircase, the ginormous crystal chandelier glittering from the ceiling and the elaborate crown molding lining the walls, and the plethora of extravagant statues and paintings on display, and uttered a silent whistle.

The Fitzgeralds flaunted their wealth like they wanted to ensure that no one forgot their social standing for so much as a minute.

After crossing an area that seemed as long as a football field, Laurel led them into a large room with a stone fireplace on one wall and floor-to-ceiling windows on the other. The den. Winter was surprised the woman had deigned to call the area something so common.

"Fitzy's friend is here!"

A gray-haired man seated in a stiff velvet chair near the fireplace slowly turned to face them. His chiseled cheekbones and square jaw declared him as Fitz's father without anyone saying a word.

Beside her, Fitz tensed like a guitar string one click away from snapping. He eyed his father with the same wariness one might show a lion roaring within a rusted cage.

"Well." Warren Fitzgerald didn't bother to rise or put down the newspaper he'd been reading. "Your mother said you'd hired someone to investigate your insane claims, but I refused to believe it until I met the poor oaf in person."

Bristling at the comment, Winter's polite smile slipped a notch. *Easy. You still need to interview this guy.*

She held her tongue and let Fitz respond to his father's infuriating opening statement. "She's hardly an oaf, Dad. This is Winter Black. She used to work as a federal agent. She's the best of the best, and she doesn't think my claims are insane."

Warren shot Fitz a withering glare before his calculating blue eyes homed in on Winter. "Used to? What, did they kick you out?"

Winter refused to be triggered by the old man's attitude. She sauntered over to the chair closest to Warren and plopped down uninvited. "They didn't. I left in very good standing with the Bureau." Her smile sharpened. "If you'd like, I can give you my former supervisor's name and his direct line so that you can reassure yourself I'm not lying? Although I can't vouch for his mood when he learns why you called."

She met his narrow-eyed suspicion with an innocent expression. *Go ahead, make my day. Ask for Aiden's number and see how well your questions about my integrity go over. I dare you.*

Fitz's dad was the first to break the stare-off as he folded his newspaper and cast it aside. "You'll have to forgive me. When Mahoney is involved in something...anything...I immediately prepare myself for falsehood and deceit. You'd do the same if you're smart."

The low blow had a visible effect on Fitz. He visibly flinched, hurt flashing across his features before they twisted into disgust.

"Mr. Fitzgerald," Winter attempted to distract the two from their silent war, "I'm aware of the issues that Fit... Mahoney has shared with you. His concerns over Sandra Smith do come off as far-fetched initially, but I believe there's truth to his story."

Warren's head whipped back to Winter. "Of course you do. My son has a knack for pulling the wool over the sharpest of eyes, especially when he's lining that person's pocket. How much is he paying you to agree with him?"

Winter battled a frustrated sigh. The more Warren Fitzgerald talked, the more validity she saw in Fitz's "devil incarnate" statement. "Mahoney is searching for someone he cares about who went missing. That's what this boils down to, sensational details aside. He hired me to assist him, and that is what I mean to do. There's been a development in his case that might cause you to alter your view on his dilemma."

"Oh? What's that?" Warren accepted a dainty porcelain cup of something, coffee or tea, she wasn't sure, from his otherwise silent wife. The china looked ridiculous in his large hand. "Are you here to tell me that this Sandra Smith person possesses magical powers, and that's how she was able to so thoroughly vanish from my son's life? I'm guessing she wiped everyone's memory while she was at it."

There was no mistaking the older Fitzgerald's words for a joke. Not even a hint of a smile played at his lips, and the air all but crackled with tension. The antagonism between father and son was so thick and real that it was beginning to seem like the fifth person in the room.

"Rats." The word shot from Winter's mouth like a bullet. "Your groundskeeper found three dead rats at the edge of your property yesterday, all with broken necks. Mahoney received a single rat at his gate, and last night, he opened a package full of rat tails. I was inducted into the rodent club this morning. Someone left a dead rat, with a broken neck, of course, at the end of my driveway. My rat had been thoroughly skinned, so that was a charming extra detail."

Cup held an inch from his mouth, Warren went silent while Laurel gasped, her plastic face as motionless as a mannequin as she lifted a hand to cover her inflated lips. Fitz broke into a smug Cheshire-cat grin, causing a low growl to rumble deep in his father's throat.

Winter tried her best not to grimace. All the wealth in the Fitzgeralds' vast fortune wouldn't pay for enough therapy to fix their dysfunction. The turmoil ran too deep, and none of them seemed particularly interested in righting—or even recognizing—the wrongs to begin with.

An hour or less. That's all the time she needed. Surely they could manage to interact like humans for that long?

"I would say that many occurrences of the same dead animal in such a small circle of individuals points to more than a coincidence. The rats might be a warning of sorts…a threat." Winter waved a hand in Fitz's direction. "I understand why you've been hesitant to entertain Mahoney's story so far, but it may be time for you to hear him out."

"You understand nothing." Warren slammed the delicate cup onto a side table, sloshing the liquid all over the surface, though the china remained intact. For a moment, Winter thought his wife might faint, though she wasn't sure if Laurel was distraught over the explosion of temper or the liquid marring the table's surface. "My son has been a trouble-making pain in the ass the majority of his life. He perfected the art of lying before he ever made it out of diapers. He's a thirty-eight-year-old man living like a twenty-two-year-old idiot."

Laurel placed a hand on Warren's shoulder. "Honey."

"I'm speaking the truth." The elder Fitzgerald shook his wife off. "I wouldn't be surprised if Mahoney is the one delivering these rats or if you were a hired actress he brought in just to beef up the fun of messing with his parents. He's pulled this type of shenanigan a million times before, for no better reason other than he got bored and needed to enter-tain himself."

As Warren rose on stiff legs, Fitz went on the defensive. "That's not fair. I've never come to you with this type of problem. I've never joked about losing a woman I love."

Warren stalked up to his son until they stood toe to toe and jabbed a finger into Fitz's chest. "That's because you're incapable of loving anyone other than yourself, you ungrateful little shit!"

The angry rasp of his breathing filled the den as father and son faced off. Warren's cheeks and nose turned a mottled red while Fitz's hands fisted at his sides.

Oh boy. Where's a whistle when you need one?

Winter glanced at Laurel to see if she might intervene, but the woman just stood there like a mannequin in her long, red dress.

Great, guess that leaves me to handle this. I'm definitely upcharging Fitz if I have to break up a fistfight, though.

Warren solved the problem for her by sneering, "I'm done here," and stomping out of the room.

As soon as he disappeared, Laurel returned to life as if

reanimated. Ignoring her son's agitation as he paced the den, she flitted around straightening Warren's abandoned chair and dabbing at the spilled tea with a cloth napkin. "Can I get you some tea, Winter? Coffee? We have sugar and cream, of course. I could have the maid fetch some pastries?"

For once, Winter couldn't fathom eating a snack, fancy or otherwise. "No thank you. That's really not why I'm here."

Fitz dropped into the chair next to her and leaned close. "She doesn't care about why you're here." His whisper was almost as loud as a shout. "No one in this house does."

Laurel continued flitting around like a butterfly, clearly pretending to miss every word. Winter was getting the sense that the woman was excellent at pretending.

Just when Winter wondered if Fitz's mother would speak to them again at all, the woman whirled toward her son and clapped her hands. "Fitzy, I should tell you the good news. Bobby Burner's mother called earlier. Bobby came out of his coma yesterday. She's absolutely beside herself with joy. He can't remember much yet, but the doctors are hopeful that, with time, he'll be able to recall his assailant's face."

Winter's attention shifted to Fitz. "Assailant? Someone you know was attacked?"

"An old friend." Fitz lowered his eyes to the floor, his shame apparent. "Bobby owns a huge car dealership here in Huntstown. He got jumped at a Halloween party he held there a few months back and was beaten up pretty bad. With a bat, they're guessing. I haven't seen the guy in years."

Tsking him like a child, Laurel smoothed her skirt. "I suppose you didn't even call to check on him after the assault either. That's bad manners, which is something the Fitzgerald name should never be associated with."

Fitz's jaw flexed with what appeared to be a combination of annoyance and shame. "You're right, Mom. I'm an ass for not checking in. Maybe I'll go visit Bobby."

Laurel beamed as though her sage wisdom had hit its precise target. "That's the right thing to do. That's the Fitzgerald way." Her son's exaggerated snort didn't faze Laurel in the slightest. Ignoring him completely, the Barbie doll of a woman turned to Winter with a grand hostess's smile. "It's been so good to meet you, dear. You're welcome in our home anytime."

Apparently finished with both them and the discussion, Laurel bent to give Fitz a kiss on the cheek and click-clacked her way from the room. Winter and her client sat without speaking on the sofa.

Well, this visit was a giant waste of time. I wonder if it's too late to call her back and ask for those snacks?

The Fitzgeralds would be giving no helpful information or eye-opening accounts. Warren acted as though his son was a lifeform somewhere below a human being, while Laurel avoided unpleasantries altogether.

Winter's gaze wandered the den, sweeping across the huge windows to land on a portrait hanging near the fireplace. Much younger versions of Laurel and Warren stared back at her, with a little girl and a boy she recognized as a young Fitz standing stiffly by their sides.

She focused on the girl. "Your sister. Laurel-Anne? Do you think she'd be open to meeting with me? My hopes aren't high after this," she waved to encompass the den, "but if I could gain any insight from her at all, it'd be worth it."

Fitz sank even deeper into the chair and shrugged. "Sure. I'll set it up. But you'll have to meet with her alone. A, because she hates me. And b, I need to go let an old friend know that I do actually give a damn whether he lives or dies."

Hates him? Interesting.

While Fitz called his sister, Winter dug a notepad from her purse and scribbled down Bobby Burner's name and the few details she'd gathered about him during the visit. Next, she started a list of the questions she wanted to ask Fitz's sister.

Even if Laurel-Anne hated Fitz, she was still his sibling… and experience had taught Winter that siblings had an indelible way of knowing each other's deepest, darkest secrets.

19

Fitz spent the short drive to Huntstown's only hospital trying to find peace in the reality that he was a horrible person. Standing in the den while his father explained all the reasons why he was deplorable to Winter Black had been one of the most humiliating moments of his life.

While his chest burned with hate for his dad for saying such things, Fitz couldn't deny the truth in the words.

As he waited to turn into Huntstown Memorial Hospital, he checked his reflection in the rearview mirror. "But you're going to change that truth from here on out."

He vowed to be a better friend. A better son. A better man.

The light turned green, and he whipped the Porsche into the parking lot. He strode toward the dated building with purpose while a fragile ember of hope flamed in his stomach.

People changed all the time. For the worse. For the better. Granted, he couldn't get much worse, but what universal law existed that declared he wasn't allowed to improve himself?

The door greeter met him amiably and sent him to the nearby reception desk. There, he was subjected to the normal HIPAA bullshit by a man who appeared to be the same age of Jesus before finally being told that Bobby had been transferred out of the ICU a couple hours ago and was now enjoying a private room in a step-down unit.

"That's good news." Fitz was genuinely pleased for his old friend. But as happy as he was for Bobby, Fitz's gut began to churn.

What if Sandra is lying in a hospital bed right now too? What if they've labeled her a Jane Doe, and she's lost in a coma just like Bobby was? What if she never gets to see her mother again before the cancer wins out? What if I never, ever find her?

Worry after worry pummeled him like fists, leaving emotional bruises in their wake. He pushed them from his mind as best he could as he rode the elevator to the floor the elderly man had directed him to.

Focus on Bobby now. Brood later.

As he approached the step-down unit, a woman wearing a low-cut red top and skintight jeans popped out the door. Fitz immediately recognized her as Bobby's wife, though he hadn't seen her in years.

Good. Maybe she'll make it easier for me to see my friend.

Tawny Burner's eyes widened as they scanned every inch of him. "Mahoney Fitzgerald, is that really you?" Without waiting for confirmation, she squealed and launched herself at him, mashing her mostly exposed breasts against his chest. "It's so good to see you. It will mean so much to Bobby that you came."

Grimacing over the top of her head, he gave her a stiff pat on the back and prayed that she'd finish mauling him soon. "Nice to see you too." It was a lie, of course, but he supposed part of being a better man was offering niceties when needed.

When she pressed against him harder, this time pushing her stomach into his crotch, his dick didn't even stir. Tawny was just as ready for action as ever, despite her husband lying in bed like an invalid somewhere on this floor.

Nothing had changed over the years.

When she showed no sign of ending the embrace, he tried to extricate himself. Tawny only clung on tighter like a rabid koala and sniffed his neck. "Mmmm. And you smell so nice. What is that scent, Fitz? It's divine."

Tawny was one of the main reasons why Fitz had drifted away from Bobby. She'd always been an over-the-top flirt, but when Fitz, dressed in his best man's tux, had accidentally walked into the wrong church office and caught her giving the priest a blowjob on their wedding day, his understanding of Bobby's wife-to-be crystalized.

The priest had flushed tomato red during the ceremony, but Tawny played it off like a pro. No one would have ever guessed that, an hour earlier, her immaculately styled brunette head had bobbed up and down on another man's pogo stick.

Fitz never told Bobby. He hadn't known how. The very thought of him giving any man advice on women had been ridiculous even then.

What bothered him most, though, was that his reasons for avoiding Bobby and Tawny were rooted in guilt as much as anything else. Later that night during the reception, when Fitz was three sheets to the wind, Tawny had cornered him in a coat closet.

"There's only one way for us to get past today." She dropped to *her knees, her wedding dress billowing out around her like a cloud. "You need some special treatment yourself. You deserve it waaay more than that bald old priest."*

Fitz froze as Tawny reached to twist the lock on the door and yanked at his tux pants. He knew what she was doing, and he didn't want it. His lips tried to form the word "no," but her mouth closed around him before any sound came out. She found her rhythm, and his mind glazed over until he no longer cared or remembered who was providing the ecstasy down south.

She'd silenced him with the act, and they both knew it. What had scared Fitz even more was the fact that, if his best friend's wife were to corner him again with the same offer, he wasn't sure he'd react any differently.

A lot had changed in the last thirteen years. Tawny was still as attractive as ever, yet Fitz found her repulsive. It angered him that she was even still with Bobby, whom Fitz had known since childhood.

Bobby wasn't a perfect man, but he deserved better than this lying little slut.

Completely over this little show of faux affection, Fitz used a firmer grip to push her away. "How's he doing?"

Undeterred, Tawny grabbed Fitz's hand and laced their fingers as she tapped some special code into the panel by the unit's door. "Sleeping now, but come on. He wakes up often. You don't wanna miss your chance to see him."

Antiseptic odors overwhelmed Fitz as he allowed himself to be led to Bobby's room. The second he saw his old friend in the hospital bed with multiple IVs and monitors attached to his body, he yanked his hand free from Tawny's.

Stirring, Bobby's eyes fluttered open, and he blinked at his surroundings. Tawny wasted no time in telling Fitz that she'd be back before bolting after an incredibly young doctor who strolled by the door.

Reminding himself that he was no better than Tawny, Fitz pulled a chair to the side of Bobby's bed. "Hey, old buddy."

Bobby's eyes lit with recognition. "Wow. It's been a hot minute, Fitz. Thought you musta forgot my number."

Jagged lines from multiple wounds were still a bit puffy and red. Boney lumps on his cheeks and nose were still apparent even though the beating had taken place three months ago. Fitz guessed facial reconstruction wasn't a high priority when a man was in a coma. He could only imagine how bad Bobby must have looked immediately following the assault.

Realizing he was staring, he forced himself to smile. "Never forgot it, Bob. Just got busy with life."

"I get that." Bobby tried to smile, and Fitz noticed that a number of his teeth were missing, giving his face a sunken appearance and his words an exaggerated slur. "What with the baseball career, and the kids, and Jesus, keeping that woman happy...I understand. Life kinda shuffles people away from each other." He lifted a bony shoulder. "It's normal."

Though his friend's tone was light, Fitz instinctively understood that Bobby was more hurt by his absence than he wanted to acknowledge. "It isn't. I should have kept in touch. And I should have come to see you right after the attack."

Bobby managed a grin. "If it makes you feel any better, I wouldn't have known you were here anyway. Took a damn long nap. I did. Damn long."

"What was it like?" Fitz braced his elbows on his knees and leaned forward, morbid curiosity piqued. "You see any bright lights or aliens or anything?"

His childhood friend fiddled with a loose string on his blanket. "I didn't see anything. No dreams. Nothing. I'm kinda thinking there isn't anything to see after...this. It's hella depressing, to be honest."

Fitz placed a hand on Bobby's arm. "Hey, man, you don't know that. You were in a coma. You weren't dead."

Bobby's dread at the prospect of an afterlife...or lack thereof...struck a chord deep within Fitz. The idea of this shitshow fading into complete nothing was bleak. Alarmingly bleak.

Lifting a shoulder, Bobby managed a half smile. "Felt like I was dead."

"You're not." Fitz sat back in his chair, willing the tears stinging his eyes to stay put. "You've got a lot left to do, Bobby-Boy. We haven't even reached our 'sit on the porch and smoke a cigar and yell at the kids who walk on your lawn' days yet."

To Fitz's relief, Bobby laughed. A deep belly laugh, the type that Fitz guessed hadn't come out of Bobby's mouth for years before he'd taken his "long nap."

"You're right." Bobby absently traced a finger over one of the scars on his face. "All kinds of hell to raise still. Maybe you could bring yourself to visit when I'm *not* on my deathbed, and we could raise some of that hell together."

Fitz bit the inside of his mouth until it bled. He'd let Bobby down, just like he'd failed everyone else so far in his life. Bobby was worse than the others, though, because of how close their friendship had once been.

"You betcha. I'm pretty sure I could still kick your ass at pool. That'd be worth the drive to Huntstown right there."

Laughing in unison, Fitz fought the urge to hug his old pal, fearing that he might hurt him if he did...or burst into tears. Seeing the gray streaks in Bobby's hair along with his pale, gaunt cheeks and the tubes feeding into his veins hit him hard. Adding in how badly he'd betrayed his friend all those years ago, and it was just too much. Fitz's insides were cracking, and soon, the floodgates would open.

"Pool it is." The plan brought a giant smile to Bobby's damaged face. "I'm gonna hold you to that."

"You won't have to. We're gonna do it differently this time. Life's too short." Unable to bear the small talk any longer, Fitz stood, his eyes misty and his heart aching. "Anyway, I've gotta run, but I'll catch you again soon. Promise."

Swiping a lone tear from his cheek, Fitz turned and prepared to flee.

He was still a few steps away from the door when Bobby called after him. "Your dad still givin' you the same hell he always did?"

Fitz froze in his tracks while flashes of Warren Fitzgerald screaming insults at him as his friends looked on was like a physical assault. The visions were so disjointed and vivid that, for a moment, he wondered if he was experiencing a seizure. He drew a deep breath, waiting for the images to calm before turning to face his old friend. "Some things never change, I guess." He added a chuckle he didn't feel to take the edge off the words.

"That's right." Bobby's choked-up voice betrayed his emotions as he lifted a finger in Fitz's direction. "But some things *do* change. Don't let that asshole convince you that you're nothing. He doesn't have that power over you anymore. You're a good guy, F..." Bobby's voice broke completely on his name. He inhaled a long breath. "I've always known that. You're a good friend."

Managing to squeak out a barely audible, "Thanks," Fitz bolted from Bobby's room and headed for the nearest lavatory, where he immediately locked himself in a stall and broke into sobs.

20

I watched from a different minivan as Mahoney Fitzgerald exited the hospital with puffy eyes, a red nose, and a hint of a grin. Wrath blazed through my stomach at the sight, but I refused to look away.

"You son of a bitch."

He didn't deserve to smile just like Bobby Burner didn't deserve to breathe.

Because I was always thorough, I'd had the forethought to create a Google alert on my phone, set to notify me anytime Bobby Burner's name was mentioned on the internet. When I'd received an alert last night, I couldn't believe what the news clip had said.

"Local entrepreneur and minor league baseball star Bobby Burner miraculously woke from his coma two days ago..."

I hadn't been able to sleep all night, knowing that Bobby was awake. As the night passed into the morning, I'd devised a plan to make sure the bastard didn't live another day.

As excited as I was, it had been difficult to act normal all morning, but I'd managed to not raise any suspicions as to just how enraged and excited I was. I'd spend the morning with Wally, and right after his lunch, I'd hit the road.

As I was heading to the hospital, the tracking device I'd left under Mahoney's Porsche beeped, telling me that he was on the move. That hadn't been a surprise since I'd known he'd visited with his parents earlier. I almost hadn't even looked at the tracking app, as I'd been sure he was heading back to his house.

I'd been wrong.

His tracker stopped moving at Huntstown Memorial Hospital...my exact destination. Had he seen the news of Bobby's magical awakening and thought a little high school reunion was appropriate since he was in town?

Knowing those two men were in the same room together was like tossing gas onto the fire of my hate. I could imagine it now...chatting...smiling...shooting the shit. Acting as if they didn't have a care in the world.

How had this happened? How had I been so weak to not finish him?

Bobby Burner was never meant to live through his beating, yet he'd had the audacity to do so anyway. Maybe it was the money running through his veins that bought him more time on this planet, but all the fortune in the world wouldn't keep me from sending Bobby to his grave this time around.

I'd only waited in my minivan a few minutes while those two privileged idiots had their little reunion, my anger flourishing into a fiery hot rage with every passing second. Mahoney had bought Bobby another few minutes of life, and he would be punished for that.

First, though, Bobby needed to pay. I'd created a plan for his eventual wake-up day the moment I learned he'd lived through my attack. For a while there, his prognosis was touch and go. The doctors couldn't guarantee that he'd ever regain consciousness.

I'd hoped for his recovery, though. Prayed for it. And the universe had chosen to reward me.

Now, I could experience the pleasure of killing him all over again.

As my gaze followed Mahoney's path through the parking lot, excitement buzzed beneath my skin. Dude-bro time was over. Finally.

Wondering if he could feel the wrath of my gaze on his skin, I smiled as he lifted a hand and rubbed the back of his neck. Apparently, he could.

Good.

I kept my gaze on him as he climbed into his "I've got a little dick so I must drive a powerful car" Porsche and drove away. "Don't worry, motherfucker. You're well on your way to getting exactly what you gave me all those years ago."

A lifetime of suffering. Complete and total ruination. Unmendable heartbreak.

Mahoney Fitzgerald was flying straight toward rock bottom. Do not pass go. Do not collect two hundred dollars.

Right after I took care of a little problem first.

Checking the visor mirror, I held up the hospital badge I'd purchased anonymously from a disgruntled nurse after learning about Bobby's coma. The eagerness with which wronged workers willingly sold out their employers was amazing. With my curly brunette wig and expertly applied makeup, I bore more than a passing likeness to the woman's tiny square photo.

"Good enough."

As long as no one paid too much attention to me, I'd be fine. And luckily, Huntstown General was just small enough to not employ the intense security measures of a city hospital while still busy enough to camouflage my path through the building.

I climbed from my vehicle, smoothed my brand-new

baby-blue scrubs, and strode into the facility as though I'd been doing so for years. The door greeter, who with his stooped posture appeared to be at least one hundred and five, offered a friendly "hello." The front desk receptionist glanced at me with extreme disinterest as he spoke to someone on the phone. A passing nurse nodded without looking up from her clipboard.

This is going to be much easier to pull off than I'd planned.

During the one-hour drive to Huntstown, I'd stopped at a run-down gas station and used the ancient outdoor pay phone to place a call to the hospital. A single phone call to a hacker I kept on retainer, and I'd managed to obtain Bobby Burner's room number in about five seconds flat.

Money had its benefits. Especially when you needed to get a quick murder out of the way.

When I poked my head into Bobby's room steering a rolling vital sign monitor, Tawny Burner sat at his bedside, yawning as she flipped through a *Vogue* magazine. She was every bit as beautiful in person as she'd appeared in the numerous press photos of her and her husband that graced the internet and local news.

My gut instinct suggested that she was also a moron.

And a whore.

"What's this?" Tawny's exquisite eyebrows arched, and her glossed lips formed a pout. "He *just* fell back asleep. The doctor said he's supposed to sleep as much as possible. You're not going to wake him up, are you? Why would you do that?"

She flicked a dismissive glance at the baggy scrubs that I'd layered sweats underneath to add size to my body, along with my ugly wig. The smug little smile that followed told me that she'd rated my appearance and found me wanting.

I dug my nails into my palm, being careful not to puncture the latex of the gloves I wore. My original plans hadn't included murdering Tawny Burner, but I was open to alterations.

"Mrs. Burner," I hit her with the kindest smile I could muster, "I'm just here to check vitals. I'll be as quiet and gentle as possible, and promise he won't be waking up."

When she processed my last statement, suspicion creased her forehead. I gave her props for that. "Are you new? I've been here nearly every day for three months, and I've never met you."

Dammit. Counting on Tawny to be an air-headed bimbo was one of the main building blocks to reaching my objective. Is it possible she does *have a functioning brain?*

I brushed my hand over the supplies in my pocket and tried to tame the rush of anxiety billowing through my body. *Easy does it. You've come too far to turn back now.*

Giggling, I grabbed the clipboard on Bobby's bedside table and pretended to scan the latest notes and figures. "Definitely not new. Sometimes I feel like I *live* here. I'm just helping cover the floor. We're shorthanded today."

Despite my nonchalance, Tawny's stare bored into me like an electric drill. "Still, I think—"

"Oh." I smacked a hand on my forehead. "I almost forgot to tell you that a delivery arrived for you and Bobby at the front desk. A ginormous bouquet of flowers that are out of this world beautiful."

That caught her attention. "For *both* of us?" She placed a hand on her chest. "The kindness of people, I swear. It's just such a beautiful thing."

Her misty eyes cleared in a hot second as a fresh-faced physician stopped at the door. "Tawny, I—"

His mouth snapped shut the moment he spotted me standing in the room.

Tawny practically leapt to her feet, smoothing her hair on the way up. "Excuse me, whoever you are…" She waved her hand, clearly having already forgotten my supposed purpose for being at her husband's bedside and raced for the door. "I'll be back shortly."

I wonder if she'll regret leaving her husband alone to be murdered so that she could go chase another man? Will that one mistake haunt her for the rest of her life? Are the Tawny Burners of this world even capable of eternal remorse?

Her hasty retreat out the doorway made me highly doubt it. If anything, Tawny would feel relieved that she was free to act as loose in public as she'd no doubt behaved behind the scenes throughout her entire marriage.

And, of course, Bobby was sure to have a sizeable life insurance policy in place to guide his grieving widow through the lonely nights.

A warm blanket of relief fell across me as Tawny closed the door behind her. When I was sure we were alone, I turned to glare down at the man I planned to eliminate from this planet...again.

"Well, Bobby," I spoke just loud enough for him to hear me, "your wife just got super-duper lucky. I almost had to murder both of you."

When his mouth twitched, I held my breath.

Okay. No more goofing around. Bobby doesn't need a soliloquy. He needs to atone for his sins.

I replaced the clipboard, studied Bobby's IV bags, and spotted the morphine among the rest. My poor Wally had required intravenous medication countless times in his short life, leaving me regrettably familiar with the machines.

Wally deserved the relief while this bastard didn't.

Pressing the pause button, an alarming three-second beep sounded as Bobby's morphine drip came to a halt. One glance at his slack mouth and the drool streaking to his chin assured me that his la-la land respite prevailed. No doctors or nurses or security came running. Yet.

My pulse quickened. *Hurry the hell up.*

After removing the cap from the injection port, I pulled a syringe from my pocket. Inserting my own needle into the tube, I delivered a lethal dose of pain medications and liquid rat poison straight into Bobby's veins.

The asshole wouldn't be aware that he was dying, and that part of the plan was regrettable.

I much preferred to view the fear in his eyes as he took his last breath.

My bad, though. I'd already had that opportunity, and I'd failed. There was no one to blame but myself, and this time, I'd leave no wiggle room for another remarkable survival story.

Breathing out a relieved breath, I indulged in one last look at the piece of shit formerly known as Bobby Burner. "Burn in hell, asshole."

In less than ten seconds, I reattached the cap, and un-paused the IV pump. Rolling the vitals monitor in front of me, I sauntered from Bobby's room feeling lighter than I had in months.

Nothing like ridding the world of an asshole to serve as a little pick-me-up.

I made a quick, last-minute decision to take a side exit, but I was still close enough to the reception desk for Tawny's appalled whine to reach my ears. "You better find that delivery. How could you have lost it so quickly? Who hired you? Where's your manager?"

Biting my lip to hold in the laughter, I only released it once I was cruising down the highway with Huntstown in my rearview mirror. The Burner family's day had just taken a massive turn for the worse.

On the flip side, I felt much better.

"One down, two to go. Then you'll really have reason to celebrate."

21

Winter arrived at Huntstown Seafood Restaurant ahead of schedule, wanting to be seated and prepared for her encounter with Laurel-Anne, who had agreed to meet after her hospital shift ended at four.

The hour was a bit early for dinner, but according to Fitz, Laurel-Anne's shift as a psychiatrist at a busy Austin hospital always started at six in the morning, and she was in bed by eight o'clock every night. He claimed she was both a stickler for routine and a seafood addict.

Fine by Winter. She didn't care if they were meeting for communion at a crack house where Laurel-Anne served as the resident witch doctor. She wanted to talk to the woman and see if a single person in the Fitzgerald household might possibly have a single good thing to say about her client.

Insight into Fitz's past was what she sought, and his sibling was bound to have some.

Good or bad.

She placed an order for the crab cake appetizer and an iced tea, her server disappearing into the back of the restaurant just as an attractive blonde woman wearing gray slacks and a soft blue button-down top stepped through the entryway.

Winter did a double take. Fitz's sister could have been his twin. Tall, blonde, and graced with the same attractive, symmetrical features, she caught Winter's eye and waved, weaving her way to the small table without waiting for the hostess to seat her.

"You must be Winter." Laurel-Anne slid into the chair across from her. "Fitz had only good things to say about you."

She lifted a hand, catching the attention of the nearest server and requesting "the usual." There was no entitlement in Laurel-Anne's tone. Just friendliness and familiarity.

Winter hesitated as she floundered for a safe icebreaker. Fitz hadn't shared many complimentary details regarding his sister. "Fitz says you're an early riser."

Laurel-Anne chuckled before her expression grew sober. "I'm sure he said a good deal more than that, if I know anything about my brother. Fitz has never been one to mince his words."

"Families are complicated." Winter's lame attempt to smooth over such a personal and awkward situation fell flat between them. Grimacing, she tried again. "Look, I understand. Trust me."

Cocking her head, Laurel-Anne examined Winter with a psychiatrist's gaze. "I did a quick search on you, and your brother came up. Whatever complaints I have about Mahoney will more than likely seem unimpressive by comparison. That's fair, but my issues aren't insubstantial."

Much sooner than Winter could have believed was possible, the server arrived with their orders. Winter's crab cakes sat on an elaborate bed of greens, creating a picture that was almost too pretty to eat.

Laurel-Anne's usual meal was far more complicated. A small plate of oysters and mini baguettes paired with a seared salmon filet, roasted asparagus, and a bottle of sparkling water. She poured the liquid into a flute, thanking the woman by name.

"I take it you come here a lot?" Winter speared a piece of the cake with her fork.

"Oh," Laurel-Anne sipped her water, "just every day that I work. I love good food but never have time to make my own. The life of a doctor, I suppose."

"Makes sense." After another bite of crab cake, Winter was ready to get down to business, uncomfortable as it was. "I guess you're aware that I had a meeting earlier today with your family. Safe to say that your parents don't believe much of what Fitz is telling them as of late. Especially your father."

Her brows knitting together, Laurel-Anne lowered her fork without touching her salmon. "Fitz's story is, pardon my French, complete and utter bullshit. He lies. That's what he does. My mother and father would be fools to take him seriously, and with all due respect, an accomplished professional like yourself will soon grow tired of his games."

Setting her own fork on the plate, Winter analyzed Laurel-Anne's statements. "You don't believe Fitz is capable of telling the truth? Ever?"

Laurel-Anne let out a heavy sigh, relaying what sounded like decades of familial turmoil. "I'm a psychiatrist. I could never make an *official* diagnosis for my brother, as I'm incapable of giving an unbiased opinion. Acknowledging that fact, my honest opinion as a doctor of mental health would be to diagnose him as a pathological liar. A sociopath."

Winter fought the barrage of memories attempting to flood her mind. "Would it be safe to say, after his lifetime of lies, that someone might have it out for your brother?"

"Yes." Laurel-Anne eyed the oysters but ate nothing. "I couldn't even begin to imagine a world where no one wanted revenge on Fitz. He's never respected any authority or shown our parents an ounce of remorse for the hell he put them through. He was a headache for his teachers and class-mates alike."

I can only imagine, but Fitz isn't soulless.

"He did have friends, correct? He didn't grow up as a social pariah, from what I've gathered."

"Rich kids always have friends." Laurel-Anne declared her certainty as a matter of fact. "So do rich adults. That doesn't mean the privileged individuals aren't assholes. It just means that people are drawn to them, if for no other reason than in the hopes that some of that privilege might overflow into their own lives. Unfortunately for Fitz's acquaintances, chaos seems to be the most common 'benefit' of spending time with him."

A clatter near the bar distracted them both for a moment and drew Winter's attention to the clock over the dangling wine glasses. Almost five. She managed to eat another bite of her order before curiosity outweighed her appetite. "Could you give me specific examples of the chaos Fitz wreaks on his companions?"

Laurel-Anne's blue eyes hardened. "Two of his ex-girl-friends have ended up in my mental ward, both suffering from severe depressive episodes. One of them tried to kill herself before she was brought in. I couldn't treat them, of course, but I knew who they were, and I can only guess at the barbaric way my brother must have broken things off with those poor women."

Winter tried to filter the information through an impar-tial investigative lens. "That is awful...but it doesn't neces-sarily mean Fitz committed any heinous acts. Breakups are hard."

"He's paid for three abortions for three different women." Laurel-Anne tightened her grip on the fluted stem. "I'm as pro-choice as they come, but the fact that Fitz officially denied having impregnated any of them is despicable. He has a ten-year-old son he's never met in Michigan. That ex refused to get an abortion and moved as far away as she could. Best decision she ever made."

Stunned, Winter envisioned a ten-year-old version of Fitz. "Has he ever tried to—"

"No." His sister didn't need the rest of the inquiry. "He was relieved that she wanted nothing to do with him. She never asked for a cent of child support, and he never gave her one."

Winter fought against the mounting disgust in her chest. She hadn't thought for a second that Fitz's past was exaggerated, but she wouldn't have pegged him as a man who abandoned his own child.

Laurel-Anne dabbed her lips with a napkin. "At least two of his 'friends' went through messy divorces after he got a little too chummy with their wives. He's had highly successful employees leave his firm and cite him as the sole reason for their departure. And if you wonder how I know about those things, it's because he told me. Fitz thinks his playboy lifestyle is hilarious. He's proud of it."

If there was a proper response to give in the moment, Winter's brain refused to conjure it up.

"My parents," Laurel-Anne's volume rose, "aren't the kindest people on the planet, as I'm sure you've discovered, but they tried to do right by Fitz. They paid his way out of numerous traffic tickets, drug possessions, and disorderly conduct charges, all in the hopes that he would grow up someday. He was never grateful for any of it. Fitz is a taker, and I hope you realize that before he's swindled something away from you too."

Winter straightened in her chair, a small wave of indignance flushing her cheeks. "Thank you, but I'm not so easily
swindled."

Another long sigh escaped Laurel-Anne. "I believe you.
The problem is that, from what I read, you *are* a good person,
and people like my brother…they feed off people like you.
You need to make sure that you truly question everything
Fitz is alleging, as well as what's taking place around you. If
he's involved, you can't take anything at face value."

"I see."

Warren Fitzgerald's words rattled through Winter's head.
*"My son has been a troublemaking pain in the ass the majority of
his life. He perfected the art of lying before he ever made it out of
diapers."*

"Do you? Because as much as I'd like to witness my
brother experience even an ounce of karmic payback," wrin-
kling her nose, Laurel-Anne pushed her plate away, "I guarantee you that this is just another self-indulgent, narcissistic
scheme he's pulled together simply because he can."

Fitz's sister snatched her purse off the chair, which
screeched as she scooted away from the table. Her jerky
motions prompted an uncomfortable weight to settle on
Winter's shoulders.

You upset her. Well done.

"I can't thank you enough for taking the time to meet
with me."

Laurel-Anne's ponytail whipped as she shook her head.
"Don't thank me. Just please, be careful. I wish you luck." She
pulled a shiny gold card from her purse. "And this is on me."

Wanting to argue the bill, Winter knew it was useless as
Laurel-Anne handed the hostess her card. When she exited
the restaurant, Winter poked at her crab cakes for another
few minutes before tossing her napkin on her plate and gathering her bag.

There was a lot to examine in the information that Laurel-Anne had shared, but only one sentence caused a shiver to feather across her skin.

"Just please, be careful."

22

Winter surveyed the multi-colored labyrinth of sticky notes she'd created on her very own whiteboard with a disproportionate amount of satisfaction.

Aiden would be proud.

Shaking her head, she dismissed all thoughts of Richmond that might send her spiraling down a black hole of homesickness and focused her attention on Fitz's messy life.

An entire half of the board was devoted to categories of people Fitz had hurt and/or angered. The ex-girlfriends he'd sent into major depressive episodes, the women whose abortions he'd financed, the woman who was out there somewhere raising his son.

She intended to press Fitz for specific names and expected that conversation to be something of a nuclear bomb drop on his composure. If she could drag the information out of him, an infinitely long list of telephone calls would follow.

And it wasn't just the women she'd be investigating. Anyone who cared deeply about these women—their parents, siblings, and spouses they'd acquired after Fitz had been a part of their lives—would all have reason to harbor ill-will toward Mahoney Fitzgerald.

"Next up, ladies and gentlemen," Winter lowered her eyes to the "Ex-Coworkers" section, "we have bosses, colleagues and contemporaries, and miscellaneous business associates who may have watched their marriages or careers crumble to pieces after a Fitz-storm blew through."

That list offered information that was easier to access. Fitz might never admit to screwing the CEO's wife at a former firm, but Winter could research his work history and associated paths of destruction with more phone calls.

Bzzz. Bzzz.

Winter grabbed the vibrating phone, and her heart grew in her chest. "Hey, stranger."

"I'm on the way." Noah's familiar deep voice wrapped around her like a hug. "Figured I should let my adorable little wife know. That seems like a proper married person thing to do."

Dropping into her desk chair, Winter tossed a rainbow of crumpled neon notes into the wastebasket. "Adorable? *Little?*"

Noah chuckled. "Oh, of course, what I meant to say was confident. Strong. Terrifying."

Lips twitching, she scrunched her nose. "Terrifying? Really?"

If her husband were there, he'd be dodging the paper wads she chucked at his head. As it was, she could only laugh along with him. The happy sound bubbling out of her throat momentarily drowned out the endless, screeching drama of Fitz's case.

"Be there soon." Noah's words mingled with background traffic noise. "Love you."

"Love you more."

Winter ended the call before he could one-up her declaration and returned her attention to the board.

The real question is, where do you start? In a sea of pissed-off people, who's carrying the red flag of "most likely to screw with Fitz"?

"And why," Winter pinched the bridge of her nose, "am I still inclined to believe Fitz about Sandra Smith despite everything his sister told me?"

Though her list of people to trail was growing longer by the minute, following Fitz himself could prove enlightening. Winter's instincts—sixth sense and all—had led her astray before. She certainly wasn't immune to liars.

Especially not sociopathic ones.

Thou shalt not reminisce over past interactions with the deranged.

Winter reached for her phone to call Fitz. She'd dig the info out of him with a pickax if necessary.

Sudden pulses of pain at her temples interrupted the plan.

"No." Winter scrambled for the package of tissues in her top drawer. "*No.*"

She'd wanted to leave her gift, her curse, behind in Virginia...but that just wasn't in the cards. The throbbing intensified to stabs, and blood trickled past her tissue, over her lips.

No...not now...

Winter's throbbing forehead smacked into the desktop...

A little girl with flaming red hair stood sobbing at the top of a steep staircase, peering up at a faceless, tall man. The man held a belt and roared while raising it overhead. "You little rat! Look what you did!"

Leather lashed down, striking the child once, twice, three times as the little girl screamed and covered her face.

"Look what you made me do!"

The girl's screams faded as Winter pushed herself back into a seated position. Viewing her office through blurred eyes, she swiped at the pool of crimson on her desk. A quick touch to her forehead found a bump already forming from her face-plant.

As the pain and dizziness subsided, Winter grasped at the thought teasing her brain and went statue-still.

Little rat. He called her a little rat.

Despite still feeling a bit off-center, she grabbed her phone. Dialing Fitz, she attempted to calm her racing thoughts.

"Hello?" Fitz's tone was heavy with concern. Was he expecting bad news? Like how she was dumping him as a client.

Which is exactly what I should do.

She didn't, of course, because she was too interested in the mystery of what was happening if nothing else. Did she believe Fitz? No. Like him? Hell no. Did she want to connect all the dots on this case? Absolutely yes.

Winter could talk to him over the phone, but she wanted to see his face. Needed to witness his reactions. "I'm on my way to your house."

As she finished cleaning up the bloody mess, she holstered her weapon and grabbed her messenger bag. Hurrying to her car, two questions circled through her mind.

Who is that little girl, Fitz? And what did you do to her?

23

Fitz spent the hour following the surprise call pacing his foyer. Winter Black hadn't asked to come over. She'd made a declaration of intent, informing him that she was on her way.

This is bad. This is really, really bad.

Beads of sweat dripped down his back as Fitz considered calling his sister. She'd just met with Winter a few hours ago, and the stories she may have told—all of which were true—could have done more harm than good for his case.

If Winter became so disgusted with his past that she quit, he was back to square one. The square where everyone assumed he was half-baked and fully nuts.

The front gate buzzed. Fitz yelped like a feral dog and charged toward the intercom. "Yeah?"

"It's me."

Fitz smacked the gate release with a trembling hand, opening the entrance for Winter. She'd be at his door in less than a minute. Just one minute.

Sixty seconds of infinite nightmares.

He studied her expression in the surveillance camera as she climbed from her car and approached the front door.

Intense. But not angry. Not unfriendly.

His confidence in the observation dwindled when he showed her into the foyer. There was a new wariness in Winter's piercing blue eyes that betrayed her altered view of him. Whatever narrative Laurel-Anne shared had taken due effect.

Nerves caused him to spit out the first words that came to mind. "Did your dinner prove enlightening?"

Winter's stiff posture became even more rigid. "You could say that. I learned a lot about your views on women. And children."

Vomit rose in Fitz's throat, and he barely managed to swallow it down. "Oh."

"Putting aside your history of epically bad breakups," Winter's nose scrunched in apparent disgust, "I was surprised to discover that you were also a deadbeat dad."

Emotion swelled in his throat. *Carli. Her name was Carli. And she wouldn't even consider the abortion. Not even for a second.*

"That all happened in my twenties." He had no defense or desire to create one. "I was a dick. I can't deny it. But there's not much I can do to turn back the clock now. What happened, happened."

"You could take responsibility for your own child." Winter stepped toward him, her face a tight mask of anger. "You could do the right thing. It's not too late."

Fitz pictured the young boy he'd helped create. The kid's name was Jaxson, and he was the spitting image of Fitz as a kid. Fitz knew because he often looked up his ex and their child on social media.

Too often.

"His mother would never..." His voice cracked hard, and he lifted his fist to his mouth until his throat loosened enough that he could speak. "She wouldn't let me see him even if I begged. Trust me. And I don't blame her. I essentially...abandoned her. Them. But the time for 'making things right' is long gone. That ship sailed after...after how I treated her."

Winter shook her head. "If you don't try, you'll never forgive yourself. And neither will your son."

Son?

The word sounded so foreign. Mahoney Fitzgerald wasn't capable of being a father. That kid was better off never coming near Fitz or his family. They were poisonous, and no amount of money would make up for the emotional damage that experiencing the Fitzgerald bloodline in person would inevitably wreak on Jaxson.

As Fitz struggled to formulate a response, Winter switched gears. "If we're focusing on revenge, I'm more concerned with your coworker relations. Pissing off people in the stockbroker world is a bad idea. Those individuals have the actual money and power to make you pay."

Fitz was less worried about stockbroker cohorts than the reel of angry husbands that flashed through his mind. "Well, if you're wanting that list of suspects, you'll be here all night."

Winter shot him a sharp glare. "That will not be happening."

He flinched. He hadn't meant the statement as a come-on, but every word that slipped past his lips was now tainted with Laurel-Anne's tell-all session.

You mean tainted with the truth, don't you?

Fitz fought off a shudder of humiliation. "That's not what I—"

"A little girl," nostrils flaring, Winter's volume rose with each word, "with bright red hair. Flaming red. Who is she? How do you know her?"

"What?" He eyed the living room doorway, longing to bolt

from the room. He was unnerved by his P.I.'s unfaltering intensity as she circled the foyer.

Winter halted, her crossed arms and narrowed eyes sending a bolt of fear through his body for reasons he couldn't articulate. "Redheads usually stand out in a crowd. *Think*. Did you grow up with one? Are you related to one? Did you date one?"

"No." Fitz's pulse pounded in his ears. "Ew. I don't date redheads. Not my type."

"Ew?" Winter's countenance grew severe, and for a second, he thought she really might kick him in the balls. "My best friend has red hair, and she's gorgeous."

"Is she single?"

Dammit.

The jibe passed his lips by habit…a split second before he could filter it. Winter's fists clenched at her sides, and Fitz braced himself for a punch.

Wouldn't be the first time a woman's tried to knock me out.

Instead, his private investigator took a deep breath and slowly blew it out. "I need you to stop being you for five minutes and focus. Somewhere, somehow, sometime…your path crossed with this little girl. Maybe she was older when you knew her, but she most definitely had bright red hair."

Indignance pricked at Fitz. "I don't get why you're on this ginger binge. Is it something Laurel-Anne said? Because you seem like a different person after speaking with her."

As if she were a balloon slowly deflating, Winter leaned against the wall, shoulders slumped. "This has nothing to do with Laurel-Anne that I know of. Although to be fair, you're the one who seems like a different person after my discussion with your sister."

Embarrassed, frustrated, and sick of himself—of his entire shitty existence—Fitz threw his hands in the air. "I haven't hidden what I am from you. And if this was just about me getting what I deserved from one of the thousands of people who rightfully hate my guts, I'd shut my damn mouth and take it." Determination burned a path through his chest. "I'd let them destroy me, but I'll be six feet underground before I let anyone destroy Sandra."

✳

WINTER GROWLED and resisted the urge to flick Fitz on his stupid-rich forehead.

His default answer to all her inquiries—and seemingly to life in general—was to play dumb. He didn't know. He couldn't remember.

There was a slight chance that Fitz was telling her the truth. Or...he was the true master of manipulation that Laurel-Anne had claimed he was.

Regardless, there wasn't a doubt in Winter's mind that the red-haired girl from her vision was significant to Fitz's case somehow. Her gift didn't always provide the clearest of answers, but it hadn't completely misfired either.

"Okay." She clapped her hands together. "Let's focus. You haven't dated any redheads, so we'll assume you knew her as a child. In grade school maybe? I get that it's been three decades since you were running around pissing off your elementary school teachers, but you're going to have to dig deep."

Fitz pressed two fingers to his temples. "You want me to dig deep into my days as a prepubescent asshole? Right. All sorts of clear memories stored up in my head about that."

Sarcasm dripped from his words. Winter narrowed her eyes, wishing she could shoot actual daggers. "Being a smart-ass isn't going to save Sandra. I'm asking you these questions for a reason, even if you don't understand what that is." Despite her best intentions, her voice rose. "You want me to figure this mess out for you? Then *help me do it!*"

"Okay! Geez." Fitz raked his hands through his hair before pointing at the ceiling. "Yearbooks. My mom kept all my yearbooks for me growing up. They're upstairs in a box. Just have a seat in the living room, stop asking me questions for five seconds, and I'll go get them."

Now we're getting somewhere.

If Fitz couldn't recall his own history, photographic evidence might fill in a few blanks or at the very least jog his memory. And maybe a certain redheaded child will appear on the pages.

Mentally crossing her fingers, Winter settled into a chair facing its own giant coffee table and prepared herself for a visual feast of private school privilege. Fitz's living room, though decked out with high-end furniture and all the latest electronic wonders, emanated a desolate, chilling aura. No color, no photos. No personal touches.

"It's like a cemetery in here." A shiver rippled through her muscles. "During a funeral. In the rain. At night."

"Wow, tell me how you really feel." Fitz rounded the corner, lugging a sizable box. "Did you just compare my house to a cemetery? And do you always talk to yourself?"

As he plopped the container beside her chair, Winter lifted a shoulder. "I call it like I see it."

"I'm aware." Fitz's forehead creased with wrinkles and apparent resignation. "You have a good time with those. I'm going to take a shower, then I can answer the eight million questions you'll come up with in the next ten minutes."

For someone desperate to save his girlfriend, Fitz was shutting down fast. Winter had expected as much after bringing up his less-than-flattering past—especially the part about the abandoned child—yet she still worried that her client might retreat too deeply into himself and leave her with an unsolvable case. Hopefully, the shower would do him good.

While Fitz withdrew to lick his wounds, Winter dug into the box like a treasure chest. Guessing at the age of the girl from her vision, she pulled out his kindergarten through fifth-grade yearbooks and flipped to the page showcasing Fitz's final year of elementary school.

Dammit. All the pictures of the children were in black and white. Not helpful.

A half hour later, she shut the fourth-grade yearbook and tossed it on top of the fifth-grade volume.

No little redheaded girl. Well, at least that she could tell based on the lack of color.

She grabbed the next book, her pursed lips holding back a multitude of curse words as she flipped through the world of Fitz's third-grade academic experience. Maybe he couldn't remember the redhead because there truly hadn't been one. At least not at school.

He was cute back then—shaggy hair, twinkling eyes, a few freckles, and crater-deep dimples—appearing as innocent and sweet as any other eight-year-old. Nothing could save him or his classmates from the outdated hairstyles and fashion trends they'd proudly displayed, but third grade Fitz didn't appear to be the demon-seed hellion his family had described.

"You look like a normal kid." Winter glanced at the boxful of history awaiting her perusal. "Or at least like a normal snotty, spoiled-brat rich kid."

Reentering the room with a wet head and fresh clothing, Fitz let out a mirthless chuckle. "I really need to start announcing myself from down the hall. Maybe then I can avoid your snappy monologues. 'Snotty, spoiled brat'? Did you ever consider going into the field of motivational speaking?"

Chuckling in spite of herself, Winter flipped the page and spotted a picture of Fitz with two of his friends in soccer uniforms. The boys all had their arms thrown around each other and were grinning from ear to ear. "Were these your best friends?"

Fitz sauntered toward her and crouched to survey the image. "Yeah. You could say that."

Tears glimmered in his eyes. Actual tears.

"Did something happen to them?" Winter tapped the photo. "Why does this picture make you sad?"

Fitz shook his head. "Not sad. Regretful, maybe." He straightened, backing away from the pages of memories as though they were laced with the plague. "That's Bobby Burner and Roosevelt McGee. We were thick as thieves back then, but I kinda fell out of touch with them."

Winter frowned. *Bobby Burner. Why does that name sound fam—*

She shot up in the chair. "Bobby Burner, as in the guy your mom was discussing this morning? The one who was assaulted?"

"Yeah." A wistful half-smile played at his lips. "I went to visit ole Bob this afternoon. Hadn't seen him since...since his wedding, I guess. Jesus. Isn't time the weirdest damn thing?"

Judging from his softened tone, Winter guessed that Fitz and Bobby had undergone something of a hatchet-burying session during their reunion. "Didn't you say that Bobby was assaulted about three months ago?"

"Yeah, I—"

Fitz's phone erupted into ear-splitting crow caws. "Sorry." He yanked the device from his shirt pocket. "That's my mother's personalized ring tone."

Winter bit her lip, refusing to break into the laughter that desperately wanted out. Asshole or not, Mahoney Fitzgerald's sense of humor was alive and well.

She continued to flip through the yearbook pages as Fitz spoke to his mother, only looking up when he gasped.

"What?" Fitz sank to his leather couch, the phone pressed to his ear. "But I just…I just saw him. Are you sure?"

Internal alarms flared like lightning in a black sky. Winter rose, studying Fitz's ashen complexion and the glistening tears returning to his eyes with growing trepidation.

Fitz tapped at his screen and dropped the phone onto the couch. He stared at the floor. "He's dead."

Winter took slow, steady steps toward him. "Who's dead?"

"Bobby." Fitz lifted his gaze, tears now streaming down his cheeks. "Some type of IV overdose. He's just gone. *Gone.*"

"Fitz," Winter stood beside him and placed a hand on his shoulder, "I'm so sorry."

His brow furrowed. "There's suspicion of foul play. They think someone may have killed him."

Forget think. Winter was certain of foul play.

"It could have been the same person who tried to off him before. Maybe they came back to finish the job."

"Why?" Fitz's hands balled into fists. "Why would anyone want to kill Bobby…*twice?*"

Dozens of questions swirled through Winter's skull.

"Fitz…" she waited until he met her gaze, "what time were you with Bobby Burner today?"

Swiping at his eyes, he glanced at his watch. "I don't know exactly. Why?"

Winter ignored the question and asked another of her own. "Did your mother know Bobby's time of death?"

Fitz shrugged. "She didn't say. Why are you ask…?" The question died on his lips as realization lit his eyes. He raised his hands as if to ward off a blow. "No! Just no. I never—"

Before he could run down the path of denial, Winter

clapped her hands together. "Listen to me." She counted the seconds until Fitz's breathing steadied. "I need to know, because, believe me, the police will want to know the answers to those questions too. You may be one of the last people to see Bobby Burner alive. That puts you on the suspect list."

As if his bones had turned into sand, Bobby practically melted back into the couch. "Are you serious?"

She didn't pull the punch. "Very. I need you to look at the GPS in your car or on your phone and note down the exact times you arrived at and left that hospital. In the meantime, I'll try to learn more about your friend's death."

If she were still a Fed, that information would be at her fingertips. Now, she'd have to get creative.

And she needed to get out of there.

What if Mahoney Fitzgerald had offed his friend? Had he done the same thing to Sandra? And who was next?

Not me.

Returning to the yearbooks, she hefted the box onto her hip as another thought occurred to her. If Fitz was as innocent as his currently devastated looking body seemed to suggest, then something bigger might be going on.

"The other boy in that picture. Roosevelt? You need to get in touch with him. Make sure he's doing okay…just to be safe."

"You think he might not be?" Fitz fumbled for his phone. "I don't think I even have his number anymore. He's got a body shop in Austin, but nobody is going to be there this late."

"Leave a message." Winter hesitated, hating herself for the sliver of sympathy in her chest that made her question leaving Fitz alone in such a shaken state. "I'm taking the yearbooks. You should stay put tonight. Lock up. Batten down the hatches."

Fitz didn't move from his position on the couch. "Bobby was a good guy. He didn't deserve this."

The ghosts of every dead victim from Winter's past screamed through her brain as she made her way toward the front door. "Of course he didn't." She hollered over her shoulder. "But somebody else thinks he did. We have to find that somebody, Fitz, and *soon*. I'll call you in the morning. Remember to lock up and set the alarms."

She stepped into the darkness with a shiver. Midnight approached, and Noah would likely be asleep by the time she arrived home. Winter imagined what it would be like to reach their house and find he'd dissipated into thin air. The love of her life…gone without a trace.

Shuddering at the idea, she hurried toward her car. A tiny dark shape scurried behind the tires.

She froze, her stomach clenching.

No. No more rats. I'm done with the rats. Done-diddy-done-done-done!

Goose bumps shot down her arms as she inched closer. The creature scurried out and glanced her way, its eyes reflecting the light from Fitz's windows.

"Cat." Her body went limp with relief. "You're just a cat."

The feline ran off, and Winter rushed to climb into her car and leave the Fitzgerald premises. Logic dictated that there probably wasn't another furry visitor waiting around to scare the living bejeezus out of her, but she floored the gas through the front gate anyway.

24

Noah peeked at the kitchen clock for the umpteenth time. Ten minutes to midnight. Winter had sent a text earlier relaying her afternoon vision of the little redheaded girl, her impromptu trip to Mahoney Fitzgerald's home, and that it might be a late night.

Midnight was a tad later than he'd expected.

Unable to relax, let alone sleep, he'd attempted to assist his wife's investigation by running a few of the names from her whiteboard through federal databases. His job description might not include helping Winter any longer, but lightening her load came naturally.

He'd uncovered next to nothing.

The front door creaked open and shut. "Is that my husband still awake at midnight on a *weekday?*"

Noah grinned as Winter entered the kitchen, dropping a cardboard box on the floor. "I was tryin' to help you out, darlin'. I must admit, though, that all I've done is confirm the incredibly clean legal slates of a few Texan stockbrokers and CEOs that Mahoney rubbed shoulders with. Not so much as a single sealed file to throw some shade on one of these people."

"We should get some sleep." Winter squeezed his shoulder and immediately contradicted herself by leaning over to view his screen. "Who are you running now?"

"Dr. John Newberry." Noah's fingers flew across the keys. "He's looking as squeaky clean as the rest of them so far."

"Wait." Winter pointed at a highlighted box in Newberry's work history. "Click that."

Noah obeyed, opening a vague addendum and reading it aloud. "We hereby release Dr. John Newberry from all medical duties and/or privileges as head surgeon at Bogey State Medical Center. This termination is final. No filed appeal shall be accepted or considered by the hospital board."

Winter was practically lying on Noah's shoulder now. "That's dated just five months ago. Dr. Newberry got fired five months ago from one of Texas's most prestigious hospitals, and there's not even a reason listed?"

"That's weird as heck." Noah reached for the nearest chair and yanked it toward them. "Sit. I'm not a surfboard."

Winter plopped in the seat and began typing on his laptop. "Maybe we should dive a little deeper into Peaceful Acres's employees. Can you pull up the facility's website for me?"

Chuckling, Noah nudged the computer her way. "Pretty sure you're pulling that one up yourself."

"Bam." Winter threw her hands up in triumph. "There they are."

Peaceful Acres's "Meet Our Medical Staff" page displayed the typical group photo full of scrubs and smiles. Nothing about the staff screamed suspicious, odd, or even interesting.

Winter scrolled down the page. "The receptionist is new, and she isn't in that picture, which means it's old. But not over five months old because Newberry is front and center.

Fitz couldn't remember any specific nurses' names due to his inability to care about anything but himself, and I haven't spoken with any nurses at all. This lists a 'Maude Little' as head nurse, so let's start with her. I wanna know when she got the position and where she came from."

Noah raised an eyebrow. "You really believe Fitz was there? You think he's telling the truth?"

Pausing for a moment, Winter chewed her lower lip. "I just can't figure out any reason why Fitz would create such an elaborate lie. This goes beyond screwing with people for fun. The entire mess is too much work. The labor would cancel out the entertainment for someone like him."

Her fingers resumed their rapid key-clicking, and Noah watched—lovestruck—as Winter ran Maude through the database. Nothing beat having a front-row seat to his wife in stealth mode. She had no clue as to how beautiful she was when she was on the hunt, which made her all the more attractive.

"Boom." Winter slapped the table in triumph. "Maude Little's work history shows that she was let go from her position as head nurse at a Waco hospital just four months ago. Shortly after that, she started at Peaceful Acres."

"Any listed reason?" Noah didn't particularly believe Mahoney's story, but the Peaceful Acres faculty was beginning to raise some flags.

Winter shook her head, eyebrows arched with suspicion. "Nope. That's two employees...the two highest ranking employees at Peaceful Acres...that were fired for undocumented reasons immediately before joining the hospice facility staff."

Noah released a giant yawn. "Shady."

"Absolutely." Eyes flitting to the clock, Winter grabbed his hand. "Something awful happened today to one of Fitz's old friends. Bobby Burner died and—"

"Didn't he used to be in the minor leagues?"

"Used to. Yes." Winter cringed, squeezing his fingers. "He was assaulted a few months back by an unknown assailant and just woke up from his coma two days ago. This afternoon, he had an IV overdose of some sort. Bobby's dead, and they suspect foul play."

Knots twisted tight in Noah's stomach. "You think it's related? That whoever murdered Bobby has it out for Mahoney too? Maybe they have something to do with Sandra's disappearance?"

It was Winter who yawned now. "It's possible. Fitz and Bobby were tight with another guy—Roosevelt McGee—growing up. I told Fitz to get ahold of him. Warn him. But that doesn't seem like enough."

Noah knew Winter's next step because it would have been his own. "You think you need to go talk to this Roosevelt guy yourself."

"Yes." Closing Noah's laptop, Winter rose from the chair and stretched her arms high. "He might not listen to Fitz, for one thing. They haven't spoken in years. And Roosevelt might have some insight into the red-haired girl's identity. It's worth a shot."

Tapping his fingers against the tabletop, Noah couldn't ignore the unease stirring in his gut. "Have you considered that this Roosevelt fella could be the killer? You might be walking right into a trap."

Winter planted a kiss on Noah's forehead. "I have, and I'm prepared for that scenario. I was a federal agent, you know. I have some skills."

"Yeah, yeah." Joking about danger wasn't about to appease him. "You're also alone now. No partner. No backup. And if someone actually killed Bobby Burner, they might be interested in a lot more than messing with Mahoney...or anyone he's hired to work for him."

"Duly noted, Agent Dalton." Winter grabbed a water bottle from the counter. "I'll probably make a stop at Peaceful Acres first. Poke around and see what reactions I can get out of the staff. If I'm lucky, Patricia Smith might even be awake and able to chat."

"That's a good place to start." Noah still didn't like it.

Winter ran a hand through his hair, reading his mood as usual. "I'll be fine. Promise. Now, come on, let's go to bed. It's already tomorrow, and I've got investigative yearbook homework waiting for me after the workday ends."

"Sounds fun." Noah flipped the kitchen lights off and wove an arm around his wife's waist. "If we're lucky, maybe we'll wake up in the morning to a driveway that hasn't been graced with a rat corpse."

"Reach for the sky, babe." Chortling at her own humor, Winter seemed unaware of just how concerned Noah truly was.

She wasn't scared in the least. Simply determined and fearless. That was why he loved her...and also the cause of massive, recurring bouts of anxiety that he'd learned to keep to himself.

Noah threw the covers back while Winter switched into sweats and a t-shirt. Seconds away from pulling her close, he tried to ignore the dark cloud hanging over his head.

The general nature of her case—the idea that Sandra Smith had evaporated altogether—had triggered painful, disturbing flashbacks of Winter's own vanishing act when her damn brother took her hostage.

Noah could leave the past in the past, but he wouldn't deny the emotional scars from that nightmare to anyone. And despite his general misgivings about Mahoney, if the man was telling the truth, it was safe to say that Noah understood his agony better than anyone.

25

Winter pushed through the entrance doors at Peaceful Acres Hospice Care at exactly ten in the morning. Visiting hours were open, and regardless of her being a different type of visitor, she took full advantage of the open-door policy.

Poppy sprang up to greet her. "You're back. Is everything okay?"

The question seemed absurd. Poppy was aware of who Winter was, what she did for a living, and the client she was working for. It was a clear and safe bet that everything was not okay, but Poppy seemed like a "glass full" kind of person and most likely avoided—either consciously or unconsciously—seeing anything bad in her world.

"Nice to see you again, Poppy." Winter bypassed the inquiry altogether and fought to keep her tone light and friendly. "I wondered if you could tell me what happened to Peaceful Acres's previous receptionist?"

"Honestly?" Poppy tilted her head as though she was concentrating very hard. "I don't know. No one ever really told me. I guess I assumed that she transferred."

"Hm." Believing Poppy if for no other reason than the woman seemed too dull-witted to lie, Winter gave her an encouraging, conspiratorial grin. "Maybe you could give me her name?"

Poppy's eyes went wide as she began fidgeting with a button on her cardigan. "Oh, I can't do that. I'd get fired. You'll have to speak with Dr. Newberry if you want that information. I can page him again?"

Maybe Poppy was brighter than Winter gave her credit for. Since she had planned on speaking with the man anyway. "That'd be great."

If Dr. Newberry had appeared swiftly during Winter's first visit, this time, he must have teleported. He burst through the door, rushing to greet her.

"Winter Black." He held out a hand, as friendly as ever… on the surface. His smile was a little too brittle, his pupils a bit too dilated for her to take his welcome at face value. "How can I be of service to you today?"

"I have questions." Winter noted the sheen on the doctor's forehead and wondered at its source. "About your employees. Current and former."

Casting a side glance at Poppy, Dr. Newberry gestured toward the door he'd just used. "Why don't you come with me to my office? I could take a few minutes from my day for the sake of a former federal agent."

The flattery held an undertone of panic. While Winter was well-used to mixed reactions from those she requested to interview, it was too early in this particular situation to tell if Dr. Newberry's apprehension was due to guilt or simple nervousness at the idea of a Fed digging into his business.

Former Fed. Just your friendly neighborhood private investigator here. Nothing to get too worked up about, folks.

Ushering her into his office, Dr. Newberry took a seat

behind his desk with a pleasant smile still in place. Yet all the feigned calm in the world couldn't hide the fact that many things about the doctor's private workspace were off. Wrong.

Aside from a laptop, his desk surface was clear. Not a pen or stapler or family photo in sight. The beige walls were equally bare. No plaques or motivational quotes or landscapes.

No certificates. Not even a high school diploma to boast its owner's name.

Sliding her gaze around the room, Winter spotted a briefcase by the door with an overcoat resting on top. Beside it, a suitcase stood on its little whirly wheels. "Going somewhere?"

Though his posture tensed, his smile widened by several degrees. "I have all the time in the world for you. I've done some research on you since we last saw each other. I didn't realize you were *the* Winter Black. You have a tremendous reputation that you should be quite proud of."

The former damp shine on Dr. Newberry's brow had morphed into glistening beads that began a slow crawl down his temples.

Winter considered sitting in one of the two chairs facing the doctor's desk and decided against it. She preferred the power position of standing in this instance. "Thank you for the compliment, but I'm no more impressive than any other former agent. Anyway, I wanted to ask you about your former job as the Bogey State Medical Center head surgeon. That's a very desirable position for any physician. What made you decide to come to such a small facility like Peaceful Acres?"

Dr. Newberry's gulp echoed off the empty office walls. "I-I was seeking a change of pace. I have a family, and this job allows me much more time to spend with them."

Good answer. Total bullshit, but you get an A for effort, Doc.

"Interesting." Winter tapped a finger on her chin. "Because official records indicate that you were let go from Bogey State. Not that you chose to leave. Those are two very different sets of circumstances, don't you think?"

"Okay." His cheeks flushing, Dr. Newberry's smile disappeared. "You've done your research. My former employers did what was best for me at the time. I needed to…to get myself in line. I had a very minor addiction issue that caused much more concern than necessary."

The admission was the exact fuel for fire that Winter had hoped for. "So, that minor addiction of yours. What was it? Drugs? Alcohol? Hookers? Little girls?"

Dr. Newberry stood, slamming a hand on his desktop. "It was nothing of that sort! How dare you suggest such atrocities."

Yawning to show just how unfazed she was by his outburst, Winter lifted her shoulders. "Just trying to get to the truth."

"Gambling." The doctor's jaw flexed with his growing anger. "It was a simple matter of me gambling too much, and it's none of your damn business."

"You forget," she couldn't help grinning now, "that I'm in the business of making things that are none of my business my business. And I'm sorry, but I highly doubt your addiction issue was 'simple' in any way, considering you lost your job over it. I mean, that's the kind of scandal that could ruin a career."

Flaring his nostrils, Dr. Newberry was the dictionary definition of indignant.

Winter stepped closer to the doctor's desk. "Have you ever heard of a minor league baseball player by the name of Bobby Burner?"

Newberry's crimson cheeks turned ghost white as he sputtered out a cough. "I haven't, and I'm not sure what this line of questioning has to do with anything. Do you really have a valid need for my assistance? Because you aren't an actual law enforcement officer, and I certainly have no reason to waste my time on such conversations. I'm a busy man."

"Well," Winter kept her tone amicable, "you did say that you had all the time in the world for me. Let's talk about your head nurse, Maude Little. Were you acquainted with her before you began your job at Peaceful Acres? It seems you both started here around the same time."

"No." Dr. Newberry held her gaze steadily, his lip curling into the beginnings of a sneer.

She'd be getting kicked out soon anyway, so there was no need to stop now. "Are there any employees here today who I can speak with that were working at the facility before you came on as head physician?"

The doctor huffed, throwing his hands in the air. "There are not. We've been experiencing a large amount of employee turnover recently. Now, I'm afraid I must end this meeting. I have an appointment to get to."

Storming toward the office entrance, he waved Winter into the hallway and promptly shut the door behind her without so much as a "bye."

Of course, Newberry expected her to leave, but he hadn't given that specific suggestion, and Winter wasn't done just yet. Instead, she crept back to the reception area and headed for the hallway the doctor had taken upon her first visit when he went to check on Patricia Smith.

The hall was doorless until it came to a T, with four doors down both the right and left sides. Winter went left, aware that her time was short and no one in hospice care would likely appreciate a P.I. popping her nose into their rooms.

The first room was empty, which at the very least narrowed things down. Peeking into the second doorway,

Winter caught sight of an elderly man sound asleep on his bed.

At the third door, voices carried from inside.

"Let me just help you up, Mr. Woodsmall. We'll get you a change of clothes, some fresh sheets, and a clean bedpan."

Definitely not the right room.

The last option presented with a wide-open doorway and a bald woman leaning against a stack of pillows on her hospital bed. The patient was awake...and staring blankly at the wall.

Winter took a few steps into the room. "Patricia? Patricia Smith?"

Large blue eyes shot Winter's way, widening as they registered her presence. "Y-yes. I'm Patricia. But...oh my. You shouldn't be in here."

At the strange greeting, Winter came closer. "I'm sorry, ma'am. I'll only take a minute of your time. My name is Winter, and I—"

"I know who you are." Patricia wheezed between every word. "You have to leave this situation alone. Please. I'm begging you."

The dying woman's plea gave Winter a moment's pause. Patricia's see-through skin stretched tightly across a face that had decayed to mostly bone and veins. Her bright, lucid gaze seemed to be the only part of her body still possessing life.

She doesn't have much time left. Are you really going to push an issue with a terminally ill woman who's lying on her actual deathbed?

"I'm so sorry." Persisting seemed like Winter's only viable option, though she kept her tone soft. If the woman got more distressed, she would leave then. "I can't go yet. And why...why is it so important for me to leave this situation alone? What do you know about what's been happening?"

Patricia lifted an emaciated hand to her forehead. "Please. I don't know anything. Let it go."

Anger at Fitz for having ever put her in such a position coursed through Winter's every cell. "What do you actually know about Sandra Smith? Mahoney Fitzgerald? What's going on with Dr. Newberry and this place? You can trust me, Patricia."

Chin trembling, the dying woman shook her head. "I don't know anything."

Before Winter could respond, Patricia glanced at the door and closed her eyes, as though she'd fallen asleep. Or hadn't been awake to begin with.

"Winter Black." Dr. Newberry's voice boomed behind her. "You have no right to walk around my facility harassing my patients. If you do not immediately leave the premises, I will be forced to call the authorities. The *real* authorities."

She'd expected a day would come when she desperately wished for her badge and the power that came with it. Yet, as Winter obediently made her exit from Peaceful Acres, she understood that nothing could have prepared her for the magnitude of the moment's sting.

Though she'd been met with general respect so far, she'd just as easily been dismissed when her questions hit too close to home or her presence became unwanted. Winter accepted that even her initial success might have more to do with her former federal agent credentials than her private investigator license.

How could she—or any P.I.—expect to solve a case when doors so quickly closed in her face?

She missed the authority. The ability to force an issue to its conclusion.

But you aren't the first private investigator in the world to run into a wall, and you're in the lucky majority considering the resources you still have through your husband. You're being a big baby.

"Whining isn't a part of the job description." Winter climbed into her car and slammed the driver's side door. "Shut your mouth and make it happen."

26

Winter stomped the gas pedal as she flew down the highway. The visit to Peaceful Acres had stirred up a deep agitation in her chest. Patricia Smith had information she was too scared to share. Dr. John Newberry was flat-out lying about...possibly everything.

What those two had to do with Fitz or Sandra Smith or Bobby Burner's assault and murder was unclear. But there was a common denominator somewhere, and Winter was determined to suss it out.

Eyes on the road, she called Fitz on speakerphone.

"It's me." His tone was strained and exhausted. "Still alive over here."

"Excellent." Winter's knuckles whitened as she clenched the steering wheel. "Let's try to keep you that way. Did you get ahold of Roosevelt?"

Fitz huffed in frustration. "No. I left him a message at his shop last night and a few this morning. But you have to remember, I haven't spoken to Roose in years. Decades. The version of me that he remembers isn't necessarily someone you rush to get back in touch with."

Winter bit her lip, wanting to tell Fitz that the current version of himself wasn't much to write home about either. "Keep trying but stay put. Don't leave your house for anything. Doors locked. Alarms on."

"Um." Fitz wasn't a pro at hiding his fears. "Is there something I should know? Another new development? 'Cause you sound...extra stressed."

Envisioning Dr. Newberry's wrath-filled glare, Winter still had no proof to back up what she now regarded as true. "I believe you, okay? Someone *is* messing with you. And I think Dr. Newberry and Patricia Smith—maybe everyone at Peaceful Acres—are involved. Just have to nail down the how."

"God." Fitz's voice trembled. "I just want Sandra to be okay. I just need to know what's happened to her. I need to know she's *alive*."

Winter pitied her client, even though she firmly believed his poor behavior over the years still had something to do with the case. "We'll find her. For now, one of us needs to speak with Roosevelt. I was on my way to his shop, but I'm thinking if he's not answering your calls that he might not even be there. I'll try his house first."

"You have the address?" Her client's doubtful timbre rang loud and clear. "I tried to google him, and I found nothing but the shop information."

"He might be unlisted." Winter guessed Roosevelt couldn't live too incredibly far from his workplace. "But I can get around that. I'll call you afterward."

Ending the call, she immediately dialed Noah, and despite being at work, he answered on the first ring. "You okay?"

It wasn't the normal banter-ish hello her husband usually shared, but Winter couldn't blame him for being on edge. She was on edge too. "Could you find an address for me? It's most likely unlisted. Roosevelt McGee."

Noah's computer keys click-clacked away in the background. "Will you please be careful approaching the home of a man who may or may not be responsible for Bobby Burner's death? And Sandra Smith's disappearance...and about one too many skinned rats in our driveway...and Mahoney Fitzgerald's impending future in the looney bin."

"Or..." Winter appreciated her husband's concern, but she didn't have time to entertain it. "Roosevelt is in serious danger and may have information that proves vital to the case. Address, please."

While Noah spouted off the information, Winter entered it into her GPS, keeping one hand on the wheel and both eyes on the road. She'd been right. Roosevelt's home was less than five minutes from his mechanic shop.

"If you get time, run a deep background check on Patricia Smith. Not just her but her family. Close friends. All their criminal records and finances. I have to get the backstory on this woman."

"Darlin', I'll take my lunch break and do it right now."

Grateful that her partner was still her partner even when they weren't partners, Winter exhaled a breath of relief. "Thank you. I love you. Call you soon."

Ten minutes later, Winter pulled into the driveway of a modest ranch-style home in a quiet middle-class neighborhood. Roosevelt may have grown up in the elite mini universe that was Huntstown, but he'd certainly taken measures to make that fact unobvious.

Winter climbed the three simple steps to the McGees' front door and rang the bell.

"Coming!" A female voice carried through the house before a petite, sweet-faced brunette opened the door. "Can I help you?"

"Hi, ma'am." Winter strove to keep her expression stress-free. "I'm Winter Black, Private Investigator. I was hoping to speak with Roosevelt McGee?"

Taking a step back, the woman's features flooded with concern. "He's at work. I'm Liz, his wife. You said you're a private investigator? What's this about? What's happened?"

Smiling to calm Liz's nerves, Winter gave her best "no worries" speech. "Just a routine part of a case I'm working. Your husband isn't directly involved, and he certainly isn't in any trouble with the law. Maybe I'll try back later."

Liz crossed her arms, frowning at the reassurance. "He isn't *directly* involved? What does that mean?"

Winter recognized that she'd utterly failed at doing anything other than doubling Liz's concern. "It just means that I'm working on an investigation that he might have information about. I won't know for sure until I get a chance to speak with him. Please, don't worry."

The wrinkles on the woman's forehead grew deeper. *I never could have made it as an actress.*

"Are you sure?"

Sure about what?

That Roosevelt was or wasn't involved in some elaborate scheme to drive his old friend crazy? Or that he might be in trouble? Winter didn't have time to give Roosevelt's wife any additional information or reassurances.

"Thank you for your time." Handing Liz her card, Winter backed down the steps, giving her a reassuring smile. "You have a nice day."

Winter pitied the woman, who stood frozen at the doorway, helplessly watching as she hightailed it to her car and backed out of the driveway.

"He isn't in any trouble with the law…maybe." Winter entered McGee's Motors into her GPS. "His trouble could be much much worse…also maybe."

The maybes threatened to drive her insane.

Noah's concern was that Roosevelt was dangerous—possibly a killer—but Winter feared that the man was *in* danger of being killed himself.

And she still couldn't for the life of her piece together why.

27

Roosevelt McGee scrubbed at the black oil staining his fingers. After fifteen years of working on cars, he'd come to accept that his hands would never be completely clean again. His wife seemed okay with that reality, and that was all that mattered at the end of the day.

Keeping Liz and his two kids happy.

He headed toward the front reception area and flipped the "open" sign to "closed" before grunting in approval at the tidy counter and neatly lined customer waiting chairs. Every wall in the building was lined in solid brick that he'd painted white with his own two hands. Simple. Cost-effective. A nice place to have his quiet lunch.

He'd started this business with his own money, and while there was a hell of a lot more of it at his disposal, he'd kept the shop efficient and flash-free. Proud of himself for having stuck to the goal—creating a modest world where he could live an honest life—Roosevelt allowed himself a pat on the back.

Growing up, his parents had been a miserable, raging trainwreck. His father was a coke-snorting philanderer, and his mother a full-blown alcoholic. Being filthy rich hadn't made a flip of difference in their familial hell.

Roosevelt was certain that the money had actually made things worse.

"When you've got everything you could ever want, there's nothing left to do but be miserable."

His mutters were heard by no one as he ran the shop alone. There was a priceless peace in not having to deal with another living soul while he fixed the automobile messes that people brought him. Roosevelt preferred the company of the local classic rock radio station over human interaction.

He didn't even answer the shop's phone. If it was important, they'd leave a message. If they needed service, they'd leave a message.

If they wanted a piece of his time…well, he had enough to go around, and they'd leave a message.

Liz and the kids could get ahold of him on his mobile, and the rest of the planet just wasn't that incredibly important to Roosevelt. He kept his circle—his worries—to a minimum.

Yet here comes good ole Mahoney Fitzgerald, like a bullhorn in a nursery.

His old friend had left at least ten messages on the shop's phone in the last twelve hours. Roosevelt had stopped counting and listening to them altogether an hour or so ago.

Liz kept up with the news, and she'd informed him that another old friend, Bobby Burner, had passed away in the Huntstown hospital yesterday. Roosevelt hadn't been surprised. After Bobby's attack a few months back, which blew up the headlines for a bit due to his local celebrity status, Roosevelt had assumed that his old buddy had pissed the wrong person off.

That's what money did to a man. Made him stupid and got him in deep shit.

Fitz had to be calling about Bobby's death. The three of them had been tight growing up, their relationship getting even stronger as they made their way through college. That was round about when Roosevelt had the epiphany that he wanted to be a different man. A better man.

He'd distanced himself from his buddies and all the rich assholes in the village of privileged idiots that was Huntstown. Shortly after, he'd met Liz, and they'd built a nice life together in Austin.

Roosevelt trudged to his desk. "And all I want now is that tuna salad sandwich in the fridge and an ice-cold Pepsi. Damn you, Fitz."

It was best to get the call out of the way. Collapsing in his beat-up office chair, Roosevelt reluctantly put the phone to his ear and dialed his old friend.

Fitz picked up on the first ring. "Roose? Oh my god. What took you so long? Listen. I think we're in trouble, man. I'm guessing you heard that Bobby died, but what you don't know is they're saying it was *murder*. Someone killed him, and I think that same person kidnapped my girlfriend. You might be in some serious danger too."

No "hello," just a breathless Mahoney spewing out a crazy spiral of gibberish warnings. The guy sounded like he was three days into a bad acid trip.

Nothing's changed at all for Fitz.

"Hey." Roosevelt took advantage of Fitz's pause for oxygen to get in a word. "I did hear about Bobby, and it's really a bad deal. Bobby's always had a way of pissing off the wrong people, so as much as I hate to say it, I wouldn't be surprised if someone did kill him. I don't know what that has to do with your…girlfriend disappearing or why you think it has anything to do with me. I haven't talked to Bob in years."

Something like a frustrated pig squeal emitted over the line. "That's what I'm talking about! I hadn't talked to him either, but this shit isn't about now. It's got something to do with the past, Roose. And we were the three friggin' muske-teers for damn near twenty years. Something we did is catching up to us. I know I sound insane but—"

"You do." Roosevelt didn't have the time or patience for this bullcrap anymore. "You sound one hundred percent deranged, and I've got work to do."

"Do you know any redheads? A little girl, maybe?" Fitz wasn't done spitting nuts yet, and his line of inquiry gave Roosevelt pause. "Or anyone with red hair but especially a little girl. Do you?"

"What in the actual hell?" Roosevelt's nose crinkled with disgust. "That's one creepy freakin' question, Fitz. I don't know what kinda mess you're in or what drug bender you're on, but my best advice would be to get some help and call me when you're sober. They have doctors for this kinda thing."

Ending the call, Roosevelt ran a hand through his thin-ning brown hair. Here they were, facing their forties, and Mahoney was still acting like he'd never made it past his junior year in college.

"Something we did is catching up to us."

Yet Fitz hadn't said what. Or who. Or why.

Mahoney wasn't a bad guy per se—he'd grown up with an absolute dickhead for a dad—but he'd always been a sucker for party drugs, particularly hallucinogens. He was either hitting rock bottom or suffering brain damage from having already hit his lowest point.

And the little girl shit? Roosevelt wasn't touching those questions with a ten-foot pole. He only hoped the redhead was part of Fitz's delusional trip and that his old friend hadn't delved into darker hobbies since they last spoke.

Processing back through the disturbing call, Roosevelt headed for the mini fridge in the garage where his tuna and sent-from-heaven soda were waiting. With his hand on the door, he came to a conclusion. "Fitz always has and always will be a mess. The dude sounded like a certifiable lunatic. I'll never—"

"You're right. He is."

Startled to his core by the voice behind him, Roosevelt whirled just in time to see the baseball bat coming at his head. One hard crack dropped him on the concrete floor, where he struggled to stay conscious even as warm blood gushed down his face.

Fitz was telling the truth.

"You're right." The cold edge to the laughter that followed nearly loosened his bowels. "You're absolutely right."

Roosevelt blinked, trying to focus on his assailant, his hands raised to ward off another blow. "Why…?"

The laughter stopped, replaced by a triumphant voice. "Mahoney Fitzgerald sounds like a lunatic. Everything is working out perfectly. I knew I could do this." The bat raised over his assailant's head. "*I knew it.*"

Wondering if he would ever get a chance to apologize to his old friend for brushing him off like a bug, Roosevelt decided he already knew the answer to that question before the bat landed another blow.

28

Justice had been served.

Well...almost.

Using all my strength, I thrashed the bat into Roosevelt's midsection and listened to the air shoot out of his lungs before he curled into a ball of misery. I could end it now, but I needed a few more moments to enjoy the triumph I'd created with my own two hands before landing the fatal blow.

I wouldn't make the same mistake I did before. I'd learned that lesson.

"You know," I knelt beside his blood-covered head, being careful to not step into the pool of red so I could gaze into the one eye that was able to open, "I considered letting you off the hook. You were the least awful in your little trio of assholes, and you seemed to make a real turn-around as an adult. I mean, that house you live in? Nobody's *ever* gonna guess how many zeros are behind the numbers in your bank account. You tried so hard to be humble, didn't you?"

Roosevelt wasn't a great conversationalist at the moment,

but that didn't mean he couldn't listen to my words. He still had ears, and for now, they could still hear.

"The problem is, humble doesn't fix anything. It doesn't undo the hands...all the sick, demented hands...that hurt me. Groped me. Invaded me." I closed my eyes against the memories of the assaults. How did something that happened so long ago still hurt so badly? I cleared my throat, swallowing the misery of the past and refocused on the present. "Humble doesn't undo the fact that *your* hands pummeled me with dodgeballs and beat me into the godforsaken fury that was the beginning of the end."

A pathetic groan was the best response he could offer. I was sure that, given the chance, Roosevelt would have apologized. I should have waited to kill him until after he groveled. Until now, I didn't know how badly I needed to hear his expressed regret.

That wouldn't happen now. Another lesson learned.

"My father's hands threw my mother to her death that day. You have no idea what it's like to watch your own mother die. To watch one of your parents kill the other. You don't know what the end really looks like, but you're about to find out."

Mumbles escaped Roosevelt's mouth, accompanied by little bubbles of blood. Internal damage...good.

I was internally damaged too.

"D...pees."

Don't. Please.

It said a lot about me and my situation that I was able to understand his gibberish. It made me think of Wally and his coos that had become a language all their own.

What would Wally think of me right now? What would my baby boy say about the bloody bat in my hands?

I closed my eyes and exhaled the guilt away, purposely steeling my heart over. "Wally can't talk. He wouldn't say a damn word because he doesn't have the capacity to do so. But your kids?" I nudged Roosevelt's limp arm with the bat. "I bet they talk up a storm, don't they? Your perfect healthy little children...so beautiful...I bet they're incessant babblers."

That had been the tipping point, actually, as far as Roosevelt's fate was concerned. I'd stumbled across pictures of his family on the internet. His wife was unimpressive at best, but those kids...a happy as can be little boy and girl, laughing while they played with bubbles.

Just like Bobby, Roosevelt's good fortune had passed seamlessly to the next generation. Meanwhile, my child had inherited the curse I'd incurred that day on the playground. My child had never even *been* to a playground.

The world was a cruel, unfair hell, and letting Roosevelt get away with what he'd done to me would be wrong. He was a rat. A fucking little rat. He was vermin, no matter what he'd tried to pretend to be as a grown man.

I was taking my well-deserved justice and doing the human race a favor by wiping him from the earth.

Another moan from the mostly dead bastard on the floor brought my straying attention back to the man. He wanted to speak so badly and couldn't. I'd felt that way many, many times throughout my life. Trapped. Horrified. Wishing I could die.

"I'm going to do you a favor and not drag this out any longer. Just know, I do appreciate that you at least recognized what a horrible piece of shit you were." I lifted the bat high, tightening my hands on the grip. "But it's time to pay your dues."

With a whistle of wind, I brought the bat down on Roosevelt's head. Over and over and over until there was nothing left but a pool of blood, mush, and bone where his face had once been. I was out of breath and crying from exertion by the time I made myself stop.

He definitely wouldn't be making a miraculous comeback in a hospital bed. I refused to make that mistake again. Roosevelt McGee was dead as dead could get.

Sweaty and breathing hard from the physical effort, I managed a smile. The scales of justice had been righted just a little bit more today. I'd done what I'd set out to do.

"Smashed my goals." I giggled—loudly enough to alarm myself—and attempted to focus. Someone would eventually find Roosevelt's body, and I certainly didn't need to be here when they did.

I had Wally to get home to. He needed his mommy.

Vibration against my hip alerted me to an incoming call. I yanked the phone from my pocket and grunted in annoyance at the name on the screen. "How can I help you, John?"

"She's figuring it out." He panted the words like a rabid dog. "I'm not sure exactly how much she knows, but she's putting it together. For shit's sake, she was a former federal agent. Of course she's seeing through this. We're in over our heads, and I'm resorting to Plan B."

"Plan B?" I wasn't aware that Dr. John Newberry had any alternate plans. He'd been screwed when he came to me and my husband begging for money to bail himself out of an ungodly amount of gambling debt. The man had even lost his job because of his addiction, not showing up for surgeries and even risking a few people's lives after gambling for too many hours and not getting any sleep.

The hospital he'd worked for was probably still dealing with the legal issues associated with their former head surgeon.

My Hank was a softie, though, and had given in to his friend's pleas without a moment's hesitation. Later, with

Hank's blessing, I'd gone so far as to offer jobless John a desirable position at the hospice facility Hank owned.

All he had to do was help me out with a little mission I needed to pull off in the background and never speak a word of it to my husband.

"Did you really think I wouldn't have a backup if this all went south?" John's scoffing tone was highly offensive. "I've handled Maude and taken care of a few loose ends. You won't be hearing from me again, and I promise you that all the money in the world isn't going to find me and my family."

I watched a fly crawl across Roosevelt's smooshed brains, probably searching for the best parts. "You're being overdramatic and making hasty decisions you'll regret. I want you to—"

"I don't give a damn what you want anymore!" He screamed—actually screamed—at me. "That P.I. won't stop until someone answers for something, and I will not be that person. I recommend that you offer her money, and soon."

When the line went dead, my jaw dropped even as I nodded in understanding. Men like John Newberry were weak. Cowards. I should have expected him to bail when the shit got sticky.

Taking one last triumphant gaze at the dead rat on the floor, I sprang into action.

I'll take care of the private investigator...but it won't be with fucking money.

Money just meant that people I thought I could trust could create a Plan B.

Another lesson learned.

29

Winter's stomach writhed for the entirety of the short drive to Roosevelt McGee's place of business. While she had no idea what to expect upon reaching the auto shop, her gut screamed that something was amiss. Part of her still believed the man was in danger, but as she gunned the car through the last yellow light, Noah's warnings reached a crescendo in her head.

"Will you please be careful approaching the home of a man who may or may not be responsible for Bobby Burner's death? And Sandra Smith's disappearance..."

Speeding into a left turn, Winter braked to a stop in an empty parking lot surrounded by field grass. The low-slung, industrial structure hosting McGee's Motors squatted ahead on a patch of concrete. A bright red "closed" sign hung in the entrance window, despite the sunny weekday afternoon and Liz McGee's certainty that her husband was at work.

Her heartbeat quickened as she envisioned Roosevelt committing heinous crimes.

Where are you, Roosevelt? Off kidnapping women? Killing old friends? Skinning your next gift?

Fighting for your life?

She stepped out of her car and scanned the one-story building. Nothing stirred, and both garage doors were shut.

Middle of the day and no one's home? Seems a little off.

Could be that Roosevelt was on a lunch break or running an errand. The lack of a car in the parking lot lent support to that theory. Based on the increased tension in Winter's body, though, her gut wasn't buying it.

Keeping her ears and eyes peeled for any signs of danger, she crossed the short distance to the front door and turned the handle. The door swung open.

So much for her meal-run theory. She could believe Roosevelt might shut down his garage to grab a bite to eat, but leave the place open for thieves to steal his expensive tools? Not a chance. Not unless he'd left in a big hurry.

Winter unholstered her revolver and cleared the reception area, her dread skyrocketing.

A doorway branched off to an office space, and beyond that, the garage itself. There was still a chance she'd find Roosevelt beneath a car. Maybe he'd closed all the doors to grab a quick break from an annoying customer, or as a private spot to smoke a quick joint and forgotten to lock the door. If so, he was about to experience the shock of his life when she walked back there with her weapon drawn.

The darkness looming from that direction didn't bode well, though.

She tightened her grip on the gun and inched her way toward the garage. Before she could get there, something scurried across her foot. Swallowing a scream, she spun in a circle. No one else was in the room.

Please, please, don't be a—

High-pitched squeaking cut her off. She jumped before completing the rest of the thought aloud.

"Rat."

Though not as thunderous or deafening as the horde from her dream, the sheer volume of animalistic sounds assured her that far more than one of the rodents awaited her in the garage.

"You know exactly what we did. You know what we are."

A shudder racked her body, and cold sweat trickled down her back.

Would they be ready for her with red eyes glowing and bloody teeth bared? Had she fallen into a vision without realizing it? A dream? A nightmare?

The point was moot. Whether awake or asleep, Winter had to face the rats.

She took a deep breath and edged closer to the scuffling, shrill din.

At first, she didn't notice anything amiss as she stepped into Roosevelt's workspace and scanned the stained concrete. Just the usual oil stains, jacks, and scattered tools. When her inspection reached the far side of the room, her skin turned icy.

The floor was moving.

Be a P.I., they said. It will be fun, they said.

Her legs tried to lock in place, but she forced them to move in that direction. The mob of rodents slowly took shape. Fifty—maybe more—furry little bodies with fleshy pink tails wiggled and bulldozed each other, all of them concentrated in a single spot.

A sick premonition crept down her spine as she approached. *They're feeding on something.*

She took a few more steps and stopped again. Work boots jutted out from the pile. Her stomach dipped. The rats were eating...but their meal wasn't a something.

They were feasting on some*one*.

And she was afraid she knew exactly who that someone was.

Her pulse pounding through her skull, Winter searched the room and laid eyes on a crowbar. Seizing it, she lunged into the pack and swiped at the ravenous beasts. As they skittered away, the rest of a human body was gradually revealed. Most of a body, anyway.

No head. Well, not anymore. Someone beat this person's head so hard that it's just one big pile of goo.

Stomach acid scalded her throat. No matter how many times she experienced the distinct horror of viewing splattered brain matter, the atrocity never became easier to process.

Taking another swing at a few of the bolder rodents that were starting to return, Winter crouched by the body. The victim's clothes were ripped and covered in blood. Big chunks of fabric and skin both were missing in spots where the rats' sharp teeth had sliced into flesh, likely corresponding with the body parts they considered especially delicious.

Shoving that horrifying thought away, Winter peered at the victim's chest. She could still make out the name patch sewn onto the shirt.

Roosevelt.

30

Noah drove like a bat out of hell toward McGee's Motors while Eve gripped the "oh, shit!" handle and repeatedly checked her seat belt. Winter had called him not even a full fifteen minutes ago, relaying the horror she'd stumbled across, and he'd sprinted from the resident agency like a madman.

Dashing after him and jumping into the truck, Eve had managed to get enough information from him to alert SSA Falkner to their swift departure as she experienced her first road trip with Noah's more turbulent alter ego.

The shop sat on a plot of land between the residential and urban sectors, an unpretentious and unlikely business space for a grown-up rich kid from Huntstown. Easy to ignore.

No one would overlook it now, however. Swarming with cop cars, two responding ambulances, and an Animal Control van, the establishment was a veritable circus show. As Noah steered into the lot, a pair of SUVs labeled with "Texas Parks & Wildlife" insignias passed him heading out to the street, followed by a large van.

At least we missed the rats.

Shaking off a crawling sensation along his skin, he navigated around the LEO vehicles and parked as out of the way as possible.

Eve let out a low whistle. "Crime scene techs are already here. A whole gaggle of 'em."

Climbing from his truck, Noah was much more interested in locating his wife. He scanned the sea of officers until he spotted her, the lone person in street clothes, speaking to a cop who appeared to be writing down every word on his clipboard.

Winter's porcelain complexion had taken on a greenish hue. Noah charged toward his wife, forgetting for a moment that he was an on-duty federal agent in his rush to embrace her.

Vivid blue eyes met his, and seconds later, Winter threw her arms around his waist, squeezing his ribs tight before releasing him. "I guess we can officially take Roosevelt McGee off of the suspect list, huh?"

Noah understood that dark humor was Winter's prime coping mechanism. "Hope nobody tells my new boss how wrong I was about the guy. I might get my badge revoked."

Winter's lips curved slightly upward but never made it to a full smile. "You gonna introduce me to your partner or what, Agent Dalton?"

Smacking his forehead and feeling like an ass, Noah slid apologetic eyes toward the woman standing patiently at his side. "Special Agent Eve Taggart, meet my wife, Winter Black-Dalton, Private Investigator."

Eve jutted out a hand, a warm smile stretched across her face. "It's a pleasure to meet you." Her gaze shifting toward the shop, Eve's expression sobered. "Although I wish it were under different circumstances."

Winter accepted the handshake and craned her head in

the same direction. "You and me both. I've heard good things about you."

"Likewise."

"You think this is the same culprit?" Noah kept his voice low. "The same person who killed Bobby and took Sandra?"

A tremble coursed through his wife's body. "Yes. And I'm one thousand percent sure it's the same person who's been leaving the rats. I'll take you to the scene."

Noah gave Eve a nod, and they both trailed closely behind Winter as she led them past the yellow tape and deep into the shop. There was no question as to where the murder had taken place. Techs and cops alike huddled near a bloodied human form near the back of the garage.

A headless human form.

Their jackets making a silent announcement of who they were, officers moved aside as Noah and his partner approached. Eve's sharp intake of breath at the brutal tragedy on the floor matched his own. Murder was never a pretty sight, but this killer had left a scene that incited a special shade of vomit.

Noah winced, imagining Winter's horror at having found the corpse. "Holy hell."

"Yep." A tall, built-like-an-ox officer, the only one who hadn't moved upon their arrival, met his stare. "I'm Detective Darnell Davenport, and you must be Agents Taggart and Dalton. Your wife said you'd be showing up. This is my scene, but I wouldn't mind some federal insight as long as you stay out of the way."

"Of course. Only here to help." Noah had already accepted that he wasn't present in an official capacity, and also that local law enforcement would be marking their territory at some point.

Best to get that part out of the way.

After uttering a grunt of what Noah took for approval,

Detective Davenport studied him and Taggart with dark brown eyes. "The victim died from blunt force trauma to the head, but I think that goes without saying."

Winter knelt on a plastic sheet beside Roosevelt's body. "This murder was so messy. Rage, excitement...probably a combination of the two...but messy as hell. There's gotta be some of the unsub's DNA here."

Noah agreed. From what he knew of Bobby Burner's assault, the assailant had delivered just enough blows to assume that Bobby was dead, leaving without so much as a fingerprint in their wake. This time, they hadn't left any room for guesswork. They'd beaten Roosevelt McGee's head to a verifiable pulp, and that took effort. Dedication.

Rage.

Whatever the killer's motivations, the amount of damage they'd inflicted on the body could lead to a break in the case. The longer any murderer spent taking out their victim, the better the chances they'd leave behind a tidbit of evidence for law enforcement to work with.

Detective Davenport gestured toward the crowd of techs around them. "The rats didn't help our cause. The little vermin contaminated the scene before we even knew it existed...but if there's any DNA to find, my team will find it. I just hope *we* find this psychopath before another victim gets their head bashed in."

Standing, Winter ushered Noah to the side. "I have to go. I can't say for sure who's in danger versus who's dangerous right now, but there are so many people involved in this nightmare..." She blew out a long breath. "I can't just hang around and wait for something else to happen."

Fighting his natural inclination to go with her, Noah tried to offer genuine encouragement. "You go do what you gotta do, darlin'. Agent Taggart and I can stay put for a while and gather whatever information comes from this."

He didn't say it out loud, but if Winter was right and the murders were connected, the FBI would probably get a call to assist on a serial killer case anyway.

Winter's posture relaxed an infinitesimal bit. "Thank you."

Noah and Eve followed Winter out of the shop. He struggled to take his eyes off her even as she drove away.

"She'll be all right." Eve's soft, comforting tone betrayed her mothering instincts. "Your wife is a tough cookie if I ever met one."

He couldn't argue with that.

Seconds after Winter drove away, another civilian car came to a stop on the street in front of the shop. Noah's stomach sank as a petite woman shot from the vehicle, frantically scanning the scene before her.

"What's going on?" She made the demand of everyone present. "Where's my husband? Where's Roosevelt?"

Two officers immediately rushed over to the woman and spoke to her in hushed voices.

Moments later, Roosevelt McGee's wife broke into inconsolable screams.

The after-lunch traffic was tame as Winter headed deeper into the heart of Austin, allowing her mind to spin circles as she debated where to go first. The case was like a baseball game, except that there were fifty bases to run, and her legs were bound in a potato sack.

"Worst. Game. Ever."

With the investigation escalating at such a breakneck speed, Winter's adrenal glands rose to the occasion, seeming to flood her system with a nonstop rush of adrenaline. Her jittery hands and twitchy legs were proof of that. Meanwhile, a sinking sensation in her gut insisted that she was a million miles behind the culprit, even though Roosevelt's body had still been warm when she'd arrived at the shop.

Gritting her teeth, she zoomed around a black pickup truck put-putting down the street.

You're not that far ahead, you son of a bitch. Just far enough to feel invincible...and that's when criminals make their epic mistakes.

The misstep *would* occur, but when? Where? After how many more people were dead?

At the next light, Winter tapped out a brief text for Fitz

instructing him to remain on lockdown. Next, she placed a call to the office in Sandra Smith's apartment building in hopes of catching the property manager who'd failed to respond to the note she'd left.

The phone rang three times, and the gruff voice that answered was anything but friendly. "Yeah?"

"Hello, this is Winter Black, and I was trying to reach the property mana—"

"Not in." The man's interruption was more like a growl. "You got Chuck. I'm the custodian here. Or at least, I think I am."

Winter's curiosity piqued. "You think?"

"Listen, lady." Chuck's growl morphed into a bark. "This building got sold yesterday. I don't know who bought it or when they're comin' in or if I even get to keep my damn job."

Her stomach twisted like a Rubik's Cube. "Chuck, I'm a licensed private investigator and former federal agent. I wonder if you could do a quick wellness check for me on the tenants of 2G? It's very, very important."

Chuck muttered a mostly undecipherable reply but seemed willing to take on the task. Her muscles wound tighter and tighter as five minutes dragged past on hold. By the time Chuck returned to the line, Sandra's apartment building appeared up ahead.

"Ain't nobody in 2G."

She frowned. "No one is home, you mean?"

"I mean, the apartment is *empty*." Chuck's obvious exasperation at putting out all that effort for nothing made his patience, likely in short supply to begin with, seem nonexistent. "You sure you got the right address?"

Sure as hell. "I'll check on that. Thanks, and have a nice day."

To her right, the driveway for the building drew closer. Winter glanced at the apartments as they flashed by on the passenger side but didn't brake. Instead, she accelerated the rest of the short drive to the Cup and Go Café.

She'd meant to stop in the previous day, but her meetings with the elder Fitzgeralds and Laurel-Anne—in addition to Bobby Burner's death—had overtaken the hours. Parking in a slanted spot near the front door, Winter mentally crossed all her fingers and toes that Shay would be working the midday shift again.

When she rushed inside, the only employee she recognized was Sue, who was filling the straw dispenser at the counter. Winter approached without hesitation. "Hi Sue, do you remember me?"

Sue's brow creased as she examined Winter. Her face relaxed a few moments later. "I do. From the other night with that handsome fella? What can I get for ya, hon?"

A nap? A mansion on the beach in the Bahamas? Infinite hours of free therapy?

Haunted by images of Roosevelt McGee's pulverized, oozing head, Winter dug deep for a convincing grin. "Actually, I'm still trying to catch Shay. I never made it in yesterday like I planned."

"Oh." Sue's features drooped with a frown. "I'm sorry, but Shay up and quit yesterday at the end of her shift. Said she finally had the money to fly back home to see her parents. Her dad's been unwell for a while now."

The news hit Winter like a gut punch. "Oh."

The property manager was gone. The family who'd *"lived in that apartment for years"* was gone. And Shay, one of the few people able to corroborate Fitz's story, had chosen to fly out of town at the precise same time?

"Ma'am?" Sue leaned across the counter. "Ma'am? I do apologize, but could I ask you to move to the side so I can take some orders?"

With a start, Winter checked behind her shoulder to find a couple waiting. "Oops, sorry. Thanks anyway."

A thick fog enveloped her mind as she headed for the exit. She'd questioned her client's mental stability since the day they'd met, but now her own sanity seemed at stake.

Without hesitation, she climbed back in her car and dialed the hospice facility.

"Hello, this is Poppy with Peaceful Acres Hospice Care, where we make every moment count. How can I help you today?"

Winter could picture the perky brunette bouncing in her receptionist chair and brimming with excitement to answer the phone—or do anything else, for that matter. In person, Poppy's unbridled energy was a little extra, but right now, Winter took comfort in the knowledge that not every person associated with Fitz's case had disappeared.

The reason clicked a heartbeat later.

Poppy didn't disappear because Poppy never met Fitz or Sandra. She's not a part of whatever this is. Probably.

"Hello again. This is Winter Black, and I'm so glad you're the one who answered." Treating the woman like a close friend seemed the best way to go. "I wondered if I could get another quick moment of Dr. Newberry's time?"

"Oh, I'm sorry, Agent Black. Dr. Newberry left shortly after your visit this morning. He said he wouldn't be back in today."

Of course he did. And stop calling me "agent."

Winter took a deep breath and quashed the impulse to scream. Barely. "How about Nurse Little?"

Poppy's giggle grated against Winter's eardrums. "Maude left for vacation this afternoon. I'm so jealous. I didn't even know she was going on vacay. Somewhere tropical, I think."

Dr. Newberry *and* Maude Little were gone? Winter experienced a fleeting twinge of sympathy for Fitz. The head-scratching disappearances over the last ten minutes were a tiny taste of the hell he'd been dealing with.

"Okay then." Winter struggled to keep her tone upbeat. "Could I speak with Patricia Smith?"

Poppy's indignant huff was answer enough. "I'm not allowed to just patch people through to patients. Especially if they aren't family. I'd have to get permission from Dr. Newberry, and like I said before, he's not here."

"What if—"

"I know you're just doing your job and digging around for information." There was a new haughty element to the receptionist's words. "But I have a job to do as well. Dr. Newberry seemed miffed after your talk with him earlier. I'd recommend you search for clues elsewhere. Have a blessed day."

Poppy hung up, leaving Winter's jaw dangling open.

With her peppy voice, the receptionist's mini tirade was akin to being told off by a mouse.

A pulse throbbed in Winter's temple as she steered away from the café and drove toward Peaceful Acres.

Go ahead, snap your little mouse teeth at me, but don't be upset when your deterrence tactics fail. What you don't realize is that I've spent the last few days dealing with rats.

32

I stood outside Wally's quarters during the tail end of his daily tutoring, unnoticed by both my son and Miss Anthony as she signed questions about the Harry Potter book he'd been reading. His radiant smile as he signed back punched the oxygen from my chest.

I froze in the doorway, indecision momentarily zapping my ability to leave.

Regardless of the many tasks awaiting me and my blazing desire to complete them, I considered staying. Just walking over to my boy, planting a kiss on his carrot-top head, and letting everything else go.

My world was sitting at that table. My heart was on display right there in front of me.

Hadn't I accomplished enough already?

"Why can't you just walk away?"

My whisper held logic. Reason.

Bobby was dead. Roosevelt was extremely dead.

And Mahoney's life was ruined, just as I'd intended. I'd taken away his girlfriend—Sandra was dead and gone and *never* coming back—his credibility, and soon, his freedom.

He loved Sandra so deeply. There was no way he was going to let the matter go. He'd keep squawking until his elitist fucking family locked him away in a padded cell to keep their "good name" intact.

A lifetime of suffering. That's what I'd wanted for the meanest bully of them all, because that's what he'd given to me.

But you're not actually suffering now, are you? Look around. You have everything anyone could ever ask for. A mansion. A loving husband. A beautiful child who thinks the sun rises and sets with you.

A lone tear trailed down my cheek as an unfamiliar sensation spread through my chest. Tingles raced up my arms. My insides radiated with warmth.

With hope.

The sound that I knew was Wally's version of an uninhibited laugh intensified that alien warmth and caused my heart to flutter-beat. I wrapped my fingers around the doorjamb, contemplating crossing the threshold. We could be happy. Hank, Wally, and I could—

A crystal-clear image of my mother's lifeless body at the foot of the staircase flashed through my mind. I stepped away from the door, leaning against the outside wall and closing my eyes.

"Please. Just let me live my life now. Please stop tormenting me."

My mother stared up at me with that same vacant, wide-eyed expression. This time, though, her lips moved, and words spewed out. "You killed me, little rat. You started this. And you *will* finish it."

Icy hands wrapped around my neck and began squeezing. Gasping for air, I clawed at my throat and opened my eyes, sure that I'd catch my dead mother choking the life from me.

I was alone in the hall. My mother wasn't there...and yet somehow, she was always present.

Shaken, I rubbed my arms and tried to calm my thundering pulse. What was that all about? Not once before today had Mom ever called me a little rat. Not in my memories, dreams, or nightmares.

Those were my father's words, and he was rotting in a prison cell right where he belonged, serving out a life sentence for the murder of my mother along with other numerous charges for the beating he'd given me that day.

The rules must have changed, though, if my mother was now delivering that hateful message. My mother, who'd always loved me. Who'd rushed over to protect me that day. Who'd died for my sake.

Purpose solidified inside me.

I'll finish it for you. You'll have your vengeance. I promise, Mommy.

I wasted no time clearing the hallway and shooting down the back stairs toward a seldom-used side door. This exit followed a cobblestone path that wound deeper into our property, leading toward the gardens...and my rat shed.

Hank referred to them as my "hobby rats." My husband assumed that I bred them to sell, and though I'd never confirmed that assumption—I hated lying to him—I'd also never told him he was wrong.

Believing that my rats were something of a therapeutic pastime, Hank fully supported the activity. He even hired contractors to build a state-of-the-art shed just for me. And them, of course.

"You're too good, Hank." I unlocked the entry to the shed. "Too pure."

He couldn't possibly have fathomed the true nature of my plans. The real reason I bred the rats. The people that I'd killed.

I'd shared tidbits of my childhood, but cursing my soft-hearted husband with the full knowledge of the hell I'd endured seemed cruel and unnecessary. He had no clue about the trio of bastards who'd taken everything—*everything* —away from me, or the multitude of abuse gifted to me in foster care.

Hank possessed a sweet soul, as did Wally. The pair of them needed to be shielded from the world's ugliness at all costs.

I lifted two carrier crates and moved toward the back of the shed where I kept the biggest and meanest of the rats. "This madness will all be over soon. I'm ending it tonight."

And then I'll be a good wife. I'll sell the rest of these creatures and never so much as glance at this shed again.

First, though, I would avenge my mother. I would avenge myself.

I couldn't rest until I did.

Ignoring the hissing of my rats as I lowered their cages into the carriers one by one, I imagined Mahoney Fitzgerald's brains gushing through his ears while his eyeballs popped from their sockets.

I no longer needed to watch him suffer for decades to come. Instead, I intended to kill him and release myself from my mother's dead stare...from my father's screams. From—

"Honey?"

Hank's voice from behind nearly blew my heart through my chest. He stood in the shed's doorway, brown eyes wide in a pale face as his gaze flitted from side to side. The rats squeaked and hissed, sensing a stranger was nearby.

I hastily lifted a crate and headed toward him...past him...to load the minivan. "Babe, what are you doing out here?"

Hank never came to the shed. He'd admitted to having a

slight fear of rodents, which worked in my favor. Even now, he couldn't bring himself to take an actual step inside.

Chuckling but still white as a ghost, he approached and planted a kiss on my forehead. "I had a break in meetings. I wanted to catch you before you went off to make your sale. Although I still find it hard to believe people pay you money for these angry little things."

That's because it's not true. I'm actually murdering people in cold blood, hon.

Grinning, I lifted a shoulder. "They're not so bad."

They'd gnaw your face off in a heartbeat is all.

Hank shook his head and retreated a step toward the house. "I also wanted to warn you that a storm is brewing. Be careful on the highway, okay?"

"Okay." I blew him a kiss. "I'll be back in time to put Wally to bed."

He scuttled away, his posture relaxing as he went.

In the distance, thunder roared across the darkening sky, and I smiled at the billowing clouds. I had no say in the weather, but in that moment, it almost seemed as though I did.

"It's the perfect backdrop for murder. Even Mother Nature is excited about wiping Mahoney Fitzgerald from her planet."

I walked back into the depths of the shed and unlocked the strongbox under my work desk, grabbing the small pistol I liked to carry as backup and tucked it into a bag I'd leave in the van in case I needed it. I'd never used the gun, as I much preferred the more therapeutic approach of beating the vengeance out of my foes.

Yet, "better safe than sorry" was a widely used phrase for a reason. Plus, unlike Bobby and Roosevelt, Mahoney had an actual detective working for him. I found it hard to believe that the Snow White-looking former federal agent wouldn't be packing heat every time she left that stupidly perfect tiny house in the suburbs. And there was no telling if she'd make a poorly timed appearance at her client's home.

Grabbing another crate, I pushed all thoughts of the pesky P.I. aside.

Tonight, I would kiss my baby boy's cheek, secure in the knowledge that I'd done everything in my power to take back what the world had stolen from us. The childhood innocence and ignorant bliss that the universe should have provided.

Anticipation rippled through my blood as I carried my furry load toward the minivan. The biggest bully of them all was about to answer for his crimes.

33

Winter fidgeted with the radio buttons, trying to find a weather report. The Texas sky loomed bleak overhead, its inky hues inspiring an uneasy whirling in her chest.

Hold off. Just hold off for a few hours, pretty please.

Another ten minutes and she'd arrive at Peaceful Acres. The phone call with Poppy made it clear that Winter shouldn't expect a warm welcome, so her plan was to sneak past the peppy receptionist to Patricia Smith's room. She preferred to perform that task—and any tasks that followed her conversation with Patricia—in dry, warm clothes. If only the weather would cooperate.

"It's not a good time to prove your lightning is bigger than everybody else's, okay?"

A peal of crackling thunder answered from above.

Smartass.

Her phone buzzed, interrupting her standoff with the storm. Winter's stomach clenched as she prepared for whatever crazy update awaited her and snatched the phone from the console.

Autumn Trent.

"Two times in three days?" Winter's muscles relaxed. "To what do I owe this honor?"

Autumn's giggle was like free therapy. "Would it offend you too deeply if I said that I was bored?"

Laughter sputtered past Winter's lips. "Not enough deranged serial killer action in Richmond or what?"

"Oh, you know," Autumn's words took on a singsong tone, "they come and they go. Today's been a paperwork day. We just sent Keaton off for coffees cause, apparently, it's a paperwork evening as well."

Winter envisioned Special Agent Keaton Holland, who'd transferred to Richmond from D.C. at the beginning of the year. A nice guy and super intelligent, but one of the most awkward human beings Winter recalled ever meeting.

"Giving the new guy coffee duty?" Winter tsked her best schoolmarm impression as she changed lanes to veer around a semi-truck. "I thought you were above such snobbery."

Autumn chuckled at the chiding. "You misunderstood. Keaton volunteered himself to make the run, wrote everyone's order down word for word, and reread each order twice to make sure he'd gotten them correct."

"Oh, boy." Winter could only imagine the struggle of keeping a straight face. "Sounds like a good time, but if you're really bored, maybe I could trouble you for a little behavioral profiler insight."

"Hit me."

Winter spit out the ins and outs of her case without a moment's hesitation. If aid was available, she would take it. Autumn's Ph.D. in criminal psychology had proven priceless before.

"What strikes me most is the rats." Autumn's analytical mind took off. "This unsub is murdering their victims with blunt force trauma but using rats to scare, shame, and even desecrate the corpses. My guess is that they're mirroring their own experiences, even communicating their emotions with the animals and creating a narrative that *should* be triggering some type of memory for your client."

"He remembers nothing." Winter tightened her grip on the steering wheel. "Whether he literally never paid an ounce of attention to the world around him and the affect he had on others, or he has actual memory loss from his drug usage…as far as this case goes, his brain is useless."

Autumn tapped away at her computer keys in the background. "The killer might *know* Fitz remembers nothing. That might be fueling their rage. He had something to do with traumatizing this person and is too self-involved to even recall a red-flag memory. That could push a fractured person over the edge."

Winter pictured the fleshy rat at the end of her driveway. "And the broken necks?"

"That could go two ways." Autumn seemed to have already analyzed the matter. "Either it's an attempt to ramp up the fear and level of threat posed to the victims because, simply put, rats are scary and gross. Or the broken neck is another significant detail of the killer's past trauma. Maybe someone they loved died in that way. It's even possible that they had their own neck broken but survived."

Spotting the Peaceful Acres business sign up ahead, Winter tapped on the brakes. "Sorry, Dr. Trent, but I've gotta go covert ops now. You're gonna have to fill that boredom hole in your soul with somebody else's problems."

"Fine." Autumn's sigh of resignation floated through the airwaves. "But just to be clear, I prefer your problems to the rest of the world's."

Winter snort-laughed at the sentimentality. "You're an odd duck, but I love you too. I'll talk to you soon."

She ended the call and parked on the far side of the hospice facility's lot, out of Poppy's direct line of view. With a little luck, the receptionist would never know she was there.

No matter the hassle of getting to Patricia's room, speaking with the woman was non-negotiable. The dying woman knew something, and unlike the others involved in Fitz's case, she seemed on the verge of breaking and spilling the beans.

She also happened to be the only one who hadn't skipped town.

Now that two men had been murdered, both with strong connections to Mahoney, Winter didn't doubt that her client might be next. The goal was no longer simply proving Fitz's sanity. Someone was *killing people*, and any details garnered from Patricia would be invaluable.

Winter crept up to the Peaceful Acres entrance and peeked through the window. Poppy sat behind the desk, talking on the phone.

Great. Now what?

Ducking back out of view, Winter chewed the inside of her cheek and tried to come up with a plan. She could check for a door around the back, but guidelines required them to remain locked from the outside. And even if she did manage to get one open, the risk was too high that she'd trigger an alarm.

No, the front door was her best bet. She needed Poppy to leave the room or at least turn away. Unless she wanted to stand outside like a Peeping Tom until the next time the receptionist left to use the bathroom, though, she'd better come up with a distraction.

Autumn. Maybe Autumn can call and use her medical mumbo jumbo to ask Poppy to go check on a patient.

Digging in her pocket for her phone, Winter leaned forward to sneak another look. Poppy rose from her desk holding a stack of papers and turned away to head toward the back. A moment later, she bent over the copy machine.

After a moment of hesitation, Winter raced for the door, blood pounding in her ears. She eased the door open and made a silent entrance.

Please, don't turn around.

Not wasting a second of her good luck, Winter dropped to the carpet and army crawled past the reception desk toward the doorway leading to the patient rooms.

You've really lost it this time. This is nuts.

Although, if she were being honest, her current escapade probably didn't rank in her top ten batshit choices of all time.

She fully expected to ram right into the legs of a nurse or orderly at any given moment but made it into the hallway and out of Poppy's sight without encountering a single employee.

Who's running this place? It's like a damn ghost town in here.

Heaving a sigh of relief, she jumped to her feet and speed-walked the rest of the way to Patricia's room. When she cracked the door open, Patricia lay still in her bed, eyes closed.

Waking up a dying woman from her peaceful sleep. Who's the world's biggest jerk? Me. It's me, folks.

With no other options, she nudged the doorstop to keep the space wide open and allow the security camera a clear view into Patricia's room. If caught, she might need the footage to prove that she hadn't harmed Patricia or damaged anything.

Hopefully, she'd be in and out before anyone was the wiser, though. She'd simply ask a few important questions to get to the bottom of Fitz's case and bolt...ideally with enough information to prevent more bloodshed.

Winter padded toward the bed, Patricia's poor state of health pricking at her heart once again. The cancer had eaten away at the woman until she was nothing more than a waif of humanity under a blanket. A small pile of bones waiting to die.

"I'm sorry that this is happening to you." Winter bit her lip to stave off any rebellious emotions breaking through. "It isn't fair. It's never fair."

Curling a hand around Patricia's frail shoulder, Winter gave the gentlest of squeezes.

Nothing.

She prepared to follow up with a light shake to Patricia's frame when the truth of the matter smacked her in the face like a cold blast of hurricane wind.

The woman's chest wasn't rising and falling as it should.

No...please no.

Winter pressed two fingers to Patricia's carotid artery with one hand, grabbing her wrist with the other. Holding her breath, she remained motionless and waited for the steady throb of a heartbeat to put her fears to rest.

34

F itz focused on the ceramic tiles as he paced across the kitchen floor.

...eleven, twelve, thirteen...

If someone had set out with the intention of making him lose his mind, they were doing a bang-up job of it. For the first time since Sandra's disappearance nearly three weeks ago, Fitz allowed himself to face the question that everyone else had already asked.

"Did I imagine all of this?"

He'd visited a multitude of fictitious worlds over the years, all by way of this or that hallucinogenic drug provided by random "friends" at random parties. The human brain was capable of creating magnificent, reality-bending realms, and Fitz knew this better than anyone...including his psychiatrist sister.

All the degrees in the world wouldn't provide Laurel-Anne with a bona fide technicolor experience on a mythical prismatic plane.

Not that he'd taken any recreational substances since

months before meeting Sandra. If he'd made her up, he couldn't blame it on a bad trip.

However, maybe he could blame it on one of the numerous trips before her.

"Brain damage." Fitz halted as he caught sight of his distorted reflection in the stainless-steel oven hood. "Dammit. Did I do this to myself?"

He dragged his palms down his face. What if Sandra truly was a figment of his imagination? Maybe he'd conjured up the rats, the hospice facility. Maybe Winter Black wasn't even real.

Could he trust his senses at all?

For all you know, you're in a straitjacket right now, drooling on yourself in a padded room.

Fitz struggled to inhale as his lungs turned to ice. Leaning against the counter, he closed his eyes and envisioned Sandra's sweet smile. He could still feel the soft silk of her blonde hair between his fingers. Could still smell the delicious blend of lavender and peony that had always graced her skin.

He slammed a fist on the counter. "She's real, dammit! She was here. *She was here.*"

A sob caught in his throat, and his back scraped against the cabinets as he slid to the floor.

How could he prove his sanity to his family when he was debating it himself?

Focus.

Fitz rested his forehead on his knees, gulping air to tame his raging emotions. Winter had instructed him to keep trying to reach Roosevelt and stay put. So far, he'd followed orders like an obedient dog, holing up in his mansion and hitting redial over and over until his old buddy finally called back.

"For all the good that did." Roose hadn't believed a word

of the warnings Fitz rattled off during their short conversation. Worse, he'd ignored the dozens of follow-up calls after that trainwreck of a discussion.

"And now I'm just supposed to sit here twiddling my thumbs and trust one woman to fix this entire situation for me? Trust that Winter can make Sandra magically reappear?"

He bit his lip. A premonition had gnawed at him all day, growing stronger as time ticked by.

I think Sandra might be dead. I think they killed her. I think she's gone for good.

People didn't just disappear the way she had. Someone had made damn sure to erase her entire existence from Fitz's world. Why go to such lengths if they planned on returning her safely?

"They wouldn't."

Fitz swiped at his damp eyes, his heart fracturing into a million unsalvageable pieces.

Crack!

The thunderclap made him jump. Scrambling to his feet, he ran to the living room, where the giant picture window displayed another lightning bolt splintering the night sky. The storm showed no signs of calming. Violent, monsoon-worthy winds howled through his front yard, bending the trees.

Fitz's backup generators ensured that, no matter how severe the storm grew, he wasn't in danger of losing power. His security system would protect him regardless of the size of Mother Nature's tantrum. Still, the rattling booms and flashing lights set his nerves on edge.

"You just need to sit your ass down and try to relax. This storm can't—"

D-ding. D-ding.

Fitz darted toward his security lockbox as the alarm for the front gate pealed through the halls. Adrenaline flooding

like fire through his system, Fitz patted the Glock he'd
tucked into a bellyband holster but didn't draw it. The
weapon's presence was enough to calm his quaking heart.

Who'd visit smack dab in the middle of this downpour?

Winter hadn't mentioned coming by. Actually, he hadn't
heard from her in hours.

When he reached the box and checked the monitor, his
heart stuttered to a halt.

Are you hallucinating again? Or is this real?

He squeezed his eyes shut and reopened them. The image
remained unchanged. "Oh my god."

Standing in front of his gate, drenched from head to toe,
was Sandra Smith. With terrified brown eyes and a trembling chin, she wrapped her slender arms around herself and
peered up at the camera.

Fitz slammed a palm on the gate release and raced to the
front doors, throwing them wide open before sprinting out
into the storm.

35

"No no no...you can't be dead." Winter's voice trembled with panic. "I just spoke to you this morning. Please don't be dead."

Despite her pleas, Patricia Smith didn't reply. People without a pulse rarely did.

"Shit." Winter backed away from Patricia's bed. "Shit, shit, shit."

Turning, she raced to the front desk, slapping a hand on the counter to get Poppy's attention.

The woman nearly fell out of her rolling chair. "Excuse me?"

"Patricia Smith is dead."

Poppy clambered to her feet. "Dead? But her alarm would have gone off, and Nurse Lou would have—"

"Poppy." Winter held up a hand to cut the other woman off. "Patricia. Smith. Is. Dead. Can you page Nurse Lou to the room?"

Bobbing her head, the receptionist smacked a button on the desk phone. "Nurse Bain, please report to room eight. Again, please report to room eight."

Winter nodded her approval. "Now, let's go."

Trailed by Poppy, Winter led her back down the resident hall and around the corner, past the first three doors to the dead woman's room.

They approached the bed in unison, pausing as a tall, gray-haired woman wearing scrubs dashed in behind them. "Poppy? What's wrong? Is everything okay with Patricia?"

Unable to speak, Poppy pointed at the bed.

Lou scurried past them. "Mrs. Smith? How are you feeling this evening, ma'am? Mrs. Smith?"

The nurse grabbed one of Patricia's limp wrists, her fingers groping for a pulse.

"She's dead." Winter blurted the fact from behind.

The nurse whirled. "Who are you?"

"I'm Winter Black, Private Investigator. I found Patricia like this just a few minutes ago."

Yanking the stethoscope from around her neck, Lou froze and pointed at the floor. "The monitor. It's unplugged."

Poppy gasped, raising a hand to her chest. "That's why the alarm never went off. That's why we didn't know."

Lou inserted the stethoscope ear tips and folded Patricia's blanket down. Her jaw dropped as she leaned over the dead woman's body. "Oh no. No, no, nooo."

Stepping closer, Winter spotted the cause of Lou's horror. Patricia Smith's neck displayed a ring of purplish-blue trauma.

"Someone killed her." Winter locked eyes with Lou. "Someone unplugged her monitor and strangled her to death."

Poppy's yelp echoed off the ceiling. "But she was already dying! What kind of monster kills a poor woman who's dying from cancer?"

Winter turned toward Poppy, whose face was a sopping mess of tears. "Call 911."

"You're staying, right?" The receptionist grabbed Winter's wrist. "Please don't leave us alone with this."

"I'm not going to leave," Winter assured the ghost-white receptionist, "but you need to gather all the staff together. The police are going to have questions."

Lou snorted behind them. "This is all the staff."

"Just you two?" Winter's gaze flitted between them. "You've got to be kidding me."

Poppy headed for the door. "She's not. It's just us two today. We're incredibly short-staffed. Dr. Newberry's been working on that."

Right. Winter didn't believe that for a second. Her mind spun with theories as she turned and pointed at Lou. "How long have you worked here?"

The nurse couldn't look away from Patricia's corpse for more than a few seconds at a time. "Five days."

Newbies. Poppy and Lou were both newbies, and the only employees present. Possibly the only employees that Peaceful Acres had left. Neither woman had known Patricia for a full week yet, and they certainly didn't know Fitz or Sandra.

Winter headed toward the hall. "The security camera. Whoever did this will be on that tape entering Patricia's room."

"I can't even..." Lou placed a hand over her eyes. "I don't want to see that."

Not blaming her for a second, Winter jogged toward Poppy's desk. She had to see the footage. It was the only way to know what sadist asshole had wrapped their hands around a terminally ill woman's neck and squeezed the life— whatever was left of it—out of her body.

"Did you find anything?" Winter almost jumped as Poppy laid a hand on her shoulder.

Winter shook her head. "Not yet."

She was desperate to view the video footage before the law enforcement officers arrived. Once they took over the scene, Winter knew she wouldn't get another chance.

Behind her, the receptionist sniffed and reached for a tissue. Winter glanced up at Poppy. "It's going to be okay."

Poppy shook her head, meeting Winter's gaze with a haggard expression. "No, it isn't. Why would...who could do something like that?"

So many people are capable of horrible atrocities, Poppy. This is just the first time you've ever been so close to one of those deranged minds. Well...that you're aware of.

Believing it best to keep those thoughts to herself, Winter continued to speed through the video footage, not stopping until the video glitched.

"What's that?"

Winter glanced back up at Poppy, who was hovering over her shoulder. "That's a very good question." Backing up the footage, Winter hit play just as the first cruiser entered the parking lot.

Glitch.

Stopping the footage again, Winter saw the problem. Someone had paused the camera for a fifteen-minute period that afternoon. Long enough to kill Patricia, un-pause the camera, and flee.

Dammit.

Winter bared her teeth at the computer monitor. "I knew you were a liar, Newberry, but I hadn't pegged you for a murderer."

"The police are here," Poppy whispered. "What should we do?"

Winter stood and faced the frightened receptionist. "We tell them the truth."

And they did. For the next two hours, Winter told the officers everything she knew. They'd all looked at her with a mix of incongruity and suspicion, but in the end, they seemed as puzzled as she was.

When they finally allowed her to leave the scene, she went into the restroom and dialed Fitz right away. There were developments they needed to discuss...such as someone smashing his other childhood best friend's head into mush and Sandra's mother getting strangled to death in her hospice bed.

No answer. Cmon. What could you possibly be doing?

Pacing the bathroom, she tried again. The second, third, and fourth attempts to reach Fitz went straight to voicemail too.

Winter frowned at her phone, pulling a slip of paper from her purse containing Fitz's emergency contacts. She called his parents first.

"Hello?" Laurel Fitzgerald answered with her best, breathy Scarlett O'Hara impression.

"This is Winter Black, Mahoney's private investigator. We met yesterday. I'm trying to get ahold of him, but he doesn't seem to be answering his phone. I just wanted to check if you had any idea where he might be?"

Laurel giggled as though that was the funniest question she'd ever been asked. "Oh, I'm sorry, my dear. I haven't heard so much as a peep from him, but I learned long ago not to waste too much time worrying about Fitzy. He's usually up to something silly, but he always ends up all right in the end. Stress causes premature signs of aging, you know."

Winter had entered her own private episode of *The Twilight Zone*. "Um. Okay. Thank you, Mrs. Fitzgerald."

A quick call to his sister confirmed the same. Laurel-Anne hadn't heard from him, and she warned Winter not to waste too much time waiting for Fitz to answer his phone. Her brother was likely playing a joke within the grand prank he'd been pulling.

As she disconnected the call, uneasiness wormed through Winter's gut. She didn't care what Fitz's sister said. Something was wrong.

Busting out of the bathroom, she beelined for the reception counter. "Poppy, I have to go. I need to check on...some things. You have an officer stationed at the front and back doors. They'll walk you and Lou to your cars when you're done with your shift."

Poppy's chin trembled. "O-okay. What about the people in Patricia's room?"

"Those are crime scene technicians." An empathy pang caused Winter to hesitate. "Just let them do their jobs and hang tight. I'll check in with you later, okay? You're going to be fine."

The receptionist's ghost-white features said otherwise, but Winter had no more time to give. She rushed through Peaceful Acres's front doors into the raging storm, cold raindrops pelting her as she ran to her car and set the GPS to Fitz's address.

Pulling onto the highway, Winter called Noah.

"Well, hello." Her husband's happy tone was a momentary antidote to her stressful day. "I was wondering when my stunning, intelligent wife might call."

Winter regretted having to poke a hole in his good mood. "Patricia Smith was murdered. Strangled in her bed. Whoever did it managed to pause the security cam for that precise period of time. It has to be Newberry, Noah. The police put a watch out for him, but a little federal assistance—"

"Say no more." Keys clicked. "And you are...on your way home?"

"Going to Fitz's house." Winter chewed on her lip as the windshield wipers swished back and forth. "He's not answering his phone, and what with everyone dying today, I thought I should check in on him."

"Hm." Noah's steady voice didn't betray the anxiety she knew he must be feeling. "How about you give me that address and let me be your backup for this evening?"

Winter envisioned the pile of muck that now served as Roosevelt's head. "Deal."

Sharing the address, she ended the call and continued speeding down the road. Backup was a smart idea, given the situation. And what better backup than her old partner?

Just like old times, only in Texas...and with rats.

Winter hit Fitz's number to redial it again. No answer.

Come on, Fitz, pick up the phone. Where are you?

Keeping her eyes glued to the road through the rain-streaked windshield, Winter clenched the steering wheel in a death-grip and pressed harder on the gas.

36

The rain beat down on us as Mahoney, shuddering with emotion, pulled me into his arms and smothered my face in kisses. "You're not a figment of my imagination." His breath was warm on my skin. "You're real. You're *real.*"

I placed my hand to his cheek, gazing into his eyes with all the love I could force myself to emit. "Yes, I am. And I've missed you so very much."

Rain sluicing down his face, he glanced around. "How did you get here?"

By my mommy van, dickwad.

"I walked." I forced my lower lip to tremble. "I had to get to you."

Clammy hands cupped my face. "I'm so very glad you did."

His body shuddered against me so hard that my bones rattled, but I didn't care. I gave him a few moments to slobber all over me again before pulling away. "It's so c-c-cold out here." I wrapped my arms around myself and faked an exaggerated shiver. "C-can we go inside?" Feigning weakness, I leaned against him heavily.

I needed this to be over with.

"Of course." He draped an arm around me, as if that appendage would protect me from the storm. "Let's get you dry."

The storm nearly drowned out his voice. Like the idiot he was, he scooped me into his muscular arms and headed toward the house.

Soon. Very, very soon.

Once inside, he set me on my feet, cupped my cheeks, and showered me with more kisses. "Sandra." Another kiss. "Sandra, I thought you were dead." Another kiss. "I thought you were gone forever."

His voice broke, and he started to sob.

My skin crawled as he blubbered all over me, but I didn't jerk away. I forced myself to stand still and return his kisses, even though the sensation of his lips on mine made me want to rinse my mouth out with acid.

Just stay calm. It's almost over now.

After what felt like hours, he pushed me back so he could scan my body like an X-ray. "Are you hurt? Is anything...broken?"

I shook my head, chattering my teeth for effect. "I d-don't think so, but I'm still cold. Could you get me a towel? And I think I might have left some clothes here. Could you get those too?" I lowered my eyes. "Unless you threw my things away."

He pulled me closer into his arms. "Never. I would never do that."

I forced a shiver. "Thank you, my love. We can talk when I'm warm."

Mahoney's bedroom was upstairs and at the far end of the house, so sending him on that errand to find my clothes would give me the extra time I needed.

"Yes, yes, anything you want. We need to get you out of

those wet clothes before you catch pneumonia. Gimme a minute. I'll be right back."

He bolted from the foyer, heading for the stairs that led to his bedroom and its giant walk-in closet.

The second he disappeared, I turned and ran to his game room. A pool table, several vintage arcade machines, and a wall full of every baseball bat he'd ever touched from tee-ball to the minors greeted me.

Such a beautiful array of weaponry just begging to be used.

We'd laughed a lot in this room. One night, I'd even beaten Mahoney at darts. And the pool table...well, we'd used it for activities far more strenuous than pool.

Another shiver pulsed through me, a real one this time. Letting Mahoney Fitzgerald grope and violate me was the worst part of this entire operation. It was a necessary evil, though. Before any of the plan could work, I had to ensure he fell in love with Sandra.

You weren't cheating on Hank. You were just acting. Like a star in a Hollywood movie.

My conscience continued to twinge. Another wrong I blamed on Mahoney.

With pure hatred pumping through my veins, I stalked forward and yanked his senior-year slugger off the wall.

Tonight is when Mahoney Fitzgerald graduates to Hell.

Getting my hands on one of his bats had been easier than I'd thought. I couldn't have arrived at his gate carrying a two-foot piece of wood, after all, so securing one once I was inside had been a primary goal.

Padding to the living room in my sopping wet sneakers, I waited just inside the door. A few seconds later, Mahoney's footsteps signaled his descent down the stairs. When his feet hit the bottom landing, I smiled and did what Mahoney had taught me to do. I bent my knees, planted my back foot, and raised my makeshift weapon.

Hey batter batter batter...

The second he appeared through the doorway, I swung with every ounce of my might and landed a solid connection with his face. In that instant, two things happened at once. The bully's nose exploded in a spray of blood, and he dropped to the floor like a puppet whose strings had been cut.

Swing, batter.

High on endorphins, I smashed the bat against his right knee for good measure. Just to make sure the bastard stayed down.

I was a very good lesson learner.

Pleased with myself, I tossed the bat aside and picked up a warm Egyptian cotton towel to dry my face. Phase One was complete. The subject of my torment was down. Now, on to Phase Two.

Opening the crossbody purse still hanging by my hip, I pulled out a few zip ties. Though I wasn't worried about him waking anytime soon, I had learned my lessons and didn't plan on taking any chances.

Dragging Mahoney to one of the stately columns that rose from floor to ceiling was a bit more challenging than I would have liked. And once there, I debated as to whether I should leave him on his back or sit him up. I didn't want him to drown on his own blood, after all.

In the end, I left him prone but propped a pillow under his neck to help with drainage. Dragging his arms over his head was more of an effort than I would have liked, but in only a couple minutes, I'd managed to zip tie his wrists together on the other side of the column. Pulling the heaviest chair I could find over to his feet, I zip tied each of his ankles to a leg.

The position was probably hell on his shoulders. Good.

Time for Phase Three.

Less than fifteen minutes later, I'd endured the storm's wrath to pull my hidden van closer to the house because I needed easier access to my furry little friends and the other implements I planned to use. From the way the sweet babies squeaked inside their cages, they were as eager to get to the next step as I was.

I smiled at their sweet faces. "Soon, babies. Dinnertime is very soon."

37

Hammering pain pounded Fitz's skull while agony screamed through his right leg. Even his shoulders hurt, and his hands were numb.

Have I been hit by a bus?

Opening his eyes took more effort than the simple act ever should, but the blurry world revealed itself to him soon enough. He was on the floor in his living room. His arms were tied around a marble column while his legs were tied to a heavy chair. And...he was naked.

What the hell?

Yanking at the restraints, he yelped as his shoulders howled in objection at the movement. Arthritis from years of playing baseball had left many of his joints a complete mess, and having his hands tied above his head while he lay prone on the hard floor was quickly becoming unbearable.

But that wasn't his biggest problem.

His biggest problem had just moved into his line of vision, wielding a bat like an avenging angel. In the band of her jeans was his Glock.

Shit.

Fitz licked his dry lips. "Hey, babe. You could have just told me you're into bondage. I've always wanted to play with that."

His joke fell flat.

"Hey, *babe*." Sandra threw her head back and laughed. "Be careful what you wish for." She patted the gun at her waist. "I brought my own, but I have to admit...your gun is bigger than mine. And as they say, size matters, so I think I'll play with yours."

Fear like he'd never known took a bite out of his gut as he stared into the face of the woman he loved. The woman he no longer recognized.

"Who...are...you?"

A sneer twisted her perfect lips. "I'm your beloved girl-friend, Sandra, of course. Oh, and I also happen to be the person responsible for your old pal Roosevelt no longer having a head."

Her face swam in and out of focus. "R-r-roose?"

"Yes, R-r-roose." Her tone was a mockery of his. "And what I mean is, he's dead. I smashed his head into a pile of mush. I'm the one who offed Bobby too. Snuck into his hospital room and injected him with a fatal dose of rat poison." She blinked, the picture of innocence. "That's what you do to rats, after all. Right?"

Between the ringing in his ears and the darkness bleeding into his consciousness, it took Fitz a while to process all those terrible words. When he did, he released a low moan. "Nooo."

Maybe this is all in my imagination. If Sandra doesn't exist, then none of this is real. It's all a terrible, vivid nightmare.

Only he'd never experienced a nightmare that hurt so damn much.

Sandra-not-Sandra's lips curved into an obscene grin. "Honestly, I did Roosevelt's wife a favor. She'll save at least a few hundred bucks on his funeral. Short coffins are cheaper."

When Fitz tried to speak, liquid bubbled from his mouth. *Blood.* "You're. N-not. S-Sandra."

"No shit, Sherlock." She sighed. "And it's not your fault, really, that you didn't recognize me. I've changed everything about myself that I possibly could. Multiple plastic surgeries and this beautiful bleached blonde hair."

He didn't understand. "W-why?" he rasped.

"After the horrors of my childhood, I wanted very much to be a different person. No more red hair. Why not get a new nose? A chin implant did wonders for erasing a past full of abuse." Sandra-not-Sandra dropped to her knees beside him, hovering her face just a foot over his. "Still, a little piece of me hoped you'd recognize me. It seems only fitting that the person who stole everything from me as a child should remember who I am."

Darkness crashed over Fitz in waves as she spoke, trying to drag him under. He struggled to stay afloat, dredging through his memories like a child digging in the sand.

Whose life did you ruin, Fitz? Who did you steal everything from?

He didn't know. He couldn't think. His brain felt like a demolition zone, his leg like a block of splintered ice.

Through the agonized haze, a musical sound floated to his ears.

Giggling. Sandra-not-Sandra was giggling. And there was another sound nearby. What was it?

"Let's see if this rings any bells, you narcissistic dick." The bat blurred as she twirled it. "Gaggy. Von. Dork. Remember her? You must. No one forgets a name like that."

Gaggy von Dork.

The name floated through his consciousness, and a scrawny little girl with bright red hair and pasty skin surfaced. He struggled to reconcile that image with the one of his Sandra. Gaggy von Dork and the love of his life were the same person? How?

"I d-do. I remember. M-Maggie. Her…I mean, y-your hair was…was *red*."

How did Winter know a redheaded child was part of the equation? That was a question for later. If there was a later for him.

"See, I knew you could get there. Do you remember when you punched me in the face on the playground? Remember me bleeding like a stuck pig in front of all your douchebag friends? Or how about hammering my brains with a dodgeball every chance you got? Do you remember *that*? Shall I go on?"

Sandra's—no, Maggie's—words triggered a rush of memories, along with an oily sense of shame. He'd acted like a selfish dick back then. Uncaring, entitled, with zero concern regarding the impact his actions had on others.

Even so, a crucial piece seemed to be missing. "You killed them…because…o-of d-d-dodgeb-b-ball?"

Fitz cowered as the bat swung near his head. A dull thwack reverberated through the column behind him. Sandra's surprise attack on the custom marble made him jump, causing a new course of misery to shoot through him.

The sound he couldn't recognize grew louder too. He turned his head to find the source, and his heart sank when his gaze landed on a cage filled with rats. No, not just one cage. Three.

"No, I didn't kill them because of dodgeball, you moron!" Her voice rose to a shout, and for the first time ever, Fitz wished he had neighbors. Someone close enough to hear him scream. "That day was the end of my life. Do you understand me, asshole? My father beat the living shit out of me when I finally…finally punched you back. And when my mother tried to protect me, he *killed* her."

Pulling his attention away from the cages, he tried to implore the deranged woman with his eyes. "I…what? I d-don't understand." Nothing made sense anymore. Too many facts. Too much pain. Exhaustion was closing in, tugging Fitz closer to oblivion with every breath.

Warm liquid tickled his left ear, and if his hands hadn't been bound, he didn't think he would have been able to summon enough energy to lift a single finger to check. Not that he needed to. He knew what the fluid was. Blood.

Concussion. Brain injury. Internal hemorrhaging.

Fitz was no doctor, but even he knew that, without medical attention, he could die.

If she didn't kill him first.

The world seesawed again when a rough hand grabbed his hair and yanked his head back. The bat was gone, and she was pressing his Glock to his temple.

He hadn't realized his eyes were closed until he opened them to find Sandra's nose inches away. As he stared into her face, her beautiful features leered at him, distorting into a rat's long teeth and twitching nose as they pulsed in time with his throbbing skull.

He spit out a sob. "S-top. Please."

The fingers tightened in his hair before releasing him. "I entered Hell that day while you and your fuckstick friends went on to be spoiled rich bastards without a care in the world."

"I-I'm sorry."

"I'm sorry," she mocked, tucking the gun into her pants again. "You make me sick."

In a rush, Maggie stood and strode over to one of the cages, lifting a much smaller one he hadn't noticed at first glance. Fitz watched in horror as she opened the door and a rat nearly the size of a cat ran up her arm and onto her shoulder. From its perch, it stared down at him with beady red eyes.

Nooo...no, no, no.

"I d-didn't m-mean—"

"Shut your stupid lying mouth." Maggie picked something up from a bag and turned to him. "Do you know what this is?"

Blinking to clear his vision, Fitz tried to make the lines of metal with straps attached make sense. "N-n-no."

She smiled and held what looked like a small cage with no bottom up for his closer examination. "Back in the seventeenth century, a Dutchman by the name of Diederik Sonay devised a wonderful little cage just like this to torture prisoners."

Torture? My god. Fitz's bowels turned to water.

"Turns out that rats don't like getting hot, so when the cage was heated, the rats did anything they could to escape... like tearing through flesh." Maggie held up an electrical cord. "Old Diederik didn't have electricity back then, so he had to heat his cage in other ways." She shrugged and headed toward the power outlet closest to him. "I'm all about ease, though."

The rat on her shoulder rubbed its paws together, and the damn thing almost appeared to smile.

"Don't. P-please d..." To his horror, Fitz started to cry. "I was j-just a k-kid."

"So was I!"

Her furious shriek jerked Fitz back from the edge of delirium. He opened his eyes in time to watch her lower the half cage over his naked crotch.

Nooooo!

As the horror of what she was planning registered in his brain, Fitz bucked the cage off his pelvis. Before the metal even clattered to the floor, Maggie kicked him. Then she kicked him again. And again. And again.

Unable to roll into a ball or protect himself in any way, he could do nothing but beg for mercy until she wore herself out. That didn't come soon enough.

When she was panting for breath, Fitz was sure that at least several of his ribs were broken.

Every breath was like inhaling needles.

As he writhed in pain, he was coherent enough to learn what the straps on the bottomless cage were for. After setting the metal device over his crotch a second time, she used the ties to secure it firmly to his body. The cage was warm and getting hotter as it grew tighter against his skin.

"Hungry, baby?" Maggie stroked the rodent's fur as it crawled down her arm.

When she lifted the little door at the top of the cage and dropped what might have been a piece of cheese inside, the rat followed its tasty treat.

Sharp claws landed on his most delicate skin.

As the beast took its first bite, Fitz couldn't even manage another scream.

38

W inter slammed the brakes as Fitz's wide-open, unsecured front gate came into view. On top of her ordering him to "batten down the hatches," Fitz's current state of paranoia and fear meant he'd never forget to lock his gate.

Dread kicked her in the ass. "Shit."

Grabbing her phone, she typed a hasty text to Noah.

Something's wrong here. Looks like Fitz has a visitor. Hurry.

Her phone started vibrating a few seconds later. She shoved it in her pocket without answering. "Sorry, my love. I know you'd want me to wait, but I can't do that." Not when there was a possibility that her client was in imminent danger.

Deciding to go the rest of the way on foot, Winter yanked her jacket hood over her head, unholstered her gun, and climbed from the car into a relentless deluge. Fitz's front door wasn't too far ahead, but the downpour blurring her vision and slick concrete made the path too treacherous for speed.

As Winter huffed and puffed into the last stretch, she

passed a minivan off to the side, and then the front door came into view. The remaining breath squeezed from her lungs.

Open. The door stood wide open, and light poured from the foyer onto the steps outside. Creeping into the foyer, she followed the sound of a woman's laughter.

Winter tightened her grip on the gun as she slid through the entrance and down a long hallway. The laughter was coming from the direction of his living room.

"You want some more, Mahoney?" The question was followed by the sound of metal.

Reaching the entrance to the living room, Winter peeked around the corner and swallowed the scream that barreled up her throat.

Rats. The room was full of rats.

Her mind was still processing that discovery when the laughter turned into a voice. "Who's suffering now, Mahoney? Who's the pathetic, broken little rat now?"

Agonized groans followed. "P-please. *Stop.*"

Muscles tensed and ready for action, Winter took a deep breath. She counted to three and burst into the living room.

Oh. My. God.

The image of Mahoney Fitzgerald lying on the floor with a rat chewing his dick was something Winter knew she'd never be able delete from her brain. A blonde woman stood over him, a gun in her hand and an unmistakable gleam of madness in her stare.

Winter instantly recognized her from Fitz's photos.

Sandra.

In the instant their gazes connected, the woman aimed the barrel at Fitz as he bucked and cried. Blood streamed from his nose and ear, and one eye was swollen shut. Rats skittered across his body.

Winter centered her aim on the woman's chest. "Sandra Smith! Drop your weapon!"

The woman didn't even flinch. Her focus remained trained on the man at her feet. "Sandra isn't real."

Winter crept two steps closer. "If Sandra isn't real, then tell me who you are. Tell me why you're killing people. Why do you want to hurt Mahoney?"

"Because he's a waste of a human being and deserves to die." The woman's top lip curled into a sneer. "And as a former federal agent, *Winter Black*, you should know that I'm right. Don't you dare come a step closer, or I'll blow his brains out."

The conviction in her voice chilled Winter to the core. *Distraction. You need a distraction.* "Okay, so you know my name. What's yours?"

A broken laugh spilled from the woman. "Maggie. My name is Maggie. Mahoney calls me 'Gaggy von Dork,' but you can call me Maggie."

The woman's sudden switch to a high-pitched, childlike voice sent goose bumps racing down Winter's back.

Gaggy von Dork. What an awful nickname. The kind that reeked of elementary school bullies, blatant immaturity…and Fitz. Had whatever hell Fitz and his buddies put Maggie through back then somehow fractured her mind?

Winter's stomach rolled as she and Maggie stood frozen in their deadly tableau. For once in her life, Winter wasn't sure what to do. She could aim for Maggie's shoulder and try to take her down, but not without risk. The other woman could get off a shot and hit Fitz before she fell.

She swallowed hard, nerves rattling even as her gun hand remained steady. The idea of shooting someone on her very first case as a P.I. filled her with icy dread. The private sector was supposed to bring less violence. Less shooting. Less death. Yet there she was, wading right into the thick of things again.

And then there was Maggie. A woman whose childhood bullies had apparently damaged her past the point of no return. Deep inside of Winter, a tiny part empathized with the wild-eyed woman.

Trauma ruined lives.

She extended her free hand. "Maggie. How about you give me that gun, and we can have a chat about Mahoney?" She worked to keep her voice soft and soothing. "You can tell me exactly what he did to you. How does that sound?"

Maggie's features twisted. "It sounds like you're stalling. Like you're trying to save a man who destroyed my life. And if you knew…"

Trailing off, Maggie glared down at Fitz, whose body was so still now that Winter couldn't tell if he was even conscious.

Or alive.

"If I knew what?" Winter stole another inch forward. "What do I need to know?"

Maggie burst into tears and laughter at the same time. "If you knew what he did to me…*what he took from me*…you'd pick up that bat and kill him yourself."

The notion that Fitz was capable of harming another human in an even more deplorable manner than he'd already admitted to twisted Winter's stomach into tighter knots. Her conviction wavered.

What if you were hired by the true villain of this story? What if Fitz's abuse really did snap Maggie's mind and drive her to insanity?

And if it did…why had she waited so long to take her revenge?

So many questions, but for now Winter needed to deescalate the situation. Her gaze flicked to Fitz's broken, bleeding form, and her resolve hardened. No matter what terrible acts he might have committed as a child, she couldn't stand by and let Maggie murder him in cold blood.

"Maggie, I know what it's like to want revenge. To *crave* it deep in your bones. I know what it's like for someone to hurt you so badly that the only price that seems high enough is wiping them from existence. Killing Mahoney lets him off easy, though. I can help you find your justice *and* make him answer for his crimes in court."

Fitz moaned but quickly went silent. The only sound in the room was chewing noises, and Winter didn't dare to look at the cage where a giant rodent was feasting. If they waited much longer, Winter feared that his injuries would make the decision moot.

Maggie hesitated for an instant before shaking her head. "The courts won't bring my mother back to life. There's nothing they can do that will ever make things right. But I…I can even the score."

Winter stared at the other woman and shivered, certain for a fleeting moment that she was looking into a mirror. An avalanche crashed onto her shoulders as she recalled the deep-seated pain of losing her mother at a young age.

The rats from her vision flashed through her head.

You know what we are.

She couldn't think about that right now. Focus!

"What happened to your mother, Maggie?"

The woman's chin trembled. "She was stolen from me. She was murdered. And it's his fault." She jerked the gun at Fitz, who still hadn't moved. "If he'd never existed, I'd still have a mother. I'd still have a soul. *He has to die.*"

Soul aching sobs shook Maggie's body, causing her gun arm to wobble. Winter chanced another step closer. "I know exactly what you're feeling right now, and I promise you, that ache will not disappear once Mahoney is dead. Your pain will keep eating away at your insides like a cancer. Put the gun down. Let me get you some help. You don't have to kill him, Mag—"

"The hell I don't!" Maggie's scream thundered louder than the storm outside. "That's the only way this ends. That's the only way she'll leave me alone. He has to die, and I don't care if I go with him."

Before Winter could blink, Maggie raised the gun and squeezed the trigger.

39

Noah shouted a string of profanities as he hurtled down the highway amid an absolute beast of a thunderstorm.

"She should have waited." He slammed a fist on the dashboard. "She knows damn well she should have waited for backup."

He'd attempted to call Winter multiple times after receiving and reading her text. She hadn't answered...probably because she was too hell-bent on plunging knee-deep into trouble.

Or she's dead. Maybe she used up her nine lives. Maybe you're a widower, and you don't even know it yet.

Noah hit the speed dial for Agent Taggart.

She answered on the first ring. "Howdy, partner. Thought you clocked out hours ago."

"I'm giving you an address." Noah didn't have a bantering bone in his body at the moment. "Send the cops. Paramedics. Something bad is going down at my wife's client's house in Lakeview Hills." He rattled off the street name and number.

"On it." Eve immediately switched gears. "Is she okay?"

Noah gulped down the stone in his throat. "I don't know."

His partner asked no more. Her keys jangled in the background. "I'm coming too. It's about an hour and fifteen minutes from my house. I'll see you there."

Eve ended the call before he could protest, but Noah didn't care. It couldn't hurt to have her assistance on the scene.

The devil on Noah's shoulder progressed from whispers to shrieks.

What kind of scene do you think you're in for? Remember Roosevelt's smashed-in brains? Do you? Do you remember what kind of psychopath your wife is dealing with?

Winter's return to the land of sociopaths appeared to be in full swing. Would this one kill—

"No." The word wrenched from his lungs. "My wife is alive. Winter is alive."

And if she isn't...they can put me six feet under right beside her.

WINTER SQUEEZED the trigger fractions of a second before Maggie, sending the woman's pistol flying across the room.

Maggie whirled on her, snarling and hissing like the carpet of rats swarming around them. Winter was ready. She charged, tackling the other woman to the floor and pinning her arms behind her. Rodents scattered like roaches in the light, squealing at the commotion as Winter fought their kicking and screaming owner.

"I know what you are!" Maggie's vicious shriek stabbed at Winter's eardrums. "I know what you did. I know what you took from that little boy!"

Visions of Timothy Stewart bound and gagged on a brain-splattered RV floor assaulted Winter. She could still count the glistening tears that had rolled across his duct-taped mouth while he stared at his dead parents.

Stop. You did what you had to do.

She swallowed down a mixture of rage and sorrow. "You don't know anything about me."

Drool slid from one corner of Maggie's mouth as she sneered. "I know you're a murderer."

Flipping Maggie onto her stomach, Winter zip-tied the woman's hands together before dialing 911. Noah had probably already done that, but she needed to add another type of emergency services to the list.

Animal control.

Though Winter wanted to run screaming from the house, she kept her voice calm as she explained the situation. Even as she did, Maggie's words echoed with a terrible finality in her head.

I know you're a murderer.

The worst part? Maggie wasn't wrong.

40

W inter showed her ID to the guard standing just inside Lakeview Hills Hospital. Security had ramped up considerably at all the local hospitals since Bobby's passing, and even more so after news of the attack on Mahoney Fitzgerald spread across the countryside.

Continuing to ride the unbelievable lucky streak that had graced him for his entire life, Fitz escaped the run-in with Margaret von Gork with his head—and most of his penis—still attached. Less than a dozen rat bites punctured his skin to remind him of the furry horde his ex-girlfriend had unleashed.

She *had* gifted him a broken knee, a fractured nose and cheekbone, a concussion, and a series of rabies shots, but in comparison to Bobby and Roosevelt's fate, Fitz was beyond fortunate.

Striding down the halls of the intensive care unit, Winter halted at Fitz's room and rapped three times.

"Come in." Fitz's gravelly voice was a foreign sound.

Winter entered, approaching the hospital bed and her wounded client with a small smile. "Bandaged up like that, you almost look tough. Like a war veteran or an extra in an action film or something."

Fitz blinked at her through the one eye not swathed in gauze. "Stockbrokers can be cool too, you know."

Laughter sputtered past Winter's lips. "Right."

He closed his eye, sighing heavily. "So, tell me everything. I've been in this bed for damn near twenty-four hours, and no one has explained anything to me. All I'm sure of is that the day Maggie punched me back on the playground, her entire life went to hell."

"I spent all day speaking with the police and the Feds." Winter tugged a visitor's chair to Fitz's bedside. "There's a lot to sort out. It's going to take some time to fill in all the blanks surrounding Maggie and the murders, but I can give you the basics."

Fitz kept his eye closed. "Shoot."

"She really has been through hell." Winter empathized with the woman despite her savage acts. "Her father, rotting in prison as we speak, pushed her mother down the stairs that day she punched you on the playground, and eight-year-old Maggie got to watch her die. Then it was foster care and years of abuse, both physical and sexual."

"Bobby and Roose and I...we didn't know." Fitz moaned the statement. "Everyone thought she and her family had moved away. And after a while...I guess we forgot about her altogether."

She certainly didn't forget about you.

Winter shifted against the hard plastic seat. "She married well, but her first and only child, a boy, was born deaf and nearly mute. Raising him for the last thirteen years took a toll on her, and I honestly don't think she had anything left to be tolled."

"I feel awful." Fitz ran a finger across his swollen jawline. "I caused all of this."

Placing a hand on his arm, Winter gave a compassionate squeeze. "You listen to me. Yes, you were a little asshole bully, and you should feel shitty about that fact. But it stops there, Fitz. Nothing that happened to Maggie after she went home that day was your fault."

He grunted and rolled his head to the side. She had a feeling that Mahoney Fitzgerald's mental recovery would take much longer than healing from his physical wounds. "Why now? Why wait so many years to get her revenge?"

That was a question Winter had wanted to know too. "From what she's said, she was triggered when she caught the news story of Bobby Burner's eldest son's Little League national championship win months ago. Bobby's own success as a minor league baseball player and businessman was already infuriating enough, and there he was, passing his good fortune down to the next generation of healthy little assholes." Winter smiled. "Those were mostly her words."

"So, she decided to kill us all?"

Winter shook her head. "No. She actually only planned on killing Bobby and Roosevelt based on what she said. Her plan was to destroy your life by driving you insane."

Fitz chuckled, though the sound held no joy. "She very nearly did." He frowned. "So obviously, Patricia Smith wasn't Sandra's mother. Sandra was just a lie. But how did Maggie manage to get so many people to lie *with* her?"

"She employed two classic methods of coercion. Money and blackmail." Winter pictured Patricia's emaciated face. "Patricia was dying and leaving behind a granddaughter who desperately wanted to go to college. The girl's parents are deadbeats. Patricia jumped at the chance to earn the money she needed. All she had to do was 'act' in some rich woman's play."

"And the doctor?" Fitz's raspy voice couldn't camouflage his shock. "The nurses?"

Winter lifted a shoulder. "From what I can tell, the assorted medical staff you met when you visited Peaceful Acres were in on it too. They've transferred jobs or disappeared altogether. It's going to take law enforcement a long time to hunt them all down."

Fitz stared out the window. "How did Maggie know them? Or Patricia, for that matter?"

"Her husband, Hank, is a powerful man. He owns a lot of medical facilities. John Newberry was his friend, and when John lost his job over a gambling addiction, Hank helped him pay off his debts and offered him a fresh start as the medical director at Peaceful Acres. Maggie took things from there."

"I still can't believe she has a husband." Fitz's lower lip trembled. "She didn't act married. I wouldn't have fallen in love with Sandra if I'd known about him."

Winter wondered how much therapy it would take for Fitz to process the fact that Sandra Smith truly hadn't existed. "That's the key word. Act. *Maggie* was acting. Sandra was never there. That'll get easier to accept with time."

Fitz continued to avoid eye contact. "If you say so. What about the nurse?"

"Maude Little was a regular visiting nurse for Maggie's son in their home." Winter had to give the woman credit for her impressively woven web of deceit. "But Maude got caught stealing pharmaceuticals at the hospital and lost her job. Maggie, of course, had the perfect position for Maude to fill. A job and eventual retirement in paradise in exchange for Maude's unwavering cooperation and whatever theatrical skills she possessed."

Gritting his teeth, Fitz's hand curled into a fist on the blanket. "Tell me those two assholes didn't get away."

Winter allowed herself a satisfied smile. "You'll be happy to know that, though Nurse Little made it out of the country, her computer's plane ticket receipts led the authorities straight to her. And Dr. Newberry didn't even make it out of the airport. He was stopped during a security check and identified as a person of interest in the murder of Patricia Smith."

"Killing a dying woman." Fitz spat the words. "How could anyone do that and walk around like everything was normal afterward?"

"That's one question I don't have the answer to." Winter stifled a yawn, her eyelids suddenly feeling like they weighed ten thousand pounds. "If it's of any comfort, Maggie's husband is facing the same shock as you. He had no idea what was going on inside Peaceful Acres or his wife's head, let alone that she was having a full-blown affair."

Fitz shook his head. "That's not comforting at all. It makes me feel angry and guilty. I slept with his wife, and I'm sorry for that. But Sandra…Sandra was mine."

If Fitz weren't in such a fragile state, she might have shaken him. *Sandra isn't real. She isn't real.*

As if the universe wanted to punch him for her, Fitz yawned loudly and yelped. He lifted a hand to his face. "Stupid jaw."

They hadn't even gotten to all the other people who'd been paid to take part in Maggie's revenge scheme. The owner of the apartment building, the family who'd "lived there for years," the server at the café who'd flown home…

A whole roster of individuals were involved in the ruse.

The mystery of which—if any—of those actors had known about Maggie's violent end game remained unsolved for now. Likely, the answers would come out via testimony once the court case began. As would the explanation surrounding Maggie's utilization of the rats.

Wanting to ask if his parents and sister had dropped by to visit him yet, Winter decided against it. The Fitzgeralds' family dynamic was far from healthy, and she might just twist the knife deeper by probing.

Blood didn't always mean forgiveness and love. No one was better acquainted with that fact than her.

Except for maybe Maggie von Gork.

"You should get some sleep." Winter rose from the chair and stretched her arms high above her head. "I'll check in on you again soon."

Fitz nodded, but as Winter walked toward the door, he called out one last bit of information. "I thought you should know that I'm going to do everything in my power to get in touch with my son. I'm going to be there for him as much as I possibly can. If he'll let me."

Winter's heart squeezed. In a good way. "He'll let you."

A solitary tear rolled down Fitz's battered cheek. "You think there's still time for me to be a better man?"

Biting her tongue until it bled to stave off her own emotions, Winter tossed one more comment at her very first client before exiting the room. "Are you still breathing?"

NOAH SET Winter's microwaved macaroni and cheese on the kitchen table with a flourish. "Voila, madame."

"Merci, Monsieur." Winter jabbed her fork at the pasta.

Behind her, the half-eaten blueberry pie that Ardis Ogilvie had so kindly bestowed upon them mocked his pathetic culinary attempts.

Winter seemed incredibly quiet this evening, but considering that not even a full day had passed since Maggie's capture, Noah figured the mood was to be expected.

He wasn't processing the events all that well himself.

Switching careers was solely Winter's idea, and Noah supported her decision in full. Yet he'd anticipated—and been quietly grateful for— the new profession offering his wife a substantial shift from serial killers and gore to mystery and classic, hard-nosed detective work.

Mahoney Fitzgerald's case had thrown his wife right back into the violent, unhinged psychopath arena she'd so often dealt with as a federal agent. To Noah, it seemed as if she'd never left the Bureau at all.

The one glaringly painful difference was that Noah now couldn't offer her the same level of immediate backup that accompanied her role as a Fed. By the time he'd appeared on the scene in the Fitzgerald mansion, Winter had command of the situation.

If events had gone sideways, though...he might have arrived too late.

He squirmed in his chair, antsy as hell and losing his appetite by the second.

You'll go insane if she keeps taking clients like Mahoney.

A universe where he asked his wife to take on less dangerous cases, however, did not exist. Winter would interpret the plea as an insult, and he wouldn't even blame her.

"Babe?" Winter continued poking at her food. "Do you ever think we should do something for Timothy Stewart? Just like...help him somehow? Make sure he's okay?"

He stiffened. *Where did that come from?*

"I think about Timmy sometimes, but from the sound of it, he's in good hands. He's with his uncle and has a bright future ahead of him. And...I figure that, for us, it's better to leave all of that in the past. No looking back."

If he could forget all about the night the boy had stabbed him while aiming for Winter, Noah would be thrilled.

Winter remained silent, pushing pasta across her plate while she stared out the window. Reading his wife like a book—his very favorite book—Noah knew she wasn't entirely ready to leave Timmy behind. Part of her remained in the Stewarts' RV, forever reliving the terrible events embedded upon her psyche.

Noah intended to assist in freeing her from those mental chains no matter how long the process took. Timothy Stewart wasn't her burden to carry. Not anymore.

"Hey." He grabbed the pepper shaker and doused his own pasta. "Gramma Beth stopped by earlier. She told me to tell you that skipping Sunday dinner is not an option."

Winter laughed. "I'm aware. She left me three voicemails. I guess we did promise dinner would be a weekly event if they moved to Austin with us. Did you invite Lucy?"

Just an hour ago, Noah's sister had adamantly agreed to the invitation over the phone before he'd even finished saying "home-cooked meal."

"Oh, she'll be there." Noah placed a hand on top of Winter's. "Grampa Jack is apparently going on a fishing excursion with Abe Ogilvie next week too. I think those old-timers are gonna be best friends."

"I like that idea." She glanced at the counter. "Almost as much as I like the idea of eating pie for dinner. Do we dare?"

Noah jumped from his chair like his ass was on fire. No one had to tell him twice to switch out dinner for baked goods. "We're adults, dammit. We can do what we want. As long as your grandparents don't find out."

Breaking into a deep belly laugh, Winter glanced around the kitchen, making sure the coast was clear. "Roger that. Pie dinner stays between us."

Her laughter was genuine—Noah always knew when Winter was faking—and he allowed himself a sigh of relief as he cut two giant slices. "We've got a lot of great times waiting for us in Austin. I know it's been a rough first week for you, but I'm still excited that we did this. I really feel like we're *home*."

Winter lifted her water glass, lips curving upward into

the bewitching smile he'd fallen in love with. "Cheers to that, Agent Dalton. Massive amounts of good days ahead."

"You know what they say," Noah shot her a wink and added a double eyebrow wiggle just to watch her smile again, "everything's bigger in Texas."

41

Julia Eversmeyer carefully pressed each digit of the Black Investigations phone number. Her research had turned up impressive details about Winter Black, a former federal agent who'd recently become a private investigator. Winter had a reputation. The woman was described throughout the entire internet as fearless. Relentless.

Merciless.

"Please, please, please be all of those things." Julia counted the rings, praying that Winter would answer.

Instead, her call went to voicemail.

"You've reached Black Investigations. Please leave your name, number, and a brief description of the reason for your call after the beep, and I'll be in touch."

Julia swiped a hand across her forehead as the beep sang through her brain. She fumbled for the right words even though they didn't exist.

Everything about her situation was wrong.

She cleared her throat and pressed her trembling fingertips to her temples. "My name is Julia Eversmeyer. My number is five five five, one two one two. I'm calling because...because...I need to protect my children from my ex-husband. They've been massively traumatized by our divorce, and now I...well. I believe he's...sick. Please. Help me."

Ending the call, Julia shook her head in embarrassment. She shouldn't have ended the message with a plea. Then again, there wasn't exactly a right way to wrap something like that up.

Sipping her merlot, Julia forced herself to look at the picture again. Her youngest, a five-year-old little girl, had drawn the picture with crayons and proudly presented it at the dinner table the previous evening.

A stick figure man with a broad smile was surrounded by small stick figure girls. All of them held identical objects that could have been knives, swords, or maybe needles.

The five written words below the picture turned Julia's stomach into a block of ice.

Beneath the man, the childish scrawl proclaimed *Nakid Daddy*. And beneath the females, the disturbing declaration of *Nakid notty girls*.

For a long time, Julia had suspected that her ex had a pornography addiction but stayed with him for the sake of their three children. For all those years, her decision had seemed like the right thing to do.

As it turned out, everything about her situation was wrong.

She stared at the illustration, fury flooding her veins.

If her ex-husband was doing anything close to what the picture indicated, Julia would kill him herself.

42

Timmy Stewart liked Dr. Santos. He liked her a lot. She was pretty, smelled like flowers, and almost always had a big smile on her face.

She reminded him of his dead mother.

They'd been talking for a long time. Dr. Santos said the session was only a half hour, but Timmy was sure he'd been sitting on this couch for half a day at least.

That's okay, though. She's so nice.

His uncle told Timmy that he'd be visiting Dr. Santos often. He didn't mind at all.

Or at least, he wouldn't mind as long as she didn't keep asking him questions like the one she was waiting for him to answer now.

"How do you feel about what happened with Agent Dalton...what you did to Agent Dalton...now that some time has passed?"

It was an icky question. One that made snakes wiggle around inside his belly.

He squirmed in his chair. He didn't think he could tell Dr. Santos everything.

You can tell her most of it.

Timmy stilled. He liked the idea of letting Dr. Santos get to know him. He trusted her already.

"Every time I think about what I did to Agent Dalton, I get sad." Timmy frowned, the sadness hitting as hard as ever. "I know he was one of the good guys now. And I know Agent Black didn't want to hurt my parents. Her evil brother made her do that."

Dr. Santos's smile disappeared for a second, the way people's smiles always disappeared when he talked about Justin Black.

She managed to smile again pretty fast. "Do you still think about Agent Black's brother very often?"

The answer was yes and no. He thought of Justin every day, but in some strange, foggy way that seemed like a bad dream. It felt like Justin was very far away, and Timmy liked that.

"I dunno." He kicked his dangling feet back and forth. "I try not to. He was scary. He was the scariest person I've ever met. He was going to *kill* Agent Black. He told me so. He was going to kill *all of them*."

That idea upset Timmy and made his throat all scratchy. All those agents were nice people. Good people. Killing good people was wrong.

Wasn't it?

"How do you feel about Agent Black's brother being in prison for the rest of his life?" Dr. Santos had really pretty brown eyes. "Does that make you feel safe?"

Timmy's tummy said no but his head nodded yes. People liked it when he told them he felt safe and happy. "I'm glad he's in prison. Real glad."

That was the right answer because Dr. Santos gave him her widest smile yet. Timmy wished he could share the rest of his feelings, but that was a bad idea. He was just a kid, but even he knew a bad idea when he heard one.

How could he tell the nice, pretty doctor the truth? That when he'd stabbed Agent Dalton and believed he was killing a bad guy, he'd felt...powerful? Like he was doing something important. Like a *superhero*.

His chin drooped to his chest. Why did bad people have to exist? They just hurt good people and made the world a sad place.

Timmy didn't understand why they couldn't all just die, but he knew better than to share those thoughts with Dr. Santos or anyone else.

Ever.

The End
To be continued...

Thank you for reading.
All of the Winter Black Series books can be found on Amazon.

ACKNOWLEDGMENTS

How does one properly thank everyone involved in taking a dream and making it a reality? Let me try.

In addition to my family, whose unending support provided the foundation for me to find the time and energy to put these thoughts on paper, I want to thank the editors who polished my words and made them shine.

Many thanks to my publisher for risking taking on a newbie and giving me the confidence to become a bona fide author.

More than anyone, I want to thank you, my reader, for clicking on a nobody and sharing your most important asset, your time, with this book. I hope with all my heart I made it worthwhile.

Much love,
Mary

ABOUT THE AUTHOR

Mary Stone lives among the majestic Blue Ridge Mountains of East Tennessee with her two dogs, four cats, a couple of energetic boys, and a very patient husband.

As a young girl, she would go to bed every night, wondering what type of creature might be lurking underneath. It wasn't until she was older that she learned that the creatures she needed to most fear were human.

Today, she creates vivid stories with courageous, strong heroines and dastardly villains. She invites you to enter her world of serial killers, FBI agents but never damsels in distress. Her female characters can handle themselves, going toe-to-toe with any male character, protagonist or antagonist.

Discover more about Mary Stone on her website.
www.authormarystone.com

facebook.com/authormarystone
goodreads.com/AuthorMaryStone
bookbub.com/profile/3378576590
pinterest.com/MaryStoneAuthor